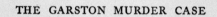

THE GARSTON MURDER CASE

BOOKS BY
H. C. BAILEY

H. C. BAILEY

THE
GARSTON MURDER CASE

The creator of Mr. Fortune writes
a novel of murder bred by murder . . . as thrilling a book
as you will ever read

GARDEN CITY, N. Y. 1930 PUBLISHED FOR

THE CRIME CLUB, INC.

BY DOUBLEDAY, DORAN & COMPANY, INC.

PRINTED AT THE *Country Life Press*, GARDEN CITY, N. Y., U. S. A.

CONTENTS

THE GARSTON MURDER CASE

CHAPTER I

MR. CLUNK

A SPRING wind was blowing down the Strand. Mr. Joshua Clunk came out of a tea shop, stopped to look at the world with benign approval, and wound his way across the jam of buses. He went on up Bow Street, a small, plump man, with the tripping step of a happy child in a hurry, not otherwise childlike. He was a harmony of gray: gray clothes which were almost black, gray moustache, and little whiskers which were almost white. His face had the colour and gloss of yellowing ivory, but from wrinkled hollows his large eyes gave a pale gray gleam. Mr. Clunk did not conceal that he liked himself. He tripped on to the murmured twitter of a hymn:

> "*But the seeds of good we sow,*
> *Both in shade and shine will grow*
> *And will keep our hearts aglow*
> *While the days are going by!*"

Near the police station two men passed him, and to the elder, a square man of some age, he lifted a hand of greeting and called gaily: "Beautiful weather!" But it was not well taken. The square man, who was Superintendent Bell of the Criminal Investigation Department, passed on with a nod and a grunt. "Who is your dear old friend, sir?" the younger, larger man asked.

"Smug little cat, ain't he?" Bell growled. "Don't you know him, Underwood? You will. He's Clunk & Clunk, Joshua Clunk."

"What, the crooks' solicitor?"

"That's the fellow. I'd say he's given us more trouble than any man that's never gone to jail."

"I suppose so," Sergeant Underwood nodded. "Sails pretty near the wind too, don't he?"

"And then some," said Bell. "Nasty little bag of tricks."

"I've never seen him before. Looks like a church-warden or a deacon or something."

"Most likely is," Bell grunted. "He would be."

If you will allow for professional prejudice, this description of Mr. Clunk was accurate enough. His father left the firm of Clunk & Clunk with a small respectable practice in people who would not pay their bills. Joshua had larger ambitions. Under his rule Clunk & Clunk took up crime. It was discovered by the small fry of the criminal profession that no lawyer could make so much of their hopeless cases as Josh Clunk. Though he failed to get them off, he would at least have a game with the police and give them a run for their money—even when money was lacking they had the run, if the case would make a show in the papers. So he attracted the more successful practitioners, the engineers of large-scale crime and its financiers, and the amateurs of talent, the respectable citizens adventuring into ample theft and fraud, learned that Joshua Clunk was the man for them.

In these days of his maturity, he did not himself take a case in the police court unless it was big enough to fill the papers. The name of Clunk & Clunk commanded respect enough for the young men from his office who had learned a portion of his bland persistence, his cynical feeling for the popular, his lack of scruple.

He worked unseen. Other solicitors might sniff at his name and counsel predict that old Clunk would end in the dock himself. All who knew anything knew there were manifold dangers in fighting Clunk & Clunk. Only the rash were confident his labours would not find out an awkward gap in the strongest case, his cunning, his intimacy with the world of crime, play tricks with it for which the law had not provided. It was commonly said that he knew more of what was going on underground than any man in London and not uncommonly believed that he was up to the neck in most of it.

But he was neither a deacon not a churchwarden. No religious denomination could satisfy the ample spirit of Mr. Clunk. His place of worship was established by his own money and called a Gospel Hall. There three times on Sundays and once in the week Mrs. Clunk played the harmonium and Mr. Clunk preached the Larger Hope, when business allowed.

The offices of Clunk and Clunk filled an old house in Covent Garden. Mr. Clunk climbed the stairs humming:

> *"There are lonely hearts to cherish*
> *While the days are going by;*
> *There are weary souls who perish*
> *While the days are going by."*

His room was a dark and silent chamber at the back, in red rep and mahogany and Brussels carpet. A gilt clock in a glass house held the middle of the white marble mantelpiece and on either side in a glass case a stuffed canary perched on artificial vegetation.

Mr. Clunk moved each of them with affectionate care a quarter of an inch, contemplated the result, sat down at his table, and rang the bell and asked his clerk for the Walker papers.

"Yes, sir. There's a young gentleman asking to see you. That Mr. Wisberry."

Mr. Clunk took the card and read, "Mr. Antony Wisberry, St. Jude's College, Cambridge," and smiled. "Dear me, yes. I'll see him at once, Jenks." He tapped his false teeth.

A large, fair youth was brought him. "My dear boy, my dear Tony! It is nice of you to come," Mr. Clunk gushed. "I am so glad to see you again."

"How are you, sir?" said Tony with less enthusiasm.

"Now sit down and tell me all your news. Have you been able to decide on anything yet?"

"I've got that job in the Rimington laboratories. Start in September."

"My dear boy, I am so glad!" Mr. Clunk rubbed his hands. "That is nice! Just when you finish at college, you step right into a good situation. With that firm you're provided for for life."

"I don't know about life. The job's all right, and I'll have a chance of doing research work. That's what I want."

"Ah, yes. You always were a worker, Tony. No joy like work, is there? But I do like to see a young man established with a settled income. It gives him a foundation, it helps him to be a good Christian, Tony. Your dear mother was so anxious you should settle to something at once. She will be happy, very happy."

Tony squirmed and looked away from Mr. Clunk's shiny face. "Well, I didn't come to talk about that," he said gruffly. "This vac. I've been going through the papers and things from the old house. Good lot o' stuff."

Mr. Clunk nodded. "I suppose so. There would be. Naturally."

"There was a pile of my father's things—notebooks and so on."

"Ah, yes. Your dear mother kept everything, no doubt. Very interesting for you." But not, Mr. Clunk's manner suggested, for him.

"It was interesting," said Tony with emphasis. "Do you know what my father was working at before he died?"

Mr. Clunk blinked in mild surprise. "Certainly— of course—but you must have been told often. He was a lecturer in the Technical Institute at Birmingham— lecturer in chemistry."

"I know that. I mean what research he was doing himself."

Mr. Clunk's large eyes opened wider. "Really, I couldn't say. I never heard anything about it. I shouldn't have understood if I had. I'm not scientific, you see."

"Well, he'd worked out a process for making hard steel with vanadium."

"Dear me!" said Mr. Clunk. "Is that important— a new discovery?"

"It's important enough. It isn't new now. But he'd worked it out more than twenty years ago."

"Of course. Yes, that would be so. It is twenty-one years this spring since your dear mother was left a widow." Mr. Clunk sighed sympathetically. "You were such a small baby, Tony."

Tony was not attracted to that phase of himself. "Don't you see," he said sharply, "it's the date that matters. He'd worked out a vanadium process by 1908, when nobody else had got one."

"I suppose it would have been valuable then?" said Mr. Clunk sadly.

"Valuable! Pots of money in it."

"But not now?"

"Now—oh, there's other ways now. Everybody's doing it."

"How unfortunate!" Mr. Clunk tapped his teeth. "Dear me, yes, how unfortunate he died then," and he shook his head and looked at Tony with bland sympathy.

"Yes, it was. Look here, the process which he'd worked out is the one that Garstons have been using for their high-speed steel. They've improved it now. But they used his way for years."

"Garstons?" Mr. Clunk repeated. "I'm afraid I don't know much about the steel trade, Tony. Is it a large firm?"

"Garston & Garston. They do about everything you can do with iron and steel. Huge concern. Lord Croyland is the head of it."

"Dear me, yes. Lord Croyland. He was Sir Henry Garston. Oh, a very wealthy man, I'm told."

"He would be," said Tony with contempt. "Millions out of the war, I suppose. And pretty thrivin' before. Well, that's how it is—Garstons had their vanadium steel on the market first about 1910, and the process they used was just the same as my father had worked out before he died in 1908, and they went on manufacturin' by that process till a few years ago. What do you think about that, Mr. Clunk?"

Mr. Clunk laughed vaguely. "My dear boy, really, I don't think, so to speak. I'm not qualified to give an opinion. Are you quite sure of your facts?"

"Yes, that's a fair question," Tony frowned. "It isn't my line, of course. I'm electro-chemistry. But there's no doubt. I've shown his notes to other fellows, and they said at once it was the Garston process."

"Dear me," said Mr. Clunk. "That is curious. But I should suppose the explanation might be that the Garston firm worked out the invention with their own chemists. They're always experimenting, aren't they, these big firms? You're going to do it yourself, Tony, for Rimingtons."

"Of course they might have got on to a process. Everybody was trying for hard steel. And there's more than one kind. But it's a jolly queer thing they should happen to hit on just the one my father had found just after his death."

"I see your point." Mr. Clunk looked at his hands. "Naturally you would think so." He opened a drawer and took out a bottle of sweets. "Will you have a fruit drop?" Tony waved them away. "I like them myself." Mr. Clunk giggled. "Just a boy still, you see." He sucked. "I think I've heard that when inventions are in the air, as you might say, a lot of people have the same ideas. It was like that with steam engines, wasn't it?—and electric light and motor cars."

"I know," Tony growled. "Of course you can say that." He stopped. He stared with concentrated attention at Mr. Clunk. "Have you any idea how my father died?"

"My dear boy," said Mr. Clunk quickly, "I never knew your father."

Tony grunted. "That was pretty queer too, wasn't it, the way he died—if he did die?"

"Really, I don't think there can be any doubt about that now," said Mr. Clunk, in a tone of consolation.

Tony frowned. "Look here—do you mind tellin' me just what you heard about it at the time?"

"Not in the least. It's very natural you should be interested." Mr. Clunk settled into his chair more comfortably. "I'm afraid I have practically nothing to tell you. You must have heard all there is to hear from your dear mother."

"She told me about it, of course, as soon as I was old enough to understand. All she said was that my father had gone away when I was a baby and disappeared. She couldn't think what had happened to him but he must have had an accident and been killed. I never bothered about it—it was pretty remote, you know—and she'd given up worrying. But now I've gone over his papers, it looks to me a very queer business."

"Did you find anything which bears on it?" said Mr. Clunk with interest. "Anything personal, I mean? Anything about his intentions?"

"No, I didn't," Tony snapped. "That's a bit odd too. Nothing but the notes of his work."

"What a pity," said Mr. Clunk. "You see, I can really give you no information about him. Now let me begin at the beginning. My acquaintance was with your mother and her family. We were neighbours in Highbury. Her father was one of my father's clients. The first I heard of Mr. Antony Wisberry was the news of your mother's engagement to him. She met him on a holiday at Llandudno, I think. He was already teaching in Birmingham. My recollection is that I was not present at their wedding. She went to live in Birmingham and for some time I lost sight of her. We met again in the settlement of affairs when her father and mother died. She was an only child. I remember thinking that she seemed happy in her marriage. She went back to Birmingham and I heard of your birth. When I saw her next, she came to this office in great distress to tell me that her husband had disappeared and ask for my advice. Her statement was that he had been in the habit of going away from time to time, giving her no explanation except that it was on business; on this occasion he had gone as usual and failed to return and she did not know where to look for him. The police of course were informed and failed to trace him; I made a number of inquiries myself and could get no information of any use. It seemed to me that your father had confided very little about himself to anyone. Well, as you know, he was never seen again and after a number of years the Court of Chancery allowed us to presume his death. That is the whole story, Tony."

"And what do you suppose happened to him?" Tony said sharply.

"My dear boy, I can only tell you, as your dear mother told you, that he must have met with an accident."

"Or foul play."

Mr. Clunk shook his head, Mr. Clunk smiled the pitying smile of mature wisdom. "Ah, Tony, Tony, don't get that into your mind. Whenever there's an unexplained disappearance, some of the bereaved always want to think there's been foul play. Believe me, it isn't true, not once in a thousand times. But once people get the idea, it runs away with them and makes their lives miserable with suspicions and brooding and bad blood. I've seen it so often, my dear boy. Don't you go that way. Take it like a reasonable fellow. It was a sad business for your poor mother, but she learned to forget it and was happy. You can't hope to find out after twenty years what actually happened to him. But you have no ground whatever for supposing foul play, no evidence of any enemies, no motive for crime."

"Isn't there?" Tony snapped. "He had this process which was worth a hatful of money—and Garstons began to work it as soon as he was out of the way."

Mr. Clunk groaned faintly. "I was afraid you were

thinking of it on those lines. Dear me, how many foolish people have said things like that to me in this room! I can only tell you, it doesn't happen. Think, my dear boy. Great firms don't murder inventors. It isn't worth their while. They prefer to swindle 'em. That is quite easy and legal."

Tony was for a moment impressed. Then his jaw hardened and he attacked again. "What do you want me to believe, then? That he died by accident somehow?"

Mr. Clunk sat up. "Tony, my friend," he said, with a sharp, contemptuous authority. "you can take it I gave the case some thought. I had a regard for your mother. I suppose you've heard that I know something about crime. Well, I tell you the only reasonable explanation of your father's disappearance that I could ever see was accident."

"And that isn't reasonable, is it?" said Tony. "Suppose he was run over—killed on the railway—drowned somehow—his body would be found, his baggage would be left about——"

"Dear me, no. Not necessarily," Mr. Clunk interrupted. "Suppose he fell overboard from a steamer at night crossing the Channel or the North Sea. It would be easily possible no one would notice the accident. And as for his baggage—my dear boy, baggage without an owner vanishes quickly and completely. When you know the world a little better, you'll see there is nothing strange in his disappearance."

The stubborn look of Tony's face—he had a considerable jaw—became less agreeable. "Lots of people you know vanish, what?" he said. "You get used to explainin' how it happened. All right. Don't mind me. Now, when you came to gather up what he left, how much was it?"

"My dear Tony," said Mr. Clunk patiently, "I sent

you not only my accounts as your mother's executor, but a full statement of her affairs. If you care to look at it, you will find that the estate left to you consists of what she inherited from her own family with the addition of what your father left. She never spent any of her capital. She always lived within her income. If I may say so, you should be grateful for her care of your interests."

Tony flushed. "Thanks very much. I am thinking about her. I don't know how she did it."

"My boy," said Mr. Clunk with emotion, "there was nothing which that dear woman would not have done for you."

"Yes, I knew my mother. Look here. My father left something under a thousand. Forty pounds a year as it was invested. She had only about two hundred a year of her own. We haven't been living on an income of two fifty. There was a good deal more came from somewhere."

"Oh, certainly," Mr. Clunk smiled. "Your education was a heavy expense, of course. From time to time, I was able to find temporary use for her capital at a high rate of interest which eased the burden. You owe me nothing, Tony. There is no obligation whatever. It was merely a matter of opportunities which offered in business. I was very glad to serve her."

Tony frowned. "That's the explanation of that, is it? Thanks. After my father's death there was money coming which doubled her income or so out of opportunities in your business. But the capital stayed the same. Well, I'm much obliged to you, aren't I?" He stood up.

"Not at all," Mr. Clunk rose also, "not in the least. It was the smallest service. And I had a great respect for your mother. You needn't bear me a grudge. I've really done nothing for you. Must you go now? Well, I've been so glad to see you. If there should be anything that I can help you to clear up, believe me, it will be the greatest pleasure. I'm always here, Tony, always here."

Tony looked at him with frank dislike. "All right," he said. "I'll remember you. Good-bye."

"Good-bye," said Mr. Clunk heartily, "good-bye. Ah, just a minute. Where will you be going now? I'd better have your address."

Tony grinned. "I shall be going to talk to Garston & Garston."

"Oh, really?" Mr. Clunk's tone was dry and contemptuous. "I shouldn't advise that."

"No, you wouldn't. That's one reason I'm going," said Tony, and went.

Mr. Clunk made little noises to himself and slowly fumbled and conveyed another fruit drop to his mouth. Jenks, the clerk, appeared with a folder. "The Walker papers, sir."

"Not now," said Mr. Clunk. "Bring me the Wisberry box." . . .

His home was a house of Victorian Gothic in yellow brick on the rural side of Highgate. Mrs. Clunk used to sit by the Elizabethan window of the drawing room and watch for his return. She noticed that he was a little late that night. Their evening meal was a high tea. He ate negligently, though she had steak pie and trifle for him and he was fond of both. But she asked no questions. She made a long story of Cook's leaving the Salvation Army and the four canaries sang to him from the four windows. "Just another cup, my dearie," said Mr. Clunk, having drunk five. "I don't mind how strong it is."

"You've such a head, Joshua," said she.

Mr. Clunk beamed at her, collected some small lumps

of sugar, and bestowed one on each canary and came back to his strong tea.

Mrs. Clunk judged that the moment for confidences had been reached. "Anything new at the office, dearest?"

"No, nothing new, dearie," said Mr. Clunk with deliberation. "Young Wisberry came in. He was asking where his mother got her money from. Rather tiresome of him."

"He might be satisfied, I'm sure," Mrs. Clunk was indignant. "He's a bit above himself, that young man. I always thought it was a pity his mother would give him such a education. Puts ideas in their heads. They want the earth, these college young men."

"That's about his measure, Maria," Mr. Clunk agreed. "Ah, well, he'll have to learn he won't get it. But we mustn't be hard on him, mustn't be hard." He chirruped to the canaries and made them sing again, and listened to them with his arm round his wife. "Come along, my dearie." He took her into the drawing room humming:

> Going by! Going by!
> Going by! Going by!
> Oh, the good we all may do.
> While the days are going by."

And Mrs. Clunk sat down to the piano and played hymns to him while he sucked peppermint lozenges and occasionally, with some thickness of articulation, sang a favourite verse.

CHAPTER II

SECRETARY AND NURSE

IT SEEMS to have been the next day but one that May Dean walked up Beachy Head. She was coming to the end of her holiday and she wanted to prove that she had recovered strength enough for something mildly strenuous.

She was a slight girl and her fairness and her small features gave her, to her disgust, a look of fragility. But she was by nature as strong as other people. In power of muscle stronger than most girls, her school would have said, and her long, capable hands suggested that she had the habit of using strength. To some force of will her bearing, her proud eyes bore witness. She climbed to the top of the headland and was a little flushed and short of breath, but would not sit down, stood facing the dark sea and the southerly wind that blew the skirt up from her knees and pressed her coat back on her slim straight body. She took her hat off and let the wind toss her yellow hair.

"Well!" she said, compressing into it regret, anger, determination. "Get on!" She turned and strode down the hill.

She did not want to leave the sea, to look at it made her feel weaker and invent excuses for staying, but she had to go. She could not do nothing for ever on sixpence a week. Back to the treadmill—if a treadmill could be found.

When she left school, being compelled to earn a living, she was sure she wanted to be a nurse. She had no great ability for anything else. The other trades taken by the girls she knew—teaching, the civil service, office work—seemed to her dust and ashes. You could feel like a woman if you were a nurse: nursing was really rather splendid: you would be so wonderful to the poor people and they would adore you. This faith carried her through some part of her hospital training, and when it failed under the ordinary realities pride told her she must go on. She learned to like the work well enough, but not enough to stay in the hospital. She wanted to be herself, not one of a regiment: she wanted to nurse in order to be somebody, not for the sake of nursing.

So she took a place on the staff of a nursing home and there was worked to the bone till she went down with pneumonia. In the first feebleness of convalescence a good Samaritan found her, an old schoolfellow who had taken it into her head to look up May Dean after years. Gladys Hurst was of those who always flourish, a large jovial damsel, everybody's friend and very shrewdly her own. At school she had been to May a little more than she was to others, but the lady's affections were not taken seriously. She came to the convalescent with eager friendship, shocked at her weakness, abusing the people who had worked her to death, ordering her to be off for a good holiday, refusing to admit difficulties, and met the confession of poverty by declaring she had money to burn. May's pride was coaxed into borrowing as little as could be stretched to cover a month by the sea.

The month was near its end and beyond it there was nothing certain. Body and mind shrank from the prospect of another post in nursing home or hospital. She did not feel strong enough, overwork had made her hate the routine and the servitude. But she could not think of anything else at which she would be worth a living wage, and wages had to be found.

She came down to the sea front of the town making dreary resolutions. From one of the seats Gladys Hurst sprang up to meet her. "Hullo, baby! Here we are again. Your landlady told me you were strolling by the sad sea waves. How's things?"

"I'm all right." May flushed. Gladys's shrewd eyes were looking her over too carefully. "Thanks awfully. I'm ever so much better, really."

"You have got a bit more vim. Not so much like the ghost of an angel," Gladys laughed. "Well, what about a spot of lunch?"

"Oh yes. Do come to my rooms," said May uncomfortably, knowing she had not enough lunch for two, nor anything fit for Gladys.

"Oh no. You come along to my pub. It's not so bad." Gladys linked arms with her. They made, as male eyes remarked, a striking pair. Gladys was of ample design, and her smart clothes proclaimed it; she was dark and florid, and the art that emphasized her eyes and her lips did not conceal itself. The pale natural colours, the straight, slim shape of May Dean set her off and were more vividly seen against her. She was quite aware of it. She looked down at May with a complacent smile. "We do go together, don't we, baby? Well, it's jolly nice to see you fit again."

"Awfully kind of you to come down," said May.

"My old man gave me a week-end, so I thought I'd put in the time looking you up. I rather like you, you know. And you gave me a bit of a turn when I found you in your little bed." She pressed May's arm and the pressure was returned.

"I don't know how I should have got on without you," said May.

"That's all right. You'd had a pretty rotten time, hadn't you? Forget it. Now then, here we are." She swept May into a hotel which, to eyes without experience of the inside of any, seemed of golden luxury. The lunch also was alarming. A cocktail could be refused, but not the wine, a simple-looking yellow wine which Gladys promised her was innocent as mother's milk and really tasted like nice grapes and yet had a subtle, disconcerting power of excitement. But the food made one want it, the food was so rich and had strange flavours that allured, even when one knew what the things were.

"Like it, baby?" Gladys smiled over a sweetbread to which the cook had added much.

"It's awfully good," said May. "I've never been to a place like this before."

"Not a bad pub. Bit of the silent tomb." Gladys looked round the other heavily respectable guests. "But they do you all right, if you stir 'em up." She contemplated the menu, which was not the menu of the hotel's ordinary lunch, with an author's approval. "I always reckon to have a good time when I get off. That's one thing about my old man, the money's all right. I give you my word. So it ought to be. He's the big noise in Garstons, you know."

May laughed. She was delightfully happy but a little dazed. "No, I don't, Gladys. What is Garstons?"

"Oh, baby!" Gladys chuckled. "What isn't it? I don't know and I know a bit and then some. Garston & Garston. Iron and steel. Put the stuff in one end as ore and take it out at the other as motor cars. Anything from a needle to a battleship—at one factory or another. And we've got about a dozen, one way and another. Sometimes I think the old man don't know what he has got. Garstons was pretty vast when he started in, but he's grabbed a lot of other firms and worked 'em into the concern. One of these men that always wants to get hold of a business and play about with it himself."

"Oh, I see," said May, trying to be intelligent. "I mean, I know the sort of thing. But it sounds very complicated and difficult. To work at, I mean. What do you do, Gladys?" A mind which thought in a golden haze tried to imagine her friend Gladys, who really had been a girl at school with her, managing steel factories.

"Me? Oh, I don't touch the business work. Personal and confidential, that's me. The old man has a batch of secretary birds of course, but the others are men. They run the manufacturing and financial. But he likes to have a woman round him for the personal touch. That's how I got in. Started in the secretary office, shorthand typist. And the old man took to Gladys." She made eyes at May in an expert manner and laughed. "He's a machine, but he's got to have a private life, poor old thing, and I run it. Not such a bad job. He knows when he's well off."

"I'm sure he is," said May. "Of course he'd like you. You always got on so well with people. It must be very interesting. I suppose he's a sort of millionaire. You must have a lot of responsibility."

"Not so jolly interesting. He isn't a gay bird. There's money to burn, of course. Plenty of responsibility. He leaves things to me. And there are some snags about. Not a soft job, being the Lord Croyland. But I'm pretty efficient, baby."

"I'm sure you are," said May, with round admiring eyes. "But I thought you said his name was Garston."

"Henry Garston, first Lord Croyland. For public services. In making a pile out of the war," Gladys laughed. "Well, what about a spot of coffee? Come into the lounge. Looks like a railway station turned into a conservatory, so they call it the palm court."

May was conducted, glad of the affectionate arm, to a gloomily comfortable corner.

"There we are. I say, I've talked a mouthful, and all about me. I came to hear about you, baby. How's things?"

"I'm perfectly all right now."

"Fit for anything, eh? You haven't put on much weight."

"Oh, I have. I never was fat, you know."

"You were not," said Gladys grimly. "Not much of any kind of fat in your job, baby."

"I don't know, it's not so bad. You do feel you're doing something some good." The coffee came. She was urged to drink a liqueur and earnestly refused.

"All right, all right." Gladys was amused. "Keep that schoolgirl complexion. So you like nursing, do you? My Lord! I always wonder how women can stick it. I wasn't born good, baby."

"It isn't being good," said May. The coffee made things clearer. "Just a job like other jobs. But it's my job."

"Yes, there's that," Gladys nodded. "I used to think business would bore me stiff. Wanted to go on the stage or something. Me for the gay life! I don't think. Now I like managing Old Man Croyland's things. It's my job, as you say. Well, what are you going to do now? Found anything to go back to?"

"Not yet. I don't quite know what I'd better do."

"Not so easy, eh?" Gladys lay back and inhaled her cigarette. "I suppose you've got to do something."

"Oh, yes, rather," said May quickly.

"Good jobs take a bit of finding in your line? They do for everybody." Gladys meditated. "You're not up to much roughing it, you know. That must have been a hell of a place you were in before."

"I shall be all right. I'm quite strong really."

"You ought to go easy." Gladys frowned. "I say—do you care for a private job?"

"Well, it depends——"

"I know. You wouldn't want to tie yourself. Might do for a bit, eh? Something to carry on with."

"Oh yes, I shouldn't mind, if it was with decent people. But what did you mean? Looking after an invalid?"

"Well, it just came into my head you might do for old Mrs. Garston. Lord Croyland's mother, you know. He's getting a bit nervous about her. She isn't an invalid but she's oldish now, something over seventy, and he wants her to have a nurse handy. How's that strike you, baby? The old lady lives at Bradstock Abbey. Ever seen it? One of England's historic mansions. Page in the picture papers now and then. If there's a shortage of bathing beauties. Ancestral home of the Garstons. They bought it by auction when Mother was a girl: as soon as they'd got money enough to be gentlemen and start a family. But it's some place, believe me. Looks like the home of ancient dukes. Kind of mixture of a castle and a cathedral with ruins complete. And central heating and running water and all the comforts. Well, Croyland thinks the old lady's getting a bit dithery and——"

"Oh, I shouldn't like a mental case, Gladys," May cried.

"Lord, she's not that kind. Nothing like it. Just old and getting weak. Crowds of servants, of course. But Croyland's idea is he'd like to have somebody who knew a bit about illness to look after her. Lady nurse is about the ticket. We haven't got on to anybody who suits.

Seen a few—ladies that aren't nurses and nurses that aren't ladies, the old man says. I hadn't thought of you, as you were down and out. But you're just the article, if you care about it. What do you think?"

"I don't know. I've never done anything like it."

"A good job, believe me. You'd be very cosy at Bradstock. A bit quiet, of course. Peace, perfect peace. But it's a lovely old place and run jolly well. Croyland will pay, you know, I'd see to that."

"You're awfully kind. I wasn't thinking about the money, Gladys. It's Mrs. Garston that matters, you see. I don't know at all what she's like, and if she didn't like me, it wouldn't do at all."

"You'd get on all right," Gladys smiled. "She's a little old thing, shy and old-fashioned. Just like you, baby. If you ask me, I should say she just wants company. Somebody to prattle to. She's lonely down there. Croyland only runs down week-ends and so on and she don't see anybody else much. There's no family, you know. Croyland's never married and he's her only son— the other one died ages ago. She feels being alone in the world now she's getting on. Mopes a bit. You'd have to see she looks after herself and keep her cheery. That's what it comes to. Like to have a try? You can always chuck it."

"I think I might like it," said Mary. "But of course it would be for Mrs. Garston to say. It would be impossible if she didn't care about me."

"Don't you worry. I bet she'll fall for you. Look here, you'd better come up to town and see Croyland. I'll fix it."

"Oh, thanks awfully. You are kind to me, Gladys."

"Not much," Gladys laughed. "It's just business. My job. I say, how's the money going, baby?"

"I've got plenty, really."

"All right, all right. Be proud. Well, I'll let you know. You can come any time, can't you?"

"Oh yes. I want to settle something."

Gladys nodded. Gladys stood up. "Righto then. Bye-bye, baby. See you soon."

A little excited, a little dazed, but not now with the wine of Château Climens, May went back to her lodgings.

In the palm court, a thick-set man with an emphatic waist and a flower in his jacket lounged across to Gladys Hurst.

"Nice bit o' bread and butter," he said.

"Sweet kid, isn't she?"

"She ought to do, if she'll do it."

"She'll do it all right," Gladys smiled.

"Good! Sooner the better." He turned away.

CHAPTER III

WARNING TO TONY

On a Cambridge first floor Tony Wisberry sat and smoked a large, foul pipe. The uncertain date must have been about a week later.

A man of much the same age but far more sedate appearance came in. Wyburn was already fellow and lecturer of his college and rather well aware of it. The room, too tidy for Tony's tweeds and sprawl, was his. But he was hospitable. "Hallo, Wisberry. Good fellow. Are you staying?"

"Only for what I can get."

Wyburn sat down. "Well, I'm sorry. I'm afraid that isn't much. I've had an answer from Masters. He says he doesn't know anyone who was in the Garston laboratories when their vanadium process was first brought into use, but it's generally understood that it was worked out by one of the Garston family—a brother of the present head of the firm."

"That's Lord Croyland. I didn't know he had a brother."

"He hasn't now. The brother died a good while ago."

"How convenient!" Tony grunted. "But how interesting."

"What's your point?"

"Quite obvious, old thing. The origin of the vanadium process is officially ascribed to somebody who can't be asked anything about it. The inference is that Garstons have got something to hide."

"You suffer from the fixed idea. There really was a brother——"

"Fancy!"

"Don't be an infant. And he was the sort of fellow who might have hit on it. He was a Cambridge man, up at Trinity about 1900. He read science and didn't stay. I gather he was unstable. But some people thought a good deal of him. When he went down his father put him into the firm. He preferred laboratories when he did anything—an odd creature with flashes of talent—and he died young." Wyburn lit a cigarette. "There you are. To my mind it explains the whole thing."

Tony put out his lower lip. "Old Man Clunk?" he inquired. "Do you happen to think it explains Old Man Clunk, George? Why was Old Man Clunk anxious to persuade me everything in the garden was lovely? What would it matter to Old Man Clunk if I tried to find out where Father went to? Why did Old Man Clunk want to persuade me I mustn't ask Garston how they got their process? And what made Old Man Clunk pay my mother double her right income? He's no giddy philanthropist."

"I agree you seem to have got a queer solicitor," said Wyburn. "One doesn't expect to hear a man complaining that the family solicitor has paid them more than the estate could produce. It's generally the other way. But Clunk had his explanation, you said."

"I should smile. Old Man Clunk as the fairy godfather! Look here. I've been asking about Clunk & Clunk in town, and their reputation is a stinker. If you've been doing the dirty on anyone, you go to Clunk & Clunk and they wangle you off. If you want to, you ring up Clunk & Clunk and they show you how. That's what the other law birds say."

"Well, I suppose that's the ordinary work of a solicitor in criminal practice."

"Criminal practice is right, George," Tony grinned. "And who would you say was the criminal that practised on my father?"

Wyburn shook his head. "No, no, I can't take it like that. Don't you see, you're not giving your mind a chance. You have a string of strange circumstances. You leap to the explanation there has been foul play, and that becomes a fixed idea. But really it explains nothing. Take the facts—your father's mysterious disappearance, the coincidence that he had worked out a process the same as that subsequently used by Garstons, which they attribute to one of the firm who is dead, and finally the generosity of Clunk to your mother. Now assume foul play. What exactly does that mean? Somebody murdered your father and sold his discovery to Garstons. But how could it be worth anyone's while to run the risk? You know very well the value of the process must have been doubtful till it had been tried on a commercial scale. That a great firm such as Garstons should desire your father's murder is preposterous. The process was no doubt profitable, but only a minor part of their business. They would have acquired it on their own terms or let it go."

"Yes, George. Old Man Clunk said that."

"But you know it's common sense, my friend. Do you suppose Clunk contrived your father's murder in order to sell the process for himself? But then it would have been his first elementary precaution to destroy any trace of it in your father's papers. He could have done that with perfect ease. Your mother entrusted him with the investigation of your father's disappearance. Naturally he would look at all private papers. It is quite incredible that if he was concerned in stealing the process he should have left the notes of it for you to find."

"I've thought about that, you know," said Tony. "The answer is, he didn't destroy the notebooks because he didn't know about 'em. They were stowed away in a box of odds and ends, my own kiddy stuff and such. I found extraordinary few of my father's papers otherwise. You might think he hadn't had any private life. That's another of the queer things, George. I should say Old Man Clunk took his precautions all right."

"My dear fellow, this is the fixed idea preferring a difficult explanation. Why should Clunk choose to be unnecessarily generous to your mother if he had anything to hide? Clearly it attracts attention to him. If you work out the theory of foul play rationally you find that, applied to one fact after another, it does not solve the problem, it makes new difficulties. But accept the obvious explanations, that the process was discovered by two people separately, as often happens, that your father did disappear by accident, and that Clunk wished to help your mother in her widowhood, both quite natural possibilities, and there is no mystery."

"No. Accept the amazin' as normal and nothing's mysterious. Quite so, George. But why did Old Man Clunk sweat to keep me quiet?"

"I want to keep you quiet," said Wyburn. "Because this sort of obsession wastes a man's brain away."

"Thank you kindly. That also is what Clunk said. No, you're a good chap, George. But Old Man Clunk isn't."

"You've formed the worst opinion of him," said Wyburn patiently. "Well, you may be right. I can't judge. The only thing certain about his conduct is that he was honest with the family capital. But on the foul-play theory you can make no plausible explanation of the facts."

"I know I can't explain them, George," Tony smiled. "The poor old brains aren't gone to pot yet. I don't say whatever happened was all planned out beforehand. Things don't go like that. Most likely one dirty trick led to another. I don't expect to find it all rational. Murder isn't a rational action. Look here. Say somebody knew my father had got hold of a good thing and passed it on to Garstons and my father cut up rough and was put out of the way. That's possible enough. Say Old Man Clunk had the job of hushing it up. That's in his line. A bit of money to keep my mother going would make Father's disappearance pass off with less noise. Or somebody may have had a sort of half-time conscience. It does happen. Anyway, anyhow, don't you see, I want to know how my father died."

"After twenty years!" said Wyburn with a sigh. "Well, what do you mean to do?"

"I mean to stir up Garstons. I hope I'm going to put the fear of God into my Lord Croyland. But the scalp I want is Old Man Clunk's." His chin came out, a smile twisted one side of his face and his teeth grated on the pipe. He stood up. "Wish me luck, George."

"I don't know what to wish you," Wyburn said, looking into his eyes. "Don't lose yourself in it. If it's taken one man's life—he wouldn't want it to take yours."

"That's all right. I'll watch it," said Tony. "Cheerio." He swung out.

CHAPTER IV

BRADSTOCK ABBEY

BRADSTOCK ABBEY stands near the sea. The small river
Brad, up which still come meritorious salmon, meets
the tide in a large expanse of water, almost landlocked,
over which there is shooting of wild duck. This is called
Bradstock Harbour, though no trade comes there, nor
ever a boat except the small craft of its own fishermen
and the few people who play at sailing on it. The lawns
of Bradstock Abbey slope down to its shore. The Cistercians who founded the Abbey eight hundred years
ago, choosing the place, after their manner, for its
loneliness, built on a limestone knoll in the midst of a
marsh. The marsh has long been dry and fertile ground,
but Bradstock Abbey remains lonely still. Its lands
spread far, from century to century they have been kept
in large farms, and the few villages which serve these
are distant and hidden. The country is gracious; drinking a soft air rich in sunshine, dark pastures and corn-
fields rise in long curves to the northern guard of hills.
All things thrive there opulently, corn and clover, sheep
and cattle; the ground breaks into flowers wherever it
is untilled, its trees grow great, it is full of life—except
the life of men. They have never been fruitful around
Bradstock Harbour.

You may walk the Abbey turf and hear on one side
the screams of the gliding gulls, on the other the chatter
of a rookery. May Dean came through this symphony
and yet felt that the place was deadly quiet. The din on

the air lost itself in the emptiness of great spaces of sunlight; she looked over miles of still water and level land on which no human creature worked or moved. She stood shading her eyes to search the sand's farther shore where a few boats lay, offering a hope of the remote company of a man doing something. But it was denied her. "Oh, heavens," she murmured with a laugh that mocked at herself for feeling forlorn, "it is empty." She turned and walked quickly away.

Where the great church of the Abbey stood is now a wild garden. The walls were long ago a quarry to rebuild the monastery into a house for the display of the wealth of the family of courtiers to which the Abbey lands were given by a generous king. Of the tall nave is left only a range of broken arches hidden deep in ivy, of the glories of the choir nothing but an oblong of black stone which some fancy was the first rude altar when the Cistercians came to the marsh, sacred perhaps before it served Christian faith. Some Eighteenth Century squire of Bradstock with ambitions for the picturesque had the fancy of marking out the plan of the church with hawthorn and lilac and laburnum. Those who came after him enriched and destroyed the design, filling up the spaces in the midst with all manner of free growing flowers.

When May came there the ruins were lost in the colour and fragrance of full spring. She made her way through the wilderness, for it has paths paved with scraps of stone and broken tiles from the church floor. She found the arches of the nave and in the thick wall of one a recess where a level stone, broad and smooth, made a seat.

There she lingered, trying to fancy what the place had looked like when it was a church. That was difficult. The surge of wild growth which overflowed it seemed what

was from the beginning and must be to the end, the
invincible reality. But she wanted her mind to be free
from the power of that, to make a vision of a great
church there and the order of its worship. It would not
come. She looked about her at the broken arches, she
told herself that where she sat must be the base of some
lost shrine or an altar which had heard the prayers of
centuries of faith. But it had no magic for her. No ghost
of a white-robed Cistercian rose before her eyes to bring
back the past.

She walked away to the house. That does not need
imagination to discover what it looked like when it was
the home of the monks. Lawns and a sunken rose garden
dividing it from the church are not now enclosed by their
cloister. But if you keep your eyes from what the Tudor
builders added on either side you may see the front of
the house as the last abbot saw it going out to die, a long
range of mellow stone with great windows, each a group
of lancets rising to a pattern of tracery, and in the middle a square tower. It has an austere dignity—while you
do not look at those blocks on left and right which were
built to be gracefully beautiful.

But you go in at the middle, and May went in to pass
between the abbot's great hall and the chapter house. In
empty, sombre magnificence they loomed like two deso-
late churches. She stood a moment listening. The house
was still and deeply silent. It always was. She had lived
her life in little homes and crowded places; she could not
be rid of the fear that in the silence of the Abbey there
was some menace. She hurried on up a staircase made for
splendid processions and came to a vaulted corridor
dimly lit by lancet windows pierced through the six-
feet thickness of an ancient wall. Here once was the dor-
mitory of the monks. To make the smaller folk of a
rich man's house comfortable, it was parted off into a

row of rooms. Two of them had been given to Miss Dean.

The evolution of the Abbey had made them queer places. Oak panelling and moulded ceilings which went up when Queen Elizabeth was young were warmed by radiators, lit by electric light, and set off by furniture of the dowdiest days of Queen Victoria.

Lord Croyland had ordained that Miss Dean must not wear nurse's uniform, and Gladys provided, vowing it came from him, money for frocks beyond her dreams. She changed from tweeds to silk and went to see if Mrs. Garston had waked from her afternoon nap.

Mrs. Garston's room was in the new part of the Abbey but not far away. The vaulted corridor of the monks led into the dark of a low pointed archway and beyond that was sunlight, a broad gallery of oriel windows and painted ceiling. Mrs. Garston's room, the first of the new part and the finest, was a spacious, stately place of tapestried walls and great windows emblazoned like the ceiling with many coats of arms. The furnishing was Tudor, most conspicuous a house of a four-poster with carved pillars and crimson curtains and a big day bed in golden brocade. By that a table on rubber-tired wheels from some modern shop of invalid apparatus bore many bottles—medicine bottles, mineral-water bottles, table bottles, bottles of scent.

Mrs. Garston sat deep in an armchair which hid her face and her body. Her maid knelt by her, putting on her shoes.

"I hope you had a nice sleep," said May.

"I did not sleep at all," a querulous voice came from the invisible face.

The maid stood up, a tall lean woman of a dark complexion and much iron-gray hair pulled back from her head to make a bulge behind. Her black dress was of an antique fashion which made her flat body seem tight-compressed. "Wide awake when I came in, Nurse," she said sharply, and stared at May.

"That will do, Jones," the high voice complained.

"Ah, you've got one of your headaches." The maid rustled to the table of bottles. "Here's your aromatic. I'll just give you some eau de Cologne to your forehead."

"That will do," the voice repeated. "Go away, Jones."

"Thank you, ma'am." Jones gave May another stare and obeyed.

"Is your head bad, Mrs. Garston?"

"Not worse than usual."

"I hope you haven't been taking anything."

"Nothing does me any good."

"I'm afraid none of those medicines will. Would you like to go down to tea?"

"I was just going down."

Mrs. Garston stood up, revealing herself as a black gown with a pallid face and thin white hair. She seemed to be without shape or substance. But she might have been no smaller than many women if she had stood erect. Her face must have had some beauty before it was shrunken and wrinkled.

"I can manage perfectly well," she said to May's offered arm, but took it and went downstairs slowly, stopping more than once.

The drawing room exhibited yet another phase of the development of Bradstock Abbey. Its windows and its proportions were Elizabethan, but in everything else it realized the ideas of beauty with which the Twentieth Century began, and so had a peculiarly faded aspect.

On a chair in its darkest corner a woman sat working embroidery. "Ah, Fanny," said Mrs. Garston without interest. "Have you been resting?"

"I never rest in the daytime. I don't sleep at night if I do."

"I don't find it makes any difference," said Mrs. Garston.

Fanny rose limply and made a fuss helping to settle her with cushion and footstool. "Are you comfortable, Mrs. Garston?" May asked.

"It will do quite well." The answer was in a tone of resignation. "Oh, you needn't go, need you?"

"I thought you would like to talk to Miss Morrow."

"Tea will be coming," said Mrs. Garston pathetically, and Miss Morrow fussed, removing her embroidery and her bag and her handkerchief to another chair.

She was a tall woman expanding into loose bulk. Twenty years before her face might have been pretty. It was become heavy and dull, expressing nothing but pity for herself. She had brown sentimental eyes. In them was the only deep colour about her, for her hair was ashen and she wore a melancholy gown of lavender and gray which gave its hues to her flaccid face.

The tea came and May ministered to them and tried to talk. She had been out—she had been looking at the ruins—the flowers were glorious but it seemed so strange. She struggled to find words for what she had felt of the overwhelming of the church by that wild life. But it was clear that she was saying nothing which meant anything to them. Yes, she had walked along the harbour. How lonely it was! No one anywhere, not even a boat out on it.

Then she saw Miss Morrow look at Mrs. Garston, and put her handkerchief to her mouth. But Mrs. Garston did not notice that. "Did you say you saw a boat?" she asked eagerly.

"No, I said there wasn't one."

Miss Morrow used the handkerchief for her eyes.

"Oh—oh, I see." Mrs. Garston's voice fell flat. "No, there wouldn't be. There never is now."

May came back to the flowers. That seemed safe at least and she laboured on, talking nonsense. Somebody had to say something or it would be too dismal. But they would not help her. They did not pretend to listen. Miss Morrow took up her embroidery. Mrs. Garston fidgeted and in a little while her plaintive voice cut into May's toiling talk: "Fanny dear, couldn't you play something?"

"If you please," Miss Morrow sighed, and rose heavily and went to fuss at the piano. It took her a long time to begin, and May's yearning to scream or throw the cups about grew almost irresistible, when the silence was broken at last by Mendelssohn at his most sentimental and with some wrong notes.

She set her teeth and tried to shut the wailing out of her mind, bidding it to think why on earth Mrs. Garston wanted the woman to stay with her and why she could want to stay with Mrs. Garston. Neither of them seemed to have the slightest use for the other except as a means to drearier depression.

These mental exercises were interrupted by the arrival of Lord Croyland. He also stopped the piano. Miss Morrow left a languishing movement unfinished and retired with her embroidery to her original dark corner.

Croyland was kissing his mother, in which she gave him no assistance. He asked how she was, and in a tone of plaintive reproof she told him she must not expect to be any better and Fanny was there.

A dreadful perception of the humour of that troubled May, but nobody else saw it. Croyland went solemnly across the room and asked how Fanny was, and Fanny's moaning voice echoed, "How are you?"

He stood between them, making noises in his throat, a man of some height and heavy shoulders from which the head was thrust forward. It had a big brow, an air of sullen determination, and the eyes were wary and seemed to be watching something distant.

"I suppose you want tea," said Mrs. Garston pathetically, and he asked for whisky and soda. It seemed to be another offence. But a gliding butler was already in the room with it. Croyland drank and thought of the existence of May.

"Well, Miss Dean, I hope they've made you comfortable?"

"Quite, thank you."

He sat down and began to talk to his mother about nothing, careful to bring Miss Morrow in. It was difficult, for she stayed in her corner, bent over the embroidery, and his mother gave him no help at all. If they did not intend to make him feel a guilty intruder, they were singularly stupid. May had some sympathy for him—he was a man—but not much. Either he was a saint to stand it or he had a very thick skin, and she did not admire either. But he did not look a saint.

Anyhow, they were making her feel wretchedly uncomfortable and there was no reason why she should stand it. She fled.

As she went back to her room by the gallery in the new building Gladys slid out of one of its doors and seemed surprised. "Hullo, hullo, baby! Where have they put you?"

"Through the archway in the old part. Rather sweet rooms."

"Good for you. Let's have a look." Gladys swept her along, Gladys surveyed bedroom and sitting room with a smile. "Quaint little shop. Dainty and dimity. Just suits you, baby." She kissed May and flopped into a chair and spread her legs. "Well, how's it going? Liking the jolly old place?"

"I don't know. The house is wonderful. But it's so queer to live in. How long have these people had it?"

"The Garstons? Oh, Pa bought it when Ma was a sweet young bride. Some time ago, eh? He did it up modern—spent a pile on it. Croyland's spent lavish too. I don't know why. I believe he hates it. He never wants to be here, and yet he's always blowing back. It's got a hold on him."

"Hates it and loves it," May said. "Yes, I can understand that."

"Can you?" Gladys looked at her sharply. "How did you mean it was queer? Being old? The pair of Westminster Halls and this tunnel place up here and the ruins and all?"

"Partly that, yes. It's queer living where you feel all sorts of things happened."

"I should shay sho," Gladys laughed. "Seen any ghosts, baby?"

"No. There aren't any, are there?"

"Never heard of 'em. You needn't worry."

"I don't. It isn't only the place being old. I've never lived in a big house and with nobody but hosts of servants. It's queer never seeing anyone and feeling they're always about."

"They are—except when you ring," Gladys nodded. "I say, have the servants been nasty?"

"Oh no. They're quite all right. Well, except Mrs. Garston's maid. Of course, she can't bear me. She's jealous."

"Old Jones. Yes, she's an old cat. Don't you mind. She hates everybody. Croyland special," Gladys laughed. "He's frightened of her, poor old thing. How do you get on with the old lady?"

"She is rather a terror. She's quite civil to me, but she has a way of putting me always in the wrong."

"I believe you! Ask Croyland. He can't ever do anything right. Does she talk much, baby?"

"Heavens, no!" May made a face. "She's forgotten how."

"Oh, you ought to get her into it. Do her good. I believe it's bottling herself up makes her so peevish."

"Very likely. I wish you'd tell me how to draw the cork. If I start talking she snubs me and then sits and sighs. It's rather ghastly sometimes. How old is she, Gladys? Seventy something?" Gladys nodded. "She oughtn't to be so feeble. I don't believe there's anything really the matter with her—except the medicines she takes."

"Dope?" Gladys said quickly. "I thought she might."

"No, I didn't mean that. She has some pain-killer drugs but nothing to make a drug habit. It's all sorts of things—a chemist's shop of stuff. She loves dosing herself and I can't stop her."

"I know," Gladys nodded. "She's always fancying she's ill."

"She always seems to be feeling injured. Has she ever had anything dreadful happen to her?"

"Not in my time," said Gladys. "I say, baby, have you got the idea there's something on her mind?"

"Oh yes, rather. I'm sure there is. I've seen people like this before. She believes she's been badly treated, or she's persecuted or something. Most likely it's a delusion. I can see she thinks I'm horrid to her. But there it is— she's sure she's a victim. It is rather queer, you know."

"What do you mean? Have you got on to what's worrying her?"

"Heavens, no. I was thinking of this Miss Morrow. She's been here all this week. Do you know her?"

"Heard of her. What about her?"

"Well, she's just the same. Younger and stronger, of course, but she has Mrs. Garston's complaint badly. She's a sufferer too. She's been badly used and it's a wicked world and nobody understands. Who is she, Gladys?"

"Oh, haven't they said anything about that?"

"They hardly say anything at all. I told you."

Gladys nodded. "It is queer. She was engaged to Mrs. Garston's other son, the young one. He died umpteen years ago. She's still keeping it up, what?" Gladys's smile was unpleasant.

"She comes to mourn with his mother still," May said in a low voice. "Poor things! How did he die, Gladys?"

"Lord, it was long before my time, you know. Suddenly—drowned in the harbour or something."

"So that was what broke them down. Both of them. Oh, it's horrible. Two women's lives all spoilt."

"You think it's that? Maybe." Gladys watched her keenly. "But they never say a word about it?"

"It is that, of course. I remember there were little things. Just now, I was talking about the harbour, and Mrs. Garston asked if I'd seen a boat on it and said no boats ever came now." Gladys made a murmur of interest. "Yes, and the other day I heard Miss Morrow say to her, 'I always have his letters'—something like that. But I thought they were just glooming. Poor things."

"Yes, poor old things," said Gladys briskly. "When's Miss Morrow going? She isn't a little ray of sunshine."

"She's only staying till Monday."

Gladys made a grimace. "That's all we are. Croyland's just come in for her. Hard lines. Well, you want to watch it, baby. Get the old girl to open out a bit.

Do her good." She stood up. "Time to change, isn't it?
Put on something fetching. Croyland wants bucking
up."

May put on the frock which she had intended to put
on. She was without any desire to do what Gladys
wanted. Gladys's tone seemed to her unpleasant in
several ways: hard, vulgar, domineering. But especially
domineering. Gladys had been very kind to her, but it
was absurd Gladys should be giving her orders. No
doubt Gladys thought she was being paid so well it
didn't matter how she was treated. But the place was
hardly endurable. Of course, now she knew about Mrs.
Garston's son, she could understand the poor woman,
she was very sorry for her. But that wasn't going to
make it pleasant living there unwanted, disliked, found
fault with all the time. If Gladys was going to come
down and tell her how to do her job, it would be impossible. And then ordering her to dress up and be bright
to please that lump Croyland—ugh! She dressed in
angry speed and so, having gone to attend on Mrs.
Garston and been rejected, arrived in the drawing
room before anyone else.

Next came Croyland. But her disgusted determination to show no interest in him was unnecessary. He
admitted by a nod that he had seen her and ignored her
existence, standing by the fire and clearing his throat.
Miss Morrow brought Mrs. Garston and he became
articulate, but without help. He stood over them making small talk while they looked anywhere but at him.
Last and late came Gladys, her high-coloured opulence
displayed in a yellow dress of some daring. She was not
repressed by any consciousness of discomfort. She swept
into Croyland's slow speech with ready chattering
answers that led him on to something like fluency.

But it was an awkward dinner. Gladys could keep

talk going, and May, being out of humour with her, was persuaded to admire her tact and help her. Her manner was respectful to the old lady, amiable to Miss Morrow. She was always addressing them and trying to interest them. She treated Croyland with a cheerful familiarity which never forgot that she was only his secretary. She gave May friendly chances to take her share. Yet it did not do. Mrs. Garston and Miss Morrow remained aloof in their gloom and with a disapproval that could be felt. Croyland was inattentive.

When the women went to the drawing room, the atmosphere, May found with incredulous surprise, was less uncomfortable. Gladys worked on nobly and had some response. Mrs. Garston was persuaded to remember Queen Victoria, Miss Morrow had heard Patti—or was it Albani?—sing "Home Sweet Home." Eyes were moist. The tact of Gladys became more admirable than ever.

But the expansive moments ended when Croyland came in. He stood at the door, as though the sound of his mother's voice frightened him, and at the sight of him she was silent.

Gladys turned with a bright smile. "Mrs. Garston was just telling us about Queen Victoria's funeral," she explained. "It must have been tremendously impressive."

"Quite. Yes, quite," he grunted.

Gladys turned back to Mrs. Garston, all eager interest. "Do tell us."

But Mrs. Garston was looking beyond her at Croyland. "You were there," she said, as if the funeral were his fault. "You and your poor father—and Alfred."

"I remember it." Croyland cleared his throat and Mrs. Garston wiped her eyes.

"All the family," said Gladys. "How interesting!

Where did you see it from?" But Mrs. Garston shook her head.

"Yes. A long while ago. Yes." Croyland moved round the room. "What about some whist? Would you like a game of whist, Mother?"

"Oh no," said Mrs. Garston faintly.

"I couldn't really," said Miss Morrow.

Then Gladys announced with a smile for Croyland that she must go and do some work.

Croyland sat down by his mother and began a painful struggle to keep on talking. May did her best for him. The man was wholly unattractive, but his efforts were pathetic. He might be a brute, which he looked, but he was at least trying to behave decently and the two women treated him as if his presence was an outrage. They might be half mad with brooding on their bereavement, but why should they turn their bitterness against him? She found herself beginning to like him, he was so gentle with them, and then, in repugnance at his patience under the intolerable, despising him.

In her sternest nurse's manner she told Mrs. Garston that she must not sit up any longer.

"Oh, really?" the high voice complained. "It makes no matter when I go to bed. I never sleep till morning."

"How dreadful, dear," Miss Morrow sighed. "I always wake up in the small hours."

"Then you had better go to bed too," May told her.

"Quite," Croyland grunted, "quite. Good-night, Mother." He kissed a cheek which turned away from him. "You must do what Miss Dean says, you know! Good-night, Fanny."

"Really!" Mrs. Garston lamented, but Fanny led her away.

It was a long affair putting her to bed. Miss Morrow came into the room and could not bear to go away; she

kept Jones, who was officious, fetching and carrying the
needless. To the ministrations of May she opposed a
limp resistance—everything was unnecessary, everything
was done wrong, each suggestion was cruel, but she
could only endure. May was not of those who bear
patiently being put in the wrong when they are trying
to do right. She departed from Mrs. Garston hot and
furious.

Back in her own room, she began to undress with a
certain violence. The door opened and Gladys lounged
in. "Hallo, baby. Breaking up the happy home?"

"I should like to," said May vehemently.

Gladys dropped into an easy chair and swung her legs
over the arm. She was in a kimono of vivid orange.

"Old lady got on your nerves?" she inquired. "Has
she been saying anything?"

"Oh dear, no! Nothing. She's only a martyr and I'm
a brute. That's all."

"Poor old girl," said Gladys, leaving vague whom she
meant. "Sent 'em to bed bright and early, didn't you?"

"It doesn't matter to you. You ran away soon
enough."

"Sorry, baby. Not my job to look after her, you
know. What happened? Anything go wrong?"

"Oh no. Only everything."

"Not a row?"

"Dear me, no," May laughed bitterly. "We don't
have rows here. We only make everybody hate themselves." She wrapped herself in a dressing gown and
sat down and lit a cigarette. "I'm sorry, Gladys. It's a
shame to fly out at you. But I don't think I could stand
many evenings like this."

"Worse than usual, was it?"

"Oh heavens, yes, far worse. Mrs. Garston wasn't
so bad alone—only dismal. But Miss Morrow's made her

resentful and reproachful. And with Lord Croyland they're both perfectly ghastly. After you went, I couldn't bear it. Gladys, what is it about him? What have they got against him? Why treat him as if he was loathsome? What's he done?"

"I say—you're laying it on thick, baby"; but Gladys was much interested.

"I'm not. But you must have seen it yourself. They can't endure him, and it's a sort of alliance between them to make him feel a worm."

"I wouldn't have said it was bad as that," Gladys said thoughtfully. "Mother doesn't like him, of course. I've not seen much of him with the Morrow. They were both down on him to-night, eh? Anything said?"

"They don't say anything. They just loathe. What has he done to them?"

"Lord, I don't know, baby." Gladys shrugged. "I suppose it's just his being alive while the other one's dead. The one they liked. That's his crime. Don't you worry. Croyland's a tough old sport."

"Nice people to live with, aren't they?"

"Cheerio. We're all going on Monday, except the old girl. When you've got her to yourself, you'll have her eating out of your hand. You have a way with you, baby. She'll love you, poor old thing. Nighty, nighty. Be good." Gladys passed away into the shadows of the corridor.

But May was left feeling that she did not want any-one to love her.

CHAPTER V

MISS MORROW'S JEWEL CASE

MISS MORROW had no home. She came to one of the old families of Sandshire, the county of Bradstock Abbey, but the house of her birth belonged to her brother, or rather to his children, and she was seldom asked to go there. But she had a sufficient income. She lived, and it was probably the best way she could live, at hotels: during the autumn and winter at a hotel in Bayswater; during the spring and summer at a hotel in Limbay, the seaside town of Sandshire which believes itself to provide the climate of the Riviera with the comfort and the morals of England.

The Victoria Hotel, which was Miss Morrow's residence, was in both those qualities eminent. It might be dingy outside—some have called it the ugliest hotel (a hard saying) on any sea—it might be dull within: but the virtue of the guests and of the cooking and of the beds was of old and just renown. Miss Morrow could feel sure that she would never have to sit near anybody who was not quite nice.

She went back there from Bradstock on Monday and by comparison was almost happy. The regular visits to Mrs. Garston were a dreadful duty which gave satisfaction afterwards in the memory of how it hurt. At the hotel there were old ladies and gentlemen who required nothing of her but an interest in their ailments and the royal family: a restful company. The other people—one did not speak to anybody who had not been there for months—were quietly worthy of the Victoria.

On a day towards the end of the week an unknown woman did speak to her. The fact—in itself disturbing— was for ever stamped upon her mind by the terrible thing which also happened that day. Miss Morrow had been sitting for her regulation half hour after lunch in the drawing room. She was about to go upstairs to prepare for her regulation walk when a woman, making apologies, asked her if she knew of a doctor in Limbay. Miss Morrow did and began to talk about him. It is one of the few subjects in the world upon which she would talk to a perfect stranger. Moreover the woman was quite a nice little creature, and humbly anxious to be instructed. It took a long time. Miss Morrow was not lucid. The little woman, though grateful, was a trifle abrupt in departing.

Miss Morrow then went upstairs. A few minutes later, the afternoon peace of the hotel was broken by peals of her bell and Miss Morrow came to the door of her room calling hysterically for her maid and the chambermaid. The decorum of the Victoria Hotel had never before been thus assaulted.

When the reason for it was given by a flustered chambermaid to a proprietor roused from his slumbers he declined to believe. For Miss Morrow declared that her jewel case had been stolen. And such a thing was also without precedent at the Victoria Hotel. In that impregnable respectability it was patently impossible.

Nevertheless the jewel case was gone.

Steeling itself to bear the horror, the Victoria Hotel sent for the police.

CHAPTER VI

INSPECTOR GUNN AND
SUPERINTENDENT BELL

Two days afterwards Superintendent Bell of the Criminal Investigation Department went down with his assistant, Sergeant Underwood, to Limbay.

The police officer in charge of the detection of crime in that part of Sandshire was Inspector Gunn, physically a contrast to Superintendent Bell, for he was long and thin and bald and of hasty movements and Bell was a square, slow man on whom hair grows thick, but in mind they were made to work together, having each a shrewd, downright way of thought and a vigorous determination.

Bell came into Gunn's office with a smile. "Here we are again! Like old times, isn't it?"

"It's fine you could come. I thought you'd be too big a man for this sort of case nowadays. I take it very kind of you."

"Not a bit. When I heard of it, I wanted to have a go at it. Very pleased to work a case with you again. How long is it since we were on that Garston affair together? Matter of twenty years?"

"That's right. Alfred Garston was drowned in 1908." Gunn grinned. "We didn't make much of that, did we?"

"We did not. Let's hope we've come on a bit since then. That wasn't our fault though."

"No, we never had a chance. But it's an odd thing

meeting you again over this case. The lady's Miss Morrow—the lady Alfred Garston was engaged to."

Bell looked puzzled, Bell looked annoyed. "Engaged? I'm getting old, Gunn. I don't remember Miss Morrow. Can't recollect her at all."

"Perhaps you never heard of her. The engagement didn't have any bearing on the Garston business. I knew about her, because she's one of the county people. Well, it doesn't matter. It had nothing to do with this case either, of course. Miss Morrow's got a bit of money and she's on her own. About half the time she stays at the Victoria here. Has the same rooms year after year. Two days ago somebody went off with her jewel case. She's frantic. I couldn't stop her offering a reward. She's putting an advertisement in the papers to-morrow. Five hundred pounds."

Bell whistled. "She has got some money."

"Very comfortable, I should say. But not to throw five hundred quid about."

"What sort of jewels were they?"

Gunn gave him a list. "There you are. And if that's accurate, it's a wonder. Took me about half a day cross-questioning her and her maid to draw it up. I should say neither of 'em has any clear notion what she really had, and as for the value—search me. She's not insured, of course. She wouldn't be."

Bell read with grunts of contempt. "Looks like the usual old maid's little lot. Sentimental value, I suppose. Might be things Alfred Garston gave her." He looked up at Gunn. "What's your idea about it?"

"Very likely some did come from him. She still thinks a lot about him. I got that when she was rambling on. She was thanking heaven she always wore her engagement ring—on the little finger now, the other one having got too fat. She told me so." Gunn gave a subdued chuckle. "Poor old girl. She's absurd and pathetic, if you know what I mean. Oh yes, this big reward is sentimental. She wants everything back undamaged."

"Wish she may get it!" Bell grunted.

"Oh, it's silly, of course. Makes us look fools too. There are some letters she's keen about in with the jewels."

"I thought so," Bell nodded.

"Love letters, I gather. Alfred's love letters. Always carried 'em round with her." He grinned ruefully at Bell. "So the five hundred quid is for the recovery of case and contents. Think you're going to earn it?"

Bell shook his head. "About these letters though. They'd be just straight love letters from Alfred Garston? See what I mean? It's not a blackmail job?"

"Can't be. You don't know her, of course. You can bet your life she never had any love affair but that one. They're his letters all right. May have been pretty warm —I shouldn't have thought so. But nobody could blackmail her with them. There was no secret about the engagement. Besides—she's been living quite open down here and in London ever since. You can't imagine any fellow suddenly thinking he could get blackmail out of her for that old affair."

Bell nodded. "Well, I didn't really. Better to have a look at every possibility though. You've got to own it's a queer sort of case, Gunn."

"How do you mean?"

"Neat bit of work, isn't it? The thief got clean away out of a good hotel in daylight with a jewel case and you haven't found any clue. Looks like high-class professional work."

"I know. That's why I wanted some of you London experts on it."

"All right. But the high-class crooks don't want

to bother with Miss Morrow's kind of stuff." Bell looked
at the list with contempt. "I'd say there's nothing there
worth their while. And they generally know what they're
after."

"What are you getting at?"

"I suppose you've looked over the servants?"

"Yes. Nothing doing. All old stagers—it's that kind
of hotel. They know one another and the proprietor
knows 'em all inside out."

"What about the window of the room?"

"Not a chance. Second floor and on the front."

"What do you think of a casual stranger strolling
upstairs?"

"I don't believe in him. The Victoria has no use for
casual strangers. The porter'd bite 'em. The office
would call the police."

"Particular kind of pub." Bell smiled.

"It is. You've got to reckon with that. Anybody
who couldn't pass for quite correct wouldn't have had a
chance."

"All right. Have it your own way. You want to put
it on one of the people staying there. Then we'd better
look into 'em."

"That was my idea," Gunn smiled. "Now the case
was in Miss Morrow's room before lunch. She says so
and her maid says so. When she went up again an hour
after lunch it was gone. There were ten people left the
hotel that day round about lunch time. Here's the list.
These four are old customers. The other six they don't
know."

Bell laughed. "Oh, you can get into this exclusive
pub without an introduction?"

"Yes. Shouldn't care to myself." Gunn grinned.
"Very genteel they are at the Victoria. But of course it's
first class and they get rich people motoring and so on."

Bell studied the names. "Colonel Grose and valet. Left his club address. Mr. and Mrs. Herbert, London; Mr. and Mrs. Meyer and chauffeur, Manchester; Mrs. Hale, maid and chauffeur, Bath. Lot of servants."

"There would be. All these people had their own cars except the colonel. He's old and so is Mrs. Hale. Quite doddery. The others, the Herberts and the Meyers, were youngish. I don't get anything particular about 'em. The proprietor says they were all quite gentry. Gentry's his strong suit. But I don't know what young people want to go to the Victoria for."

"I see. Well, it might have been somebody who didn't run away as soon as he'd got the goods. But we'd better begin with this little lot. Let's go down. I'd like to have a look at this genteel pub."

They went. The proprietor, who looked like Ibsen, was not pleased to see them, and became less pleased and still more like Ibsen when they cross-examined him about his guests. He would remember nothing that was of any use. "Look here, my friend," said Bell, "if I wanted to be nasty I should say you didn't want this theft investigated."

"I don't want you starting silly scandal about the visitors to my hotel, and I'm not going to have it. Say what you like, I'm not afraid of you. You can't bully me."

Bell looked him over with a contemptuous smile. "Wait till I begin. Your duty is to assist the police. And you're not doing it."

"I understand my duty." The proprietor was still defiant. "I'm here to give you any help I can. But I can't tell you what I don't know."

"All right. As you don't know anything about your visitors, we'll have to get it otherwise. I want to see the bills of these people—Mr. and Mrs. Herbert of Lon-

don, Mr. and Mrs. Meyer and chauffeur of Manchester."
The proprietor had no objection to that. He would get
the books at once.

When he departed Bell winked at Gunn, but Gunn
shook his head. "The old boy's all right, you know."

"I should say so. He came to heel sharp when I talked
about duty, didn't he? Just a silly ass. He was hoping
to pass it off as some thief from outside, not one of his
precious visitors, that's all. And he don't feel too sure
about 'em."

The books came and revealed that the Herberts had
stayed four nights, the Meyers only two. The Meyers
had taken expensive rooms on the first floor, the Herberts had gone to the third. The Meyers were charged
for baths each day. One bath had sufficed for the Herberts. The Meyers had drunk wine, the Herberts whisky.
One Herbert had tea each day, no Meyer. "I can't
make much out of that," said Gunn.

Bell grunted and looked up at the proprietor. "Have
you got a bar here?"

"There is no bar in the hotel," said the proprietor
haughtily.

"Hard lines. What does a man do when he wants a
drink?"

"He would give his order to the smoking-room
waiter."

"I want to see him."

A small young man who already looked old was produced. "Now, my lad, do you get many of the visitors
taking a drink in the evening?"

"There's always the regular, sir."

"Leaving them out—were you serving many last
week?"

"Much as usual, sir."

"Do they pay as they have it or put it on the bill?"

"Mostly pay—except some of the regulars."

"Did you happen to notice any of the strangers?"

"There was a gentleman in most nights. I remember 'im, because 'e 'ad gin an' bitters—which it's not usual with gentlemen after dinner. Some nights 'e'd 'ave two."

Bell lit a cigarette. "Well, what was he like?"

"Nice gentleman, sir. Quite pleasant." The waiter looked at his proprietor. "I think 'e 'ad rooms on the third floor. I 'eard 'im tell the lift boy."

"Yes, but what was he like to look at?"

"I couldn't rightly say." The waiter hesitated. "Just a ordinary gent. Clean-shaved. Lot of forehead. Not the sort you notice much. Rather spry when he moved."

"That's no good," said Bell. "All right, my lad." He sent the waiter away and turned to the proprietor. "Is there anyone in your blessed hotel who knows anybody?"

"I take it the gentleman he refers to must have been Mr. Herbert," said the proprietor, with angry contempt for a gentleman who brought to his hotel an incorrect habit in drinks.

Bell made an impatient noise. "Chambermaid of the Herberts' room. Waiter at the Herberts' table. Porter. The man at your garage. I want all them. To begin with. P'r'aps one of 'em 's got some sense."

The examination was long and tedious. The Herberts had been people singularly insignificant or the servants of the Victoria thought it improper to remember anything about the visitors. Bell gained here a little and there a little. Mrs. Herbert was young and the chambermaid did not think they had been long married. Mr. Herbert was older. The waiter said Mrs. Herbert had a quiet way with her and wore black and used to be always in the drawing room with the ladies. He had thought they did not go out much.

But the last of the string, the garage man, had a different sort of mind. He was an affable cockney, he talked nineteen to the dozen, and if all he told was true he noticed everything or more. From his chatter Mr. and Mrs. Herbert emerged real and recognizable. She was quite the lady or the lady's maid. Sharp little face, rather mousy; not much of her; fair hair and dark eyes; dressed demure and blackish; didn't mind showing all a leg though. He was free and easy: quite all right but not just the thing; bit of a bagman. Ordinary-sized fellow; rather bony; skin-and-bone face: sort of skull. Moved quick. Knew a bit about cars. His own car was an Evans-Cambridge coupé 1929; been re-painted gray. He had a go at the engine just before he left.

Bell smiled. "You've seen some things in your life, haven't you?" He gave the man a ten-shilling note. "I shouldn't wonder you might be some use to me if you can keep your mouth shut. Run away." He stood up and surveyed the proprietor. "Thank God somebody in the place has got a brain. The only good you can be just yet is to go on saying nothing. Understand? If any of this leaks out, we'll come down on you. But you'd better think about knowing something. Good-day to you." He marched out at high speed.

When they were out of the hotel Gunn caught up. "Well, I suppose you think you've got on to them," he growled. "I don't see it myself."

"How could you?" Bell soothed him. "It's knowing the people that does the trick. I know your Mr. Herbert. They all have their little ways, thank God. Drinking gin of an evening is one of his. That's what put me on to him. When the garage man talked about his skull face that settled it. We call him Billy Bones."

"Regular hotel thief, is he?"

Bell nodded. "We've had him on the list ten—ah, fifteen years. Quite in a good way of business. I don't know the woman. But Billy likes 'em fresh and fresh."

"What's your next move?" Gunn grunted.

"Eh?" Bell stared at him. "Why, we'll have to find Billy for you. I'll ring up now and tell 'em to get busy. May take a bit of time, but we'll find him."

"That's all right. I'm thinking about the evidence," Gunn grumbled. "I don't see it myself. Say you get him and this smarty from the garage identified him. What about it? You prove he was down here under an alias when the stuff was pinched and you can get it in that he's a convicted hotel thief. That's not good enough for a jury."

"Don't you worry. When we've got him, we'll make a case of it. Some of these servants will have to remember things." Bell looked knowing. "Wonderful what fools can remember when they're put through it."

"How do you mean?"

"You know the second waiter did remember seeing the woman sitting by Miss Morrow. That was keeping watch on her while Billy Bones did the trick. We want one of 'em to remember seeing Billy about on the wrong floor—by Miss Morrow's room—coming down with a case in his hand. That sort of thing. We'll get it from somebody when we work at 'em."

"I don't know. I don't much like it," said Gunn.

"What's wrong with it?" Bell looked at him with searching eyes. "You can bet your life Billy did the job."

"I daresay he did." Gunn frowned. "I don't think you're going to get much of a case." Bell did not answer at once. "You don't like it yourself," Gunn accused him.

"Do you want to know what is wrong with it?" said Bell slowly. "I told you before. It oughtn't to have been an expert's job at all. Billy's not the man to come after Miss Morrow's class o' goods. He only goes for the big stuff. And yet he did it. Well, I want to know why. There's some queer game being played and Billy's got to let us into it—or he'll go for a long stretch. That's how it's going to look to him. So we have to get some evidence ready."

"Work a bluff on him?" said Gunn. "It might do. But what game could there be? Who's going to make anything out of old jewellery and old love letters?"

"Ah! Now you're asking something," Bell grunted.

CHAPTER VII

MR. CLUNK TAKES A CASE

MR. CLUNK walked round his garden before breakfast, and sparrows chirped at him and he at the sparrows and he hummed:

> *"We speak of the land of the blest,*
> *That country so bright and so fair,*
> *And oft are its glories confest;*
> *But what must it be to be there!"*

He found two young plants of groundsel, took these in to his canaries, with beaming benevolence watched them eat, then, rubbing his hands, tripped to the paper which lay to warm by the fire. The Clunks were fond of fires.

> *"To be there! To be there!*
> *Oh, what must it be to be there!"*

he murmured, and on that second line was silent.

An advertisement in the column next to births, marriages, and deaths required his attention:

£500 REWARD. STOLEN, 4th inst., from VICTORIA HOTEL, LIMBAY. BLACK LEATHER JEWEL CASE MARKED F.M. containing diamond and amethyst brooch, pearl brooch, amethyst necklace, diamond and ruby bracelet, etc., and private papers. Above reward will be paid for information leading to complete recovery of case and contents. Apply Smith & Hawkins, Fore Street, Limbay.

Mr. Clunk tapped his teeth. It was some minutes before he turned to another page.

Mrs. Clunk rustled in brightly smiling. "Is there anything in the paper, Joshua?"

"The King seems really better, my dear," said Mr. Clunk.

"God bless him!" Mrs. Clunk murmured.

"Amen! Yes, indeed. Amen!" said Mr. Clunk, and they sat down to their eggs.

One train earlier than usual Mr. Clunk went in to town. When he ran up the stairs of his office his little feet went to the tune of

> *"You are nearing the brink of Jordan*
> *But still there is work for you:*
> *Then, what are you going to do, brother?*
> *Say, what are you going to do?"*

His letters were brought him and he looked them over hastily. "Very good. In a minute, if you please, Jenks, in a minute. I want a word with Lewis."

Lewis was a bald young man to whom prominent teeth gave the look of a simpleton. Mr. Clunk showed him the advertisement. "Did you happen to notice that, my boy?"

"Caught my eye, sir. Big reward, I thought."

"It is," said Mr. Clunk. "A very large reward."

"I mean to say, it's big money for the stuff in the list. Looks like something behind."

"Just so. I'm afraid they're not being quite candid," said Mr. Clunk sadly. "Complete recovery of contents, you notice, Lewis. Complete. A curious advertisement. Do you happen to have heard anything about the case?"

"Not me. Been kept pretty quiet. Of course, Limbay —it is off the map. Still, a hotel jewel robbery generally makes a noise. And if it's a five-hundred quid reward touch—well!"

"Quite so. An interesting case. I should like to know more of it."

"Very good, sir." Lewis went out.

Mr. Clunk did not at once return to his letters. He contemplated the stuffed canaries on the mantelpiece. He rose and turned them to take more of the sunlight. Then he rang the bell and asked Jenks for a directory of the county of Sandshire.

That night he took Mrs. Clunk to a missionary meeting. When they came home a taxi was at the door. Lewis was in the cupboard upstairs which Mr. Clunk calls his study. He writes his sermons there.

"Well, well, well," Mr. Clunk beamed. "I don't like keeping you out so late, my boy. You should have telephoned."

"It wouldn't do for the telephone, sir. I wanted to tell you Bell's on that Limbay case."

"Dear me," said Mr. Clunk. "Superintendent Bell? Is that so?"

"That's right. And the man they're looking for is Billy Bones. You know, Billy Benson."

"Benson!" Mr. Clunk echoed. "But that is very surprising, Lewis. Weren't you very surprised?"

"I was. Makes you wonder what it's all about." Lewis looked at him vacantly.

"It does indeed. But we were wondering, weren't we? Well, well, well. Quite an interesting case."

"Bell's driving it hard."

"Is he really? Dear me! Do you happen to know if Benson has been working alone lately?"

"I 'aven't 'eard," said Lewis, for whom aspirates were sometimes too much. "Sure to have a girl." The foolishness of his face vanished in a knowing grin.

"Ah, yes." Mr. Clunk shook his head. "A new one, I fear."

"He does like 'em new," Lewis agreed.

"Dear, dear," said Mr. Clunk. "But if anything occurs, Lewis—it might be useful to get into touch with the lady."

"I'll watch it, sir."

"Thank you very much, my boy. Really it's a shame to keep you up so late. You must come and have some supper with us."

"I think not, sir, thanks," said Lewis hastily. The Clunks drink cocoa at supper. "My missus will be wondering what's happened to me."

Mr. Clunk chuckled. "Not a new one, I hope, my boy?"

"Not much," Lewis grinned. "I know when I'm well off."

"Ah, too bad of me," Mr. Clunk beamed. "Tell her the old man's very much obliged to her."

He packed Lewis off and came rubbing his hands to Mrs. Clunk and Irish stew and cocoa.

"Was that the office, Joshua?" she complained. "You let yourself be worked shocking, really you do."

"Oh no, no, my dearie, no, I love the work. It's welcome." He chirped the tune of that hymn:

> "*You are nearing the brink of Jordan*
> *But still there is work for you——*

How good that is, dearie."

"You're a good man, Joshua," said Mrs. Clunk with emotion.

Two days later Lewis came into Mr. Clunk's room at the office. "They've got him, sir," he said. "Found him on the Dieppe boat last night. Took him to the Yard."

"Ah, indeed." Mr. Clunk took a boiled sweet. "Yes, we had to expect they would find him. Superintendent Bell is very thorough when he knows what he should do. A very careful, zealous officer. And they took Benson to the Yard? That is interesting, Lewis. He must be taken to Limbay if he is to be charged with theft."

"Bell wants to have some information out of him, I reckon."

"I fear so," Mr. Clunk sighed. "I don't like these police examinations of arrested men, Lewis. It's not right. It's a very dangerous practice. The poor fellow should have the protection of his solicitor."

"Yes, sir, I think I'll be able to get hold of the girl," said Lewis.

Mr. Clunk sucked his sweet. "It would be wrong to attract any attention to her," he gurgled. "But if we could give her help, that is our duty." Lewis departed briskly.

In the afternoon he telephoned to ask Mr. Clunk to stay late at the office. After dusk, when the precincts of Covent Garden were deserted, he brought Mr. Clunk a lady.

She did not resemble the nice little woman who talked to Miss Morrow or the demure, mouselike, fair-haired woman remembered by the garage man. She dressed and painted herself like a chorus girl of the fourth class. Her hair was henna red. Mr. Clunk smiled at her paternally. "Miss Montague, sir," said Lewis.

"And what can we do for Miss Montague?" Mr. Clunk beamed.

But under the examination of his large pale eyes Miss Montague was uncomfortable. "You're Clunk & Clunk, aren't you?"

"I am Joshua Clunk," said Mr. Clunk with mild pride.

"I always heard you were all right." Miss Montague looked as if the sight of him made her doubt it. "Your young man said you'd be willing to take it up."

"We're always willing to help," Mr. Clunk assured her. "Tell me about it, my dear."

"You know they've pinched Billy. I suppose they're after me too."

"Dear, dear. That's very unpleasant," said Mr. Clunk. "Now what is the charge against Benson?"

He received from Miss Montague a glassy stare. "I don't know. I don't know anything about it. See?"

"Of course not," Mr. Clunk smiled. "That's the way to take it, my dear. But if we're going to help Billy, we'll have to understand what the police are putting up against him. And if we're to keep you out of it, you must tell us how you stand."

"Go on. You know what they've taken Billy for. That job at Limbay. It's a stinking plant, I say. Just because they've had him before for the same sort of thing they put this on to him. And that drags me into it."

"Too bad," Mr. Clunk murmured. "But how would they get at you?"

"Look here. I don't know anything about the ruddy jewels. Take my oath I never saw a blink of 'em. And I don't believe Billy did either. I'm not going back on him. You've got to do the job for him, as well as me. That's what I told your young man. I'm for Billy all the time."

"I like that," said Mr. Clunk heartily. "I like that, don't you, Lewis?"

"That's the touch," Lewis agreed.

Miss Montague expanded. "I'll tell you. It was like this. Billy and me have been pals quite a while. I was out of a shop, and he was flush. We went off for a jolly old

joy ride. Billy likes a quiet place when he's not working.
So we stayed at this one-horse hotel at Limbay. I take
my dying oath I never saw him up to anything." Miss
Montague displayed modesty. "It was like a honeymoon." she sighed. "Then we came back and there was
this ad. in all the papers, five hundred reward for jewels
stolen from our beastly old pub. When Billy saw that,
he said to me, 'Look at that,' he said, 'in our own little
pub! A lot of good it is to a chap to keep off it. They'll
put that on to me now. Oh, hell,' he said, 'I'll have to
break away, Gracie. I don't want you in it. You lie low.'
And he gave me a tenner and bucked off. He was always
a sport, good old Billy." She attended to her eyes. "He
knew I'd never give him away." She looked up at Mr.
Clunk. "Now, mister. What about it?"

"That's very good and clear," said Mr. Clunk. "But
it wouldn't be at all wise to tell it to the police, my
dear."

"What do you take me for?" Miss Montague cried.

"I think you're a very sensible young woman," Mr.
Clunk beamed. "It's so much easier when people trust
me, you know. Nobody ever regretted doing that, I believe, eh, Lewis?"

"Rather not," Lewis grinned.

"Now this is how we stand." Mr. Clunk put his finger
tips together and contemplated them. "You came to ask
me to look after your friend Mr. Benson who has been
arrested. Very good. I understand that. I'll see him at
once, wherever they've taken him. But we must look
after you." He turned to Lewis. "Is she staying in a
nice quiet place?"

"Couldn't do much better, sir."

"Very good. Then you'll go back there, my dear, and
never say anything to anybody about your little jaunt
to Limbay. If the police should find you out, you

mustn't answer any of their questions. Tell them you
want to see Mr. Clunk. Understand me, don't you?
They'll be trying to trap you and if you talk you'll give
yourself away. Make 'em send for Mr. Clunk. I'll see
you through it, my dear. Good-bye. Good-bye."

When Lewis had taken her out, Mr. Clunk began to
write, thus: "Montague: at L. with B. B.——? F.
M.——?" And at that statement of the case he gazed
with his head on one side and made little noises. . . . He
locked it up and lay back and murmured in very slow
time:

> *"Oh, what are you going to do, brother?*
> *Say, what are you going to do?*
> *You have thought of some useful labour*
> *But what is the end in view?"*

He sighed and shook his head. . . .

Lewis came back. "Sent her off in a taxi, with Jenks.
She's bucked." He grinned at Mr. Clunk. "Lying
good and hard, wasn't she?"

"Yes indeed. A dear, simple soul," Mr. Clunk
smiled. "How much there is to love in human nature,
Lewis. Good-night. Good-night."

He tripped off humming another verse of that same
interrogatory hymn:

> *"Oh, what are you going to do, brother?*
> *The twilight approaches now.*
> *Already your locks are silvered,*
> *And winter is on your brow."*

He pattered along very fast.

CHAPTER VIII

MR. CLUNK FOR THE DEFENCE

In the morning Superintendent Bell was busy at Scotland Yard, clearing up odds and ends of work that he might be free to spend some days with Inspector Gunn at Limbay. He was disturbed by Sergeant Underwood.

"Old Clunk's turned up, sir: he's called asking to see Billy Bones."

"Has he, by George!" Bell flung back in his chair and stared.

"Putting it quite correct, sir. He says he's informed that Mr. William Benson has been arrested and Mr. Benson's friends have instructed him to take up the case so he wishes for an opportunity to consult Mr. Benson."

"Oh, quite correct," Bell laughed sardonically. "He would be. And I'd like to know how he heard we'd got Billy here. Josh Clunk hears too much, my lad. Didn't happen to ask him who Mr. Benson's friends might be, did you?"

"I didn't." Underwood looked uncomfortable. "I thought it wouldn't do."

"All right. I was only pulling your leg. The less you ask Josh Clunk the less you'll give away. He's told us the only thing we'll get out of him—that he's in the game. God knows that's enough." Bell glowered at his table.

"He's waiting for an answer, sir," Underwood said meekly. "What will I tell him?"

"Oh, tell him we have no knowledge of Benson. Benson's been detained at the request of the Sandshire police and taken to Sandshire. Be as smooth as butter and get rid of him. The sooner we're down at Limbay the better."

In the Limbay police station that afternoon Bell met Inspector Gunn. "You do deliver the goods, I must say," Gunn began. "Never thought you'd get him so quick. He's the man all right. Had him out for identification this morning and that smart Alec from the garage got on to him at once."

"Good. What did Mr. Billy say to that?"

"Said nothing. Looked hell."

"That's his strong suit. He worked that on me three hours yesterday."

Gunn grunted. "Your bluff's not going too well, is it?"

"Give us a chance," Bell protested. "Have you tried any of the other servants at identifying him?"

"Chambermaid. Couple o' waiters. Not too good. Chambermaid couldn't be certain. Waiters couldn't really say. Thought he might be."

"Somebody's got to do better than that." Bell's jaw shut hard. "Bring 'em down here. I'll put 'em through it."

"All right. You can try. I don't like it too much myself," Gunn frowned. "Forcing things a bit, aren't you?"

"I'm not going to let Billy Bones get away with it. I told you there was something behind this case. There is. One of the things is Josh Clunk."

"And who's Mr. Clunk?"

Bell laughed. "You'll know before you've done with this case, my lad. He——"

The station sergeant appeared begging pardon: a London solicitor, a Mr. Clunk, had come down: Mr.

Clunk was going to appear for Benson: wanted to see him in order to arrange the defence.

"There you are," said Bell with gloomy satisfaction. "That's the kind of fellow Clunk is. Wonder he wasn't waiting for Billy on the step."

"Well, what about it? We'll have to let him talk to his client."

"We shall. I wish to God I could listen to 'em."

Gunn was startled. "I say! Go easy. We can't do that, you know. Got to keep to the rules."

"I do know," Bell growled. "All the rules—when Josh Clunk's against you. And you can bet your life he won't keep to 'em. That's where the fun comes in. Go on. Don't leave his highness waiting or you'll hear of it in court."

Gunn went out to arrange the interview and came back looking pleased and puzzled. "Seems a very decent old boy. Knows the ropes. Cheery and civil. What's the trouble about him?"

"He's the nastiest little bag o' tricks in the trade, that's all," said Bell. "Look here. Clunk's the man that crime with big money behind it comes to. Why do you think he's running down here on this little job?"

"But you said this chap is an expert crook."

"I did. And how does Clunk know we've got Billy before Billy's had a chance to ask for a solicitor? Clunk was round at the Yard this morning wanting to see Billy. All we told him was that Billy was in the hands of the Sandshire police. And he comes straight here to Limbay. He knows something. I told you there was a queer game behind this jewel case. It's a very queer game that has Josh Clunk in it from the start."

"But what could there be?" Gunn objected. "That Miss Morrow hasn't got a past. She hasn't hardly had a life, you might say. There's nothing to her, except having been engaged to Alfred Garston. And what could there be about that business now? He's been dead twenty years."

"I don't know what there is," Bell growled. "You can bet your life there's something. Even if we never get near it. Come on, what we've got to do now is to make a case against Billy Bones that'll put him in a funk. Let's work over these servants. My Lord, I wish I could hear how old Clunk's working with Billy."

But if he had heard, Bell would have been much disappointed. For Mr. Clunk found his client difficult.

Billy Bones did not wholly deserve his nickname. Only people with sharp eyes would have found in his bald and prominent forehead and salient cheek bones the look of a skull. He was otherwise lean and angular but not extravagantly. For professional purposes he had cultivated an inconspicuous appearance.

But the resemblance to a skull was increased as he looked at Mr. Clunk, and he said with some truculence, "What's the game?"

"Just so. We have to make up our minds about that, my friend," said Mr. Clunk. "How did you think of taking it now?"

"Who brought you down?"

Mr. Clunk smiled. "Fancy asking that! Who would it be? Well, here I am, my boy. And you couldn't get anybody better, though I say it. Now let's see what can be done for you."

"None of your tricks. I said, who asked you to come into it?"

"That young woman's a better girl than you deserve, my lad," said Mr. Clunk severely. "You shouldn't have brought her into a thing like this."

Billy was affected. "What, have they pinched her?" he cried.

"No thanks to you they haven't. They're after her, of course. So Miss Montague came to me. She has a little sense, my friend. She asked me to defend you. That's all she's thinking about, I'm afraid. Not very much sense after all. Who else do you suppose cares tuppence what happens to you?" Mr. Clunk lay back and jingled the keys in his pockets.

"Look here," said Billy. "You look after Gracie, will you?"

"Of course I shall," Mr. Clunk snapped. "I don't let my clients down. You know that. And if I'm going to keep her out of it, I have to get you out of it. Lucky for you, you fool."

"All right. Go easy," said Billy uncomfortably. "I haven't asked you myself. What's more, I haven't got any brass for you, I tell you straight."

"Then you must be a fool," Mr. Clunk said.

"How do you mean?"

"What did you go into it for, if there was no money in it?"

"Here. Let's get this right." Billy showed symptoms of alarm. "What's Gracie been telling you?"

"My instructions from Miss Montague," said Mr. Clunk with dignity, "are that she was staying with you at the Victoria, but she knows nothing of the theft of the jewel case and is sure that you know nothing."

"That's quite right," said Billy with relief. And Mr. Clunk laughed heartily. "What's the joke?"

"I've been in business some time, my friend. Is that what you told Superintendent Bell?"

"Not half, I didn't. Told him nothing at all, blast him. I wouldn't answer the blighter." Billy turned on Mr. Clunk the obstinate, evil stare which Bell had found irritating.

"He's been in business some time too," Mr. Clunk smiled.

"What do you mean?"

"Well, my friend, didn't you think it was rather odd Superintendent Bell should take a lot of trouble over this tuppenny ha'penny lot of jewels?"

Billy wriggled. "Spiteful old dog, Bell is. Once he's had a sniff at you, he won't ever let you alone."

"Worries his bones, doesn't he?" Mr. Clunk agreed cheerfully. "You have to think about that, my friend."

"My God!" Billy glared. "He won't get anything out of me. I'm not that kind, Clunk."

"I see," Mr. Clunk nodded. "He was putting it to you, you'd get off light if you let him know where he could find the swag."

Billy grinned. "Ah. Always hand out that stuff, don't they? Nothing doing. They don't catch me with it."

"Good. I suppose he didn't let out how he came to be looking for you as soon as the stuff was taken?"

"How do you mean? The blinking swine at the garage remembered my dial. They put me up for identification this morning and the dirty dog picked me out good and quick."

Mr. Clunk contemplated his distinctive face with amusement. "Quite so. That would be easy. But it's ra-ather a strange business, my friend. I should be inclined to think someone gave you away."

"What are you getting at?" Billy stared. "You don't mean Gracie?"

"No, no, no. She would lose her soul for you, poor girl," said Mr. Clunk with emotion. "She mustn't, you know, she mustn't."

"All right, all right." Billy was uncomfortable. "I'm saying nothing against her."

"You silly fellow," said Mr. Clunk. "Don't you see, the moment the jewel case was stolen our friend Bell started to look for you. I wonder who gave him that idea. I should say it was the people who have the things. It would be very convenient for them to send you to prison for the theft." Billy stared at him with sullen interest but disappointed Mr. Clunk by saying nothing. "My poor fellow, can't you see it keeps them safe and shuts your mouth?"

"I get you," said Billy. "Very nice for 'em, isn't it?" he grinned. "I wish I knew who they were, Clunk. Do you? Got something up your old sleeve, eh?"

"Dear me, no," Mr. Clunk sighed. "I'm sorry, my friend. Nothing at all. If you don't know who was after the stuff, how should I? But I'm afraid, unless we can bring someone else into the case, it's a bad business for you."

"Here. What's the game? You're talking like old Bell."

"Don't be foolish," said Mr. Clunk austerely. "I'm talking in your own interests, Benson."

"Yes, that's what he said," Billy grinned. "Nothing doing, old man. I know nothing, see? I was just down here on a spree with my girl and they're putting it on me because I've been jugged for the same kind of thing. That's my blooming defence. If you want it, you can take it. If not, go to hell."

"I shan't do that, my friend," said Mr. Clunk cheerfully. "That's your affair, I'm afraid. Yes, I'm afraid so, Benson. Very well, I'll fight the case for you. But you're running a grave risk. You're a silly fellow."

"I don't think," Billy grinned.

Mr. Clunk showed no resentment: no more interest in the case. He made a little amiable, elderly chatter about nothing and departed. With a stare of concentrated hostility Bell watched his sprightly back go down the street. Bell also had not got what he wanted.

Mr. Clunk was staying at the Victoria with his young friend Lewis. They had a sitting room, which gave them rank above casual visitors, though not with the regular inhabitants: they were approved as people of the right sort. Mr. Clunk rang for tea, and when the Victoria produced its respectable version of that meal shook his head and sighed. Lewis came in. "Sit down, my boy. Would you like an egg or something?" he asked sorrowfully.

"Not for me, thanks," Lewis grinned.

"I'm very fond of my tea," Mr. Clunk complained, and sipped and pecked with melancholy resignation. "There's no place like home, Lewis."

"Oh, this isn't so bad, sir. They'll do you all right when you get the hang of it."

"You like it?" Mr. Clunk looked forlorn. "I'm glad you like it. It makes me feel an old man. No life in it, Lewis. No joy. These people here seem to be simply waiting to die."

Lewis laughed. "That's got 'em! So they do."

"But how sad that is, Lewis," Mr. Clunk mourned.

"Yes, sir. Did you make anything of Billy Bones?"

Mr. Clunk, having eaten everything else there was to eat, took a lump of sugar. "In a way," he said, and sucked, "in a way. He told the same story as the girl. Rather silly of him, wasn't it, Lewis?" His large eyes gleamed benevolence. "I'm afraid he doesn't trust me. Such a pity! Still, that is quite interesting. The poor fellow let out that Bell had been offering to make things easy for him if he would tell the police who put him on the job. That also is interesting. Our friend Bell, you see, has a notion that there is more in this than meets the eye. He is really quite intelligent. We mustn't

underrate Bell, Lewis. I'm afraid he is going to compli-
cate the affair for us. A most persistent creature."

"Oh, Bell's a bloodhound."

"A terrier, I should say," Mr. Clunk corrected mildly.
"An honest terrier. Very worrying. Well, I warned our
poor Billy it would be a hazardous defence to put forward that it was pure accident brought him here, a
known hotel thief under an alias, just when the jewels
were stolen. I advised him to direct suspicion elsewhere.
But the silly fellow would only persist that he knew
nothing."

"He must have been well paid for the job."

"Dear me, yes," Mr. Clunk sighed. "He told me he
hadn't a farthing. Not a wise fellow at all. He must have
been very well paid. But why, my boy, why?"

"Ah well, that's it, isn't it?" said Lewis. "It beats
me so far."

"A most interesting case." Mr. Clunk took another
lump of sugar.

"Are you going on with the defence, sir?"

"My dear boy! Certainly, certainly. I gave my word
to that poor girl. Rather a sweet girl, Lewis."

"Sticks to her man," Lewis allowed one virtue.
"What do you think the police evidence is like?"

"There's a clear identification, I gather. That's a
pity. And with the alias and Billy's unfortunate record,
it looks nasty. But our friend Bell's anxiety to get
something out of Billy before they begin suggests they're
not feeling strong. Have you picked up anything in the
hotel yet?"

"They're worrying the servants like hell."

"Really?" Mr. Clunk smiled. "Ah, that's Bell's
little weakness. Well, well. What about the lady in the
case, my boy?"

"By what I hear she's in a rare stew. She hasn't

hardly shown up since the things were stolen. Eats in her room mostly. But the servants like her all right. She's a fat old maid, been living here off and on for years. Comes of one of the county families. Keeps herself to herself. You know the kind. She had a love affair went wrong ages ago."

"Ah, poor thing." Mr. Clunk's large eyes flickered.

"Yes, she was engaged as a girl and the chap died, drowned or something. She's been sort of mourning ever since. Waiting to die, you know, like you said just now."

"Dear, dear. I don't like to hear that, Lewis," Mr. Clunk sighed. "Who was the poor fellow, do you know?"

"Name of Garston. Family has a place down here somewhere."

"Is that so?" said Mr. Clunk, and did not say any more for a moment. "Dear me, it's a sad story, Lewis."

"Yes, sir," Lewis answered mechanically, wondering what the old man saw in it: for having himself seen pieces of several explanations, he had dismissed them all as impossible. But Mr. Clunk had beyond doubt found something which he thought useful. He looked specially religious: he was humming one of his infernal hymns. The words of it, which Lewis did not know, went like this:

> "There's a land that is fairer than day
>   And by faith we can see it afar.
> For the Father waits over the way
>   To prepare us a dwelling place there.
>
> "In the sweet . . . by and by . . .
>   We shall meet on that beautiful shore . . .
> In the sweet . . . by and by . . .
>   We shall meet on that beautiful shore."

On the next morning the magistrates of Limbay had before them William Benson, alias Herbert, charged with the theft of a jewel case from the Victoria Hotel.

Miss Morrow, drooping, inaudible, and tearful, was persuaded to describe its contents and its disappearance and, much shaken, turned to leave the box. "Just a moment, Miss Morrow," the smooth voice of Mr. Clunk arose. "Only one or two questions. Have you ever seen the prisoner before?"

"I don't think so," Miss Morrow said faintly.

"You don't think so. No. What was the value of your jewels?"

"I don't know. They were very precious to me."

"Quite so. You offered a reward of five hundred pounds for the complete recovery of the contents of the case. Did it contain anything besides jewellery?"

"There were some letters."

"I see. Some letters which you valued very much?"

"I did indeed," Miss Morrow sobbed.

"Quite so. That was why you offered such a large reward?" Miss Morrow nodded. "I'm not asking you anything about them. I should deeply regret to cause you distress. But you can tell me whether they could be of any value to the prisoner?"

"No indeed. I can't think why he should take them."

"Just so. Thank you, Miss Morrow."

She was followed into the box by a stolid detective. He had seen the prisoner going on board the Dieppe boat at Newhaven, recognized him as William Benson, a hotel thief of long experience, stopped him and taken him to Scotland Yard. Mr. Clunk shot up and snapped: "What happened to him there?" The detective had no knowledge. "Did you tell him he was to be charged in this case?" The detective knew nothing about the case.

"That's why the police put you in the box," said Mr. Clunk. "He was kept in London two nights and one day before a charge was made?" The detective could not say. "Would it surprise you to hear he was told things would be easy for him if he could help the police to recover the jewel case?" The detective knew nothing about that.

"A useful witness," said Mr. Clunk, and turned sharply to stare at Superintendent Bell and Inspector Gunn. "Are we going to have anyone who dares to tell the court how my client has been treated by the police?"

"The prisoner can go into the box himself," said the solicitor for the prosecution.

"I quite understand the police are afraid to," Mr. Clunk smiled.

"Please, please," the bench boomed. "Let us get on with the case, gentlemen."

"By all means, sir, if there is one," Mr. Clunk bowed.

The garage man was put into the box and swore blithely that he knew the prisoner as a man who had stayed at the Victoria Hotel as Mr. Herbert and left in his car just after the jewel case disappeared. Mr. Clunk was carelessly genial to him. He had a good memory for faces? Remembered everybody who came to the hotel?

"There were other people—without cars—who went away after the case was stolen? Quite so," Mr. Clunk turned on Superintendent Bell. "Are we going to hear anything about them? Not convenient for the police? Very good. Now the people who had cars, my man. Some of them went away at this suspicious moment?"

"There was some," the man admitted sulkily.

"I thought so. And when the prisoner went, did you see him taking the jewel case?"

"I didn't. I didn't see him get into his car at all."

Mr. Clunk looked the man over with a bland, esti-mating eye. "And you didn't see any of the others either I suppose?"

"No, I didn't," the man growled.

"In fact anybody might have gone off with the jewel case for all you know. Thank you."

And with the other evidence which Bell had forced out of the hotel Mr. Clunk was still more destructive. The clerk from the office and the porter were turned inside out and exhibited empty. Bell's energies had in-duced the unhappy waiters to add to their memories of gin and bitters in the smoking room and Mrs. Herbert sitting by Miss Morrow in the drawing room the in-formation that Mr. Herbert used to be always going upstairs and about the corridors. They were made to confess that though they remembered him so well they had not remembered him when he was put up for iden-tification—not clearly, they explained—not exactly—not to be certain. They felt sure, of course. Only it was a bit confusing. "I see. And after the police found you didn't know him when you saw him, they told you you must remember something? Come sir, on your oath. Did any policeman question you again after the identi-fication failed? I thought so. And what were you asked? If you couldn't think of something else about Mr. Herbert? Now we have it. This story of his going about upstairs was only found for you when you had been unable to think of anything yourself?"

So Mr. Clunk bullied them and they lost their heads. "Are we going to have any more of this?" he cried to the bench in virtuous indignation, and swung round upon the solicitor for the prosecution, who was con-ferring with Bell. "Oh, get some new instructions by all means."

The solicitor arose and said the bench would probably

think enough evidence had been given to justify a remand. The prosecution would prefer, for reasons which would readily be understood, not to take the case further that day.

"My friend's reasons are plain enough." Mr. Clunk stood up smiling. "Having no evidence, the police wish for an adjournment to make some. I submit these proceedings are an abuse of the process of the court. There is nothing against my client except that he has once been convicted. The police maxim is 'Once guilty always guilty.' So they chose to arrest him out of the seventy people in the hotel and tried to get a confession out of him by methods which are an abomination to all decent men. Having failed, as a little intelligence might have told them they were bound to fail, they proceed to revenge themselves by concocting evidence against him. It has been sufficiently exposed. I ask the bench to dismiss the case."

The bench conferred. "We think there must be a remand," the chairman announced. "We are strongly of opinion the prosecution should be ready with the rest of their evidence next week."

"Bail, of course, sir?" said Mr. Clunk.

"The prisoner was attempting to leave the country," Bell said sharply.

"I think no bail, Mr. Clunk." The chairman shook his head. "It is only for a week."

"We are in your hands, sir," Mr. Clunk smiled. "It will be only for a week."

After that he went to see his client. "You're a lucky fellow, my man," he said gravely. "So far."

"Oh, you're going fine, Clunk," Billy chuckled. "Did you see old Bell's face?"

"This will go well enough. Unless——"

"I should worry!"

"Unless Mr. Bell gets on to what's behind it. I warned you, you're taking risks."

Billy's face flattened out into obstinacy. "I know my game," he said.

Mr. Clunk found Lewis outside. "Pretty good work, sir," Lewis grinned. "You'll get him off without going to trial."

"Dear me, yes, of course," Mr. Clunk sighed. "A tiresome fellow. I wish I knew what he was paid for the job." Lewis laughed. "Well, well, well!" said Mr. Clunk, and began to murmur:

> *"Go work in my vineyard*
> *There's plenty to do.*
> *The harvest is great*
> *And the labourers few."*

"Going back to town, sir?" said Lewis.

"I think not, my boy. No, we'll stay on here for the week. You might pick up something."

That afternoon Mr. Clunk left him to look for it. The office of the Sandshire *Gazette* and Limbay *Herald* received Mr. Clunk. He wished to examine its old files. The Sandshire *Gazette* until lately appeared but once a week. That shortened his search. Reaching the spring of 1908, he found among the advertisements of death:

GARSTON: on April 4th suddenly, Alfred Garston, younger son of Sir Samuel Garston of Bradstock Abbey.

It interested him much.

In the paper of April 17th, he found a report of an inquest on Alfred Garston. His body had been found on April 8th on the sands of Bradstock Harbour. The doctor said that the body had been in the water for some time and the cause of death was no doubt drowning.

The dead man's brother, Henry, gave evidence that Alfred had been last seen on April 4th, when he went out in a sailing boat alone. He was fond of sailing and kept a boat of his own at the Abbey. It was quite usual for him to go out alone. He did not come back that night but there was no immediate alarm. On the morning of April 5th the boat was found drifting capsized with sails set. The jury brought in a verdict of death by misadventure and offered their sympathy to the family.

Mr. Clunk pursed his lips. "Dear me, yes," he murmured. "The poor family."

As he tripped back to the hotel he met Superintendent Bell and waved a hand at him and chirped, "Lovely afternoon!"

"Fine!" Bell grunted. "Staying on?"

"And you?" Mr. Clunk smiled.

CHAPTER IX

TONY LANDS

LIFE at Bradstock Abbey, reduced to its simplest terms, still fretted May's nerves. Deliverance from the social delights of visitors was relief such as that when acute pain passes away to leave weariness and depression. The medical comparison was much in her mind, forced not only by professional and personal memories of illness but by a feeling that the Garston family was mentally ill and had infected her. Mrs. Garston seemed only half alive, yet alive enough to keep up a quarrel with the world. Mrs. Garston never wanted her and was always wanting her, would never do as she was told and continually complained of the consequences of doing otherwise. There was comfort in being alone, and for that May had time enough, and the beauty of the place and its strangeness gained upon her. There would have been comfort, but alone she was too lonely and yet was haunted by a sense of unseen hostility. Absurd, she told herself, silly nerves. The excellent quiet servants of Bradstock cared nothing about her: were incapable of spying on her: of any mysterious malice. One, to be sure, was hostile, Mrs. Garston's maid Jones. That sallow woman's jealousy was visible enough. A horrid creature. After an hour with her Mrs. Garston could be maddening.

She had been. May walked away to the harbour, seeking solace in the sunlight on the wide water and the murmur of the tide. The air was alive: as she came down the lawns, the freshness of the western sea met the fragrance of hawthorn and lilac. She stood by the shore and her blood quickened. The wind played with her body. Far and far across the harbour the water broke in a myriad tiny waves that laughed with light.

She pulled off her hat and gave her yellow head to the sun and wind and they made her a shimmering gray wisp of a woman crowned with a flutter of gold.

So Tony Wisberry saw her, and what he said was: "Who the devil would that be?"

His boatman spat tobacco juice. "Lots o' maids to the Abbey."

And May became aware of a boat under sail. That was uncommon, not rare enough to be surprising. She had no objection to it. It was a pretty thing. But watching it run free revived the horrid feeling of lonely helplessness. She turned away and the wretched boat went with her. It was coming close in shore. It steered for the Abbey landing place. An amazing boat. No one ever landed there.

That small jetty had amused May; it seemed like a toy, it was so bright and prim, with clean white timbers and gravel freshly raked and two banks of shrubs matching each other. A gardener being asked what it was for had explained that there was once and by rights a ferry from Bradstock to Bradstock Abbey, and that the Abbey folks used to do a bit of sailing in the old days too. But the reason for maintaining it did not appear. May had never seen a ferry ply and the Abbey kept no boats of its own.

This boat vanished in the lee of the jetty and on to the jetty a man climbed. There seemed to be a good deal of him, rather loosely made. He came to May in large, swinging strides. "I beg your pardon. Is this Bradstock Abbey?"

She did not like the look of him. He was too big

and powerful, he swaggered. And it was a hard face
with such a jaw, a bullying sort of face. "Oh yes. Didn't
you know?" she said coldly.

"Well, I did hope so," Tony smiled. "But I've never
been here before. What a ripping place!" May had
nothing to say to that. When he smiled he was not
so bad: rather like a friendly bull dog: but encourage-
ment would certainly not be good for him. "Do they
show it?" Tony persisted.

"I never heard of anyone wanting to see it." May's
blue eyes looked through him. "I should think you had
better write to Lord Croyland."

Tony ceased to smile. "Would you?" he said, and
considered her with a gaze which was not at all friendly.
"Strictly private, is it? I say, do you mind telling me,
have I come to the wrong door?"

"There's the door," May informed him. "You
haven't come to it at all yet. And I don't answer it."

"Sorry, I beg your pardon. I'm not trying to make you
talk. Well, perhaps I was. But not to be impertinent."

That did better. He was really quite a pleasant youth
when he was not so pleased with himself. "What did you
want to know?" said May with patient condescension.

But he was not to answer. The little form of Mrs.
Garston came hurrying across the turf and she called,
breathless: "Miss Dean! Oh, Miss Dean, did you see
the boat? Did the boat come into the hard?"

"Yes, the boat's there." May moved quickly to her
side and took her arm, for she was trembling. "What is
the matter?"

"Who was in it? Have you see him?"

"It's my boat, madam," said Tony.

Mrs. Garston looked at him with wide eyes and
parted lips. "You!" she said, and shook her head and
turned away and hurried on to the jetty. She gazed

down at the boat, and the boatman saw her and shifted the quid in his cheek and touched his cap. She gave a little moaning cry, flung back her head and looked across the harbour, and her face was wan and piteous. She turned and walked towards the house, slowly, feebly. May came to her and took her arm again. "Don't! Don't!" She started aside. "Leave me alone! I don't want you." She went on faster.

The two stood watching her. "I say! What have I done?" Tony whispered.

"Heaven knows."

Mrs. Garston reached the garden, passed out of sight.

"They told me there was a ferry right to land by the Abbey," Tony explained. "That's why I came over in the boat. Awfully sorry if I've made any trouble."

"It's nothing. Don't think about it."

"My name's Wisberry, Antony Wisberry. I was coming to see Lord Croyland. I'm staying at Bradstock. I mean to say, if anybody asks, you'd better know."

"Thank you." May was attracted by his new manner. He was like a nice big dog—or a nice big boy—very young of course. But what he said was rather disturbing: it compelled curiosity, if not suspicion. Nobody ever came there to see Lord Croyland. And why should he choose to come when Lord Croyland wasn't there? "Do you expect anybody will ask about you?" she said.

"Well, about what upset the old lady."

"It wasn't seeing you, was it?"

"I shouldn't have thought so. I don't look very terrific, what?" The silly child seemed to fancy he might. So, "Not in the least," she informed him.

"Good. And I don't know her from Adam."

"She isn't Adam. She is Mrs. Garston, Lord Croyland's mother. Don't you know him either?"

"Never saw him. I've been trying to for some time."

"Down here?"

"No. In London. Always drew a blank. Funny, wasn't it?" A hardness asserted itself in his face again, but May did not mind it, his eyes were so interested in her. "I thought I'd have a try here."

"I'm afraid you've drawn a blank again. There's no one here but Mrs. Garston."

"Thanks. I say, do you mind my asking you, are you one of the family?"

"Heavens no. I'm only Mrs. Garston's nurse."

"I don't know about the 'only.'"

"I do," said May.

"Look here, do you feel it's rotten of me to keep you talking?"

"You're not. I'm staying because it amuses me to —to talk to somebody."

"Well, you're not amusing me"—that attractive lopsided smile came—"but you're jolly interesting. I say, do you mind telling me your name?"

"Why not call me Nurse?" May smiled.

Tony considered her deliberately and a little more colour came into her cheeks. "It doesn't seem to express the relationship," he decided. "I don't know how you'd feel, but I should feel a fool."

"It would seem quite natural," May assured him. "That's the only relations we are."

"Nurse—and patient? You think so?"

"Well—patient nurse—and small boy asking questions."

"All right, Nurse," said Tony meekly.

May relented. His eyes were certainly gray, not blue, a warm sort of gray, nice colour. "If you feel such an infant—my name's Dean."

"Thank you." He held out a large hand. "How do you do, Miss Dean?"

"How are you?" May smiled, and, which was annoying, blushed.

"Growing up fast. Look here, I don't want to do anything like making use of you. You'd better know how I stand. I've been trying to get in touch with Croyland for weeks. I want to talk to him about some affairs of my father's, who's dead. He answers my letters by declining to answer 'em. I've called at the Garston offices in London and they put me off—he can't see me—nobody has any instructions—that sort of thing. But I'm going to see him. That's what I came down for."

"You won't see him now. He's not here, really. He never is except at week-ends."

"All right, thanks. I don't want you to tell me anything about him."

"I wasn't going to. I'm in his house and he pays me a salary."

"Sorry. I know you wouldn't, of course—when I told you I was up against him. That's why I had to tell you."

"Yes, I see." They looked at each other with the grave simplicity of candid youth. "It is—horrid," said May in a low voice.

"Rather," Tony agreed.

"I mean for you," she explained hastily.

"So did I. I say—you're all right here?"

"Oh, perfectly, thank you." She flushed. "It's a very good place. I'm fortunate."

Tony was not abashed. "I suppose I oughtn't to have said that. But I mean it all the same. I want to be sure you are all right. If that's cheek—well, don't be angry."

"It would be silly," said May with her head held high, and she did not look at him.

"I shall be staying on here for a bit," Tony announced. "Shall I ever see you again?"

"I should think it's very unlikely, Mr. Wisberry."

"Don't you ever go out anywhere?"

"No. I haven't been outside the grounds since I've been here."

"But, I say, what a life!" Tony grinned.

"The grounds are quite large, thank you."

"Open to the public?"

"I believe Lord Croyland lets anybody see the ruins who wants to."

"Good. I shall be seeing the ruins." He took hold of her hand. "I'm going to see you again, you know."

May laughed and began to say something and stopped with a red face. What was on her lips was the title of a poem by the late Mr. Browning: "Love among the Ruins." She turned it into: "Among the ruins! I think not, thank you." She tried to take her hand away. "Good-bye, Mr. Wisberry."

Tony held on. "I say, I'm at the Cock and Pie at Bradstock. When I go, St. Jude's College, Cambridge, will always find me. Don't forget: Jude's. And if you go, tell me where. Will you?"

"I've no intention of going. I'm quite happy here."

Tony looked down at her with a scrutiny which made her turn away.

"Good-bye, Mr. Wisberry." She jerked her hand free and fled.

Tony watched her till the slim hurrying shape vanished in the garden. He stared at the shadowed walls of the Abbey. "Oh, damn all," he muttered, and swung away to his boat.

From her window May watched the brown sail glide away.

CHAPTER X

HIS SECRETARY AND LORD CROYLAND

To HIS perfect satisfaction Tony established that there was an immemorial ferry right of landing on the Abbey hard and a path which was public through the grounds to the highroad. The fishermen of Bradstock, a small ancient clan, calling no man master, determined about their liberties and privileges, told him that these rights of way dated from old times when the Abbey was an abbey and folks went to church there by land and water.

Tony crossed the harbour again more than once that week. But he did not see May.

May was much occupied. Mrs. Garston had fallen into a more querulous condition. She demanded continuous attention and many things done to relieve her and complained of them all. She was certainly in pain, or believed herself to be—a difficult distinction. May could find no clear symptoms of any definite illness, except the obvious disorder of her nerves, and began to fear that more drugs were consumed than those in the foolish but harmless array by the bedside. She suspected the maid, whose jealous ministrations could not be suppressed. Mrs. Garston was always more uneasy in her presence, more enfeebled after being alone with her. But there was no proof of any drug, and, to be sure, the woman herself was enough to try the strongest nerves.

May promised herself that as soon as Lord Croyland came she would decline to go on without a doctor.

Probably that would be the end of it. For when she spoke of a doctor Mrs. Garston wept and reproached and complained beyond bearing. And it was impossible to believe that a doctor would do any good. The woman had some memory which was making her life horrible.

The death of her son long ago—perhaps it was only that, poor thing. Yet why should it make her so cruel to her other son, so bitter, such an enemy when one only wanted to help her? Oh, people might be like that who had lost someone they cared for. But to nurse a sort of hatred for twenty years—surely it couldn't be just grieving. Perhaps there was something dreadful about the death.

It was ever since she had seen Mr. Wisberry, ever since that strange rush to him and his boat, she had been so much worse. What could there be about him? She didn't know him, he didn't mean anything to her —and he had never seen her before; he said so. Perhaps she was always hoping the dead son would come back sailing across the sea. People had fancies like that sometimes. Poor thing. Then she'd be horribly disappointed, breaking her heart all over again. Yes. That would explain her. That must be it.

But he was rather queer. There was some mystery about him. Something about the past of the Garston family too. It must be. Because he said it was the affairs of his father he was coming about and his father was dead. And Lord Croyland was trying not to see him.

"Oh! I do hate it all," May murmured.

He seemed nice, quite nice. He was alive at least—a change from these Garston people, all muddled up glooming and hating. He was jolly. But there was something hard about him too. Rather frightening. He wouldn't care what he did to get what he wanted.

And, oh, horrors, he had his mystery. No. One mustn't have anything to do with Mr. Wisberry. One mustn't see him again.

She remembered uncomfortably the size of him. Great big creature. He would be horribly strong.

By the end of the week May was herself in a state of nervous irritation. It was in the afternoon of Friday. Having made Mrs. Garston lie down, she was in her own room trying to rest when the sound of a car brought her off her bed with a jump. She ran to the window and saw Gladys and Croyland arriving. A chill of disappointment came over her, though she did not know what she had hoped. Then she told herself that she was glad to see them. She could have it out with the man at last—at once. She hurried into her dress.

Somebody tried the door. "Is Miss Dean in?" the voice of Gladys laughed. May turned the key. "Hullo, hullo, baby." Gladys embraced her. "Well, how's things?"

"Ghastly."

"What? Has she got worse?"

"Oh, she's in a dreadful state. She must have a doctor."

"Do you mean she's going to die?"

"I don't know. I shouldn't think so. But I can't do anything with her. I can't be responsible."

"Go easy, old girl." Gladys looked grave. "Don't get the wind up. I should say you were managing her lovely. What's gone wrong with her?"

"How should I know?" May cried. "I don't know a thing about her. She won't let me."

"Has she heard of this case?"

"What case?"

"She hasn't said anything then?"

"Not anything with any sense. What do you mean?"

"Old Morrow's had her jewels stolen, or thinks she has. Didn't you know? It's been in the papers."

"I don't know whether she knows or not. I didn't."

"Rummy. I should have thought the Morrow told her everything."

"I haven't any idea. Perhaps it is that. Where's Lord Croyland, Gladys? I must see him."

"What do you want him for?" Gladys frowned.

"To tell him she must have a doctor. I can't go on without. I won't be responsible for her. Where is he?"

"Steady, old girl. He won't like that, you know. He doesn't want a doctor."

"Doesn't he indeed!" May cried. "Why not?"

"Well, I ask you! The old girl's all dithery. That's what you're here for. If you want doctors in, it's going to be the end of your job, baby."

"Then it's quite time they came," said May fiercely.

"Don't be silly. Of course he doesn't want a family scandal. The old girl's so queer, there's no telling what she'll say. Probably tell the doctor somebody's murdering her. You for choice."

"And do you think that's to stop me having a doctor? It's the very reason. I'm going to Lord Croyland at once."

She pushed past Gladys and made haste down the old corridor through the archway into the new part of the house.

"All right! All right!" Gladys laughed behind her. "Don't burst into his bedroom, baby. Gives the valet ideas. Try the study."

To the study they came together. Croyland was there standing by the window, shoulders hunched, staring out across the harbour. He turned, and it seemed to May's excited mind that his heavy sullen face had a look of anger and spite.

"Miss Dean wants to speak to you," said Gladys, and sat down at her secretary's table and began to open letters.

Croyland cleared his throat. "Ah. Sit down. Yes?"

"I hope you've seen your mother, Lord Croyland." May was breathless. "She's not so well."

"I thought she was worse," Croyland said. There was no feeling in his gruff voice, unless a certain satisfaction. "Do you know why that is?"

"I don't know what's the matter with her."

"Anyone been to see her?"

"No one ever comes to her."

Croyland made inarticulate noises. "Has she had any—er—any communication with anyone?"

May was furious with him. "She has letters. You don't expect me to know what's in them, I suppose?"

"No, I don't," he frowned. "Nothing new happened here, eh?"

May's temper rose higher yet. "Oh, there was a very queer thing one day. She actually saw someone who didn't belong to the house. I suppose that's never happened before."

"Who was it?" Croyland growled.

"He said his name was Wisberry."

Croyland swung on his heel and looked at Gladys. "Know anything about that, eh?"

"Not a thing," said Gladys cheerfully. "He's given up writing. Thought he'd take you by surprise, I expect."

Croyland came back to May with a frown. "Did he ask for my mother?"

"He asked for you."

"But she saw him, eh? How was that?"

"He came in a boat and she saw it and ran down from the house to meet him. She seemed to expect someone else, Lord Croyland. She was horribly disappointed when she saw him. She's been upset ever since."

Croyland made noises in his throat. It was some time before he spoke, but his dull eyes were intent on May. "She ran down to the hard, eh? Met the boat, hmph? Didn't know the fellow?"

"She didn't seem to. You had better ask her."

"Did he say anything?"

"He asked me who she was."

"Did you know him?"

"I never saw him before."

"What did he say to you?"

"He asked if you were here. I said you weren't and he went away."

"Thank you. That's all right. Thank you." He turned away. "Sorry you've been bothered, Miss Dean."

"You've nothing to thank me for," May cried. "Don't you understand, I didn't come to be cross-questioned about your business people. I came to tell you your mother must have a doctor. She must. I can't be responsible for her any longer."

"Eh, what's that? Don't mean you want to go?"

"I will stay if Mrs. Garston wishes it——"

"I wish it," Croyland growled. "You're doing very well, Miss Dean. Just what I want."

"You had better think of what she wants. And I can't stay unless she's in a doctor's hands."

"That's all right. Miss Hurst—ring up Eves. Tell him to come and see my mother in the morning. Much obliged to you, Miss Dean." He opened the door for her.

May went out feeling dazed. The victory was complete. She had exactly what she wanted. The brute made haste to give way—so much for Gladys and her threats. He did his best to be pleasant about it. A victory too complete. He must be desperately frightened. There must be something horribly wrong.

CHAPTER XI

IN THE morning May was called to Croyland's study
to meet Dr. Eves. She would not have taken him for a
doctor; he was more like an old farmer. He and Croyland seemed to know each other very well. "Er—Miss
Dean—just tell the doctor what you think—anything
you want," Croyland said. And May told at length and
Dr. Eves pursed his red cheeks, puffing and blowing.
. When she had finished he trumpeted on his nose.
"Yaas. Ah see, Nurse, ah see," he drawled. "That's
what set her baack, seeing this young fella come in
the boat." He turned to Croyland, nodding his bald
head, and Croyland rumbled. It was obvious they
shared some knowledge which made them satisfied or
content. "Eh, well, ye'll be wishing me to see her,"
said Dr. Eves, as if it were a useless formality. "Ah'll
step up, Nurse."

Mrs. Garston surprised May by receiving him with
submission. She was dreary, she said as little as might
be, but she did answer him, she let him do what he liked
with her. Though his ways were queer and clumsy to
May's professional eye, he did not leave anything undone in his examination, but it was carelessly short. He
straightened his back, grunting and puffing. "Thaat's
well," he drawled, looking down at her with the contemptuous pity of thick-skinned health for the weak.
"Do you be peaceful, ma'am, and you'll see us all out
yet. Good-day to you."

When May had him outside, "It's easy to tell her to be peaceful," she said fiercely. "She doesn't know how. That's what's wrong with her."

Dr. Eves was not impressed. "Eh, she's an old woman, my dear," he grunted. "Ah'll send you along a sedative." He lumbered downstairs to the study. "It's like ah thought, Croyland," he announced. "She'd do well enough if she'd bide quiet. Tha-at's a fact." He dropped a fat hand on May's shoulder. "Ye've a good girl here. She'll do all ye need." He chuckled as May slid away from his touch. "A good girl, eh! Well, ah must be off."

Croyland took him out.

But when May returned to Mrs. Garston there were storms. Beginning with plaintive questions why had the doctor been brought? what did May suppose was the matter with her? why couldn't she be let alone? Mrs. Garston worked up to a high pressure of martyred rage: scolding and accusing while she rejected as new brutality each attempt to soothe her and showed, perhaps sincerely, more and more distress. The maid came in alarmed, as she was careful to explain, by the noise and contributed an inflaming sympathy. May was harried to the limits of her self-control.

When at last Mrs. Garston sank into the sleep of exhausted emotion, May went out wearily to try for some respite to aching head and worried mind in the open air. She was wandering towards the ruins when she saw a little plump man with gray whiskers and gray clothes. A vague memory that she had seen him before came to her, but she dismissed it, for she certainly did not know his face. Yet it was true. That day was not the first on which Mr. Clunk had made a reconnaissance of Bradstock Harbour. He had not before come so near the Abbey. She had seen only his back and his tripping gait. But this was Saturday, on which day, Mr. Clunk calculated, visitors to the ruins would most naturally come.

A red guide book was in his hand; he tripped about looking into it and looking at the ruined arches and poring over the ground and chirping to himself, the model of the earnest tripper. But what he chirped was:

> "Shall we meet? Shall we meet?
> Shall we meet beyond the river?
> Shall we meet beyond the river
> Where the surges cease to roll?"

He saw May. "Dear me, I beg your pardon. I do hope I'm not trespassing. The guide book says visitors are kindly allowed to inspect the ruins."

"Yes, they are." May had to smile at him. He was so nervous and funny.

"Thank you so much. That's so kind. I didn't want to intrude, you know."

"You're quite all right here."

"I'm most obliged to you. What a dear old church. I'm most interested in these sweet old places." He tripped away, he vanished.

A large car had drawn up at the house. Out of it came a thick-set man with a waist and a red flower in his coat. From behind the arches of the nave Mr. Clunk watched him with opening eyes.

But May saw neither of them. She was wandering on through the garden, feeling rather better. It must be recorded that she thought Mr. Clunk a sweet old thing.

The man went into the house and Mr. Clunk, coming through the bushes like a nymph, found Lewis sitting on that smooth stone in the niche of the nave wall, smoking a cigarette in tranquil boredom.

"Car at the door, my boy," said Mr. Clunk into his ear. "Do what you can. It's Harwood."

"Oh!" Lewis stared at him a moment, sprang up and stole away.

To Gladys, sitting at her table in the study with Croyland, the butler brought the card of Mr. Gordon Harwood. She looked at it curiously and waved the butler out and took it to Croyland. "This is the man who wrote that odd letter, you know."

Croyland cleared his throat. "I'll see him myself."

"Oh, very good." She shrugged disapproval and went out. The butler led her to the old abbots' hall, where Mr. Gordon Harwood sat, making in his tailor's elegance a grotesque blot on its dignity. The butler thought her very short with him, but as she took him upstairs she looked over her shoulder and, "The old man's funking, G.," she whispered. She opened the study door. "Mr. Harwood, sir," she said with contempt, and shut the door sharply.

Mr. Harwood smiled, "Good-morning, my lord. Lovely place you have here."

Croyland grunted, "Sit down, will you? What do you want to say to me?"

Harwood drew up a chair to a confidential position. "That'll want a little time to explain," he said. "It's rather complicated, my lord. It's a delicate matter too. Now, to begin with, can I take it you know who I am?" Many large teeth glittered in a smile.

"You can take it I've made some inquiries." Croyland sat with his head down between his shoulders. "Money lender, aren't you?"

"Financial agent," Harwood corrected. "Perhaps you've heard my firm handles pretty big business."

"What kind?" Croyland grunted.

"You might call it family and personal. And we don't

care to take up anything unless we're satisfied it's important. When you're dealing with me, you can be sure there's no pettifogging tricks."

"I'm not dealing with you," Croyland said thickly.

"Not yet. This is to let you know how I stand. I believe in managing big things in a big way. That's me. Now then, my lord, here's the position. My firm has been approached by a person presenting himself as the heir of your late brother, Alfred Garston." He stopped and waited for a reply.

Croyland was in no hurry. "Want an answer, do you?" he said with contempt. "The answer is, somebody's attempting a fraud."

Harwood smiled. "Too easy, isn't it? Call it a fraud and send for the police." He leaned back and crossed his legs. "Ring 'em up, my lord. I shan't run away."

Croyland cleared his throat. "I'm waiting for you to give me the evidence."

"Yes, I thought you would," Harwood laughed. "You're no fool. I know that. And you can take it I don't play the fool either. Then we'll get on." He veiled his impudence again. "My firm has a lot of experience, my lord. I don't mind telling you, when this chap came to us our first idea was he was putting up a fraud, like you say. But when we came to look into it, we found he could make a nasty, ugly case."

"Who's your man?" Croyland growled.

"Well, naturally, he says his name is Garston. Alfred Garston."

"Naturally!" Croyland made noises. "Very naturally. My brother died unmarried."

"Think so?" Harwood shrugged. "Difficult thing to prove, isn't it?"

"I shouldn't have to prove it. You'd have to prove the marriage."

"Oh, good God!" Harwood exclaimed. "Take it I know that, can't you?"

"Twenty years after my brother's death a man claims to be his legitimate son." Croyland sneered. "Hmph! That's a poor story."

"A damned poor story," Harwood agreed. "So I told him. And if there was no more to it I shouldn't be here. But have you considered how the case would work out if you let it come into court? We were bound to look into the circumstances and we satisfied ourselves that we ought to put the claim to you privately before any action was taken. It's not our practice to force an unpleasant situation. Absolutely not. When there are awkward facts which it's not necessary to bring out we believe in settlement."

Croyland made noises. "You would."

"I do. A lawsuit isn't in our interest. We don't want to be in a big scandal. That won't do our business any good. We depend on confidence in our discretion. But it would be the devil and all for you, my lord."

"What do you mean?"

"You know what I mean. What you want to find out is how much we've got in our hands. I'm agreeable. I'll put all my cards on the table for you. To begin with, there may be a difficulty in proving our man the legitimate son of Alfred Garston—"

"There never was any son."

Harwood smiled. "That's your case. Just listen to ours. There won't be any difficulty in proving that Alfred Garston had affairs with women: with one woman in particular. We could call police evidence about that, couldn't we?"

Croyland's heavy head thrust forward. "That won't help you," he growled.

"Think not? Well, we could ask Mr. Bell—Superintendent Bell he is now, did you know?—if the police ever had any suspicion about her death. You remember her death, my lord? She was found shot in the New Forest. The verdict was murder by a person unknown. And a week afterwards Alfred Garston was found drowned on your beach. You know very well what a lawyer on a claim by Alfred's son could make of that. He'd say it was someone's interest to kill off the woman and the man. Somebody wanted to wipe out Alfred absolutely. And he'd ask the court who gained by it."

Croyland watched him with sullen eyes. "Come to the wrong man," he growled. "You want the police. Tell them I murdered my brother—and the woman —and anybody else that occurs to you. It's their affair."

"That's only silly, isn't it?" Harwood was not angry but pained. "I haven't said you murdered them. If you want to know, I don't believe you did. This is what I say, my lord: these convenient deaths wiped out Alfred and his woman and left you the only heir to the firm and everything. But if the claim for Alfred's son goes into court his lawyer will want to know what you've been paying to keep it all quiet."

Croyland's big mouth curled. "The answer is, I'm not paying you."

"Who's talking about paying me? You!" Harwood cried. "Wait till you're asked. No, you haven't been paying me. But you've been paying someone else. That'll come out, you know."

Croyland stood up. "I don't know what you mean. And I don't care," he said.

"That hits you, don't it?" Harwood rose too and came close to him. "I know you're bluffing, Croyland. Come down. Our man can prove Alfred told people you wanted him underground."

Croyland thought that out, and a look of gloating satisfaction came on Harwood's red face. But when Croyland spoke, what he said was: "I see. Thanks. Given yourself away, haven't you? And for nothing."

Harwood flinched. "I don't know what you mean," he said sullenly. Then his voice rose. "Do you want to have your mother in court asked what she knows about Alfred's death?"

"Get out," Croyland growled, and his fists clenched.

Harwood laughed relief. "I've got you and you know it. Better settle quick. Else it'll go beyond me —and hell for you."

"Beyond you?" Croyland rumbled. "There's nothing beyond you. And nothing in you. Go to the devil."

"You'll be sorry for this." Harwood drew back. Croyland's bulk was threatening. "You'll be damned sorry, my lord."

Croyland gave a growling laugh. "You fool, I know there's no son. I've taken your measure. That's all I wanted." He rang the bell, and when Gladys came pointed to the door.

With a toss of her head Gladys deigned to show Mr. Harwood the way out. But on the stairs she lingered for him to draw level with her. "How did it go?" she whispered.

"Like hell. Nix," Harwood muttered.

From the ruins, from that smooth stone in the recess of the nave, Mr. Clunk watched him climb into his big car and vanish. Mr. Clunk smiled sadly and was moved to gentle song:

> "Not far, not far from the Kingdom
>   Yet in the shadow of sin;
> How many are coming and going!
>   How few there are entering in!"

He sighed and took up his guide book and studied the plan of the Abbey and wandered about with it, an earnest antiquarian.

Thus engaged, he saw another car come to the door, a car not like Harwood's but an ancient hireling of the country; out of it came Tony Wisberry.

Mr. Clunk's face as it receded behind a rhododendron confessed surprise: an unusual thing in him, except as affectation. It was also aggrieved. "Tut, tut," he murmured, and tapped his false teeth. The annoyance vanished, the surprise remained.

Inside the Abbey there was also surprise. Once more the butler came to Gladys with a card. "His lordship is not here," she was saying when Croyland cleared his throat and turned and held out his hand. "It's that Mr. Wisberry again," she explained contemptuously.

"Hmph!" Croyland stared at the card. "Bring him up."

"Oh, very well," Gladys flounced out.

Thus Tony found himself being inspected by a full-blown young woman with bold and inquisitive eyes. He did not approve of it; or of her paint; or of her. "What can I do for you, Mr. Wisberry?" she smiled.

"Nothing, except take me to Lord Croyland."

"His lordship can spare you a minute," Gladys said with condescension, and took him upstairs talking graciously and making eyes sideways. That also was ineffective.

"Mr. Wisberry," she announced, and was going back to her table when Croyland signed her out.

"Sit down." Croyland frowned and looked him over. Tony was at his angular ugliest. "What do you want to tell me?"

"I wrote to you. Have you read my letters?"

"Answered, weren't they?"

"Some fellow wrote back that Garston & Garston could give no information about their processes of manufacture."

"I approve," Croyland said quickly. "Well?"

"That isn't an answer. I told you my father discovered the vanadium process you employed. I asked you how you acquired it. And why you began to use it just after he disappeared. I've tried to see you half a dozen times to ask you that. Now you've made up your mind to face it." He stared back defiance at Croyland's sullen, resolute eyes and his chin came out, and imitating Croyland he said, "Well?"

Croyland surprised him. "Who was your father?" The question came sharp.

"Same name as mine. Antony Wisberry. Lecturer at Birmingham Technical College. There's no mystery about me. And no secrets."

Croyland was in turn surprised. "Hmph. Mother living?" he grunted.

"She died last winter. You can verify all this."

"I will if I want to. You said your father disappeared. How?"

"He just vanished. I was one year old. My mother never knew what happened to him. That's one of the things I'm asking you."

Croyland stirred. "How the devil should I know?"

"He disappeared in 1908. Before he disappeared he'd worked out the first vanadium process which Garstons employed. When did you bring that into use? 1908 or just after. Where did you get it from?"

"Our own laboratories." The answer was quick.

Tony laughed. "Going to prove that? Who was the inventor?"

"What's done in our laboratories is joint work. If you know anything about science in industry——"

"I do. It's my job. I'm going into Rimingtons."

Croyland grunted and looked at him with keener interest. "Good firm. Young, aren't you? Just finished at Cambridge, eh?"

"I'm twenty-two. I told you. One-year baby when my father disappeared."

Croyland frowned and made rumbling noises. "About your father. You say he'd got a vanadium process. Only just found that out? Twenty-one years after—after he was lost. What started you looking for it now?"

"My mother's death. I had to look over the papers she left. I found my father's notebooks—and his process. I can prove what I say, you know."

"Can you?" Croyland's face hardened again into sullen contempt. "Prove it all, and it don't matter a row o' pins to my firm. Say your father had a process. We worked out ours. Say it's much the same. That's always happening. Bound to happen. Make a claim and we smash you. No case." He leaned forward in his chair and played with a pencil, looking at it. "That's the answer, Mr. Wisberry." He made noises in his throat, and after a moment, as if the words were forced out of him, "I'm sorry," he said.

"Are you?" Tony's jaw hardened. "I bet you'll be sorrier when I do make a claim."

Croyland sat back and the chair creaked under him. "Hmph. Threatening, are you?"

"No. I asked you for an explanation. You haven't one. So I tell you you'll have to fight it out."

Croyland gave a short, scornful laugh. "Not threatening. But if we don't pay, you'll take us into court. I see. Who told you to try that game, Mr. Wisberry?"

Tony flushed. "No one. What the devil do you mean? This is my own show."

"All alone, eh? Not consulted anyone?"

"If you want to know, I have——"

"Thought as much."

"I consulted my mother's solicitor——"

"Who is he?"

"Clunk, Joshua Clunk."

"What, Clunk & Clunk!" Croyland chuckled. "You're in with good people, Mr. Wisberry."

"You know him, do you? That's interesting too. I thought you might. He told me I should make nothing out of it. That's another reason I'm going on."

"What?"

"Yes, you don't understand that," Tony laughed. "I don't want to make anything out of it. But I'm going to find out how my father died."

"Then you've come to the wrong man." Croyland rose heavily. "I can't do anything for you. Good-day, Mr. Wisberry."

Tony sat still for a moment then sprang up. "All right. Fight it," he cried, and swung out.

Croyland sat still looking at the shut door, then lumbered across the room and filled himself a glass of whisky and soda.

Gladys came back and saw him draining it. Her black eyebrows went up. She sat down at her table and began to rustle papers. Croyland glanced at her, lit a cigar, dropped into an easy chair, and smoked and grunted.

"Is there anything else for me?" Gladys suggested. A growl of negation answered. "Thank you. Will you want the two-seater this afternoon? I'd like to get some things. Back to tea." Another growl agreed. "It's lunch time, you know." A third growl dismissed her.

For some time Croyland sat smoking. Then he went back to his desk and wrote slowly with much consideration, and what he wrote he put into his pocket.

Tony also was smoking as he drove back in his hireling car to Bradstock. Mr. Clunk, still engaged on the study of ecclesiastical antiquities, watched his departure with wistful interest, for it seemed to Mr. Clunk deplorably unreasonable that Croyland should have consented to see him.

That was, as he thought about it, surprising Tony too. If the old rascal only meant to turn him down why see him at all? Why not stand by the original refusal to discuss the matter? That looked comparatively respectable, the usual formal answer to claims. There could be no question of finding out what sort of a case he had. That was all in his letters. Perfectly futile to talk it over in order to tell him to go to the devil. Showed the blighter knew there was something beastly fishy about the business. But why let it out? He must be in the deuce of a funk. And why suddenly?

Tony could see no reason, and puzzling over Croyland's queer questions became more puzzled: being without the knowledge that another visitor had been before him with Croyland that morning, threatening claims by a nameless man and revelations of what had happened in the spring of the year 1908. But Tony was very sure that he had Croyland frightened out of his life and he bit on his pipe and chuckled.

The world was being good. Quite good. A bit difficult to know what to do next. Ought to get hold of a sound lawyer and make him get busy: drive the old rascal hard now he was on the run. No screaming hurry though. He had to see that girl again somehow. Foul that she should be in the house mixed up with the rascal and his mad old mother. Nasty business. Beastly queer house. That lump Croyland, deep as sin, and devil could tell what on his conscience—mad old woman—and that scented, painted minx, his secretary. Nice young woman for a quiet teaparty she'd be. Oh, foul, that girl should be in the hands of such a crew. He must see her. Get her out of it somehow.

Very hard to know what to do. Couldn't very well call on her. Only make a hell of a mess. Couldn't hang about the place. Try writing to her, something simple and civil, ask her to meet him.

He went back to the Cock and Pie and wrote.

While he was writing, the meditations of Mr. Clunk among the ruins were disturbed by a small cough. Mr. Clunk turned and saw Lewis. "Staying at Spraymouth, sir," Lewis said. "Grand Hotel."

"Dear me," Mr. Clunk smiled. "I wonder if Mr. Bell would like to know that, Lewis."

"Not yet, eh?" Lewis grinned.

"No, not yet, I think. It wouldn't be at all good for him. He's in such a hurry, Lewis. He does worry his cases." Mr. Clunk tripped away. "Not yet, no. He that believeth shall not make haste. How true that is, Lewis. How good for the soul." And Mr. Clunk suddenly ceased to make haste. He saw Gladys get into a two-seater. "Dear, dear, what a lot of cars there are to-day," he sighed. "Where is ours, Lewis?"

They found it, they followed Gladys down the drive. As they came to the lodge Lewis turned to Mr. Clunk. "She went right. That's the Spraymouth road," he said.

"Is it indeed?" said Mr. Clunk. "Well, well, well. We'd better go our own way, Lewis." He sighed. "There was another car, an old shabby car, hired here in the country, I think. Eh?"

"Saw an old bus going down to Bradstock—that's the village beyond the harbour."

"Dear me, what a lot of people," Mr. Clunk sighed.

CHAPTER XII

MR. CLUNK BEARS NO MALICE

MR. CLUNK'S conscience objected to his working on Sunday. This limitation however was liable to exceptions when he found himself in a place which contained no place of worship approved by his conscience. Most places have that defect. In such unhappy conditions it was not merely allowed but obligatory to work; and you might have heard Mr. Clunk chanting:

> *"Give every flying minute*
> *Something to keep in store.*
> *Work for the night is coming*
> *When man works no more."*

With that melody on his lips he came to Sunday's breakfast and asked Lewis if he was going to Chapel. Lewis hastily thought not. "I fear you're right, my boy," Mr. Clunk sighed. "Yes indeed. Well, well, well. We'll have the car then. Work is worship, my boy." Work had formed no part of Lewis's plan for the day. He agreed sulkily. In gloomy and reproachful silence he drove Mr. Clunk out to Bradstock and Mr. Clunk prattled to him of the service of modern inventions to true religion. For of old, as Mr. Clunk pointed out, a journey to Bradstock would have required one horse or two, and to make the animals labour on the Sabbath was sadly wrong; whereas, going out behind the engine of a motor, they were blameless. "Doesn't that show

we're making our world better and better, my boy?"
said Mr. Clunk. "Yes indeed. How comforting that is."

And Lewis, nodding, wondered in his saturnine mind
what dirty work the old man was up to. When he
drivelled special he always had something on his mind.

But Mr. Clunk's actions were blameless. He directed
the car, not to Bradstock Abbey, but round the harbour to the little fishermen's village of Bradstock. He
had it brought down to the beach like a man intending
nothing but the simple joys of a picnic. He wandered
about the sands, pointing out Nature's beauty. He got
into talk with a fisherman here and there. Lewis, lazily
admiring the skill of the old boy in making men who
had little but manhood in common with him talk about
their trade and their sleepy village, wondered what on
earth he was after. For the drowning of Alfred Garston
in the harbour had not been confided to Lewis. Why
Mr. Clunk should be so pleased to hear the harbour
waters were safe as nothing and no one ever had no
trouble there was beyond Lewis.

They ate their lunch on the beach. Mr. Clunk then
thought that he would look at the church. The prospect did not attract Lewis. He lay on the sand and
drowsed, and Mr. Clunk tripped away. The village
church was small but of a grave dignity, built by the
monks in a good age. About it were the graves of many
of the rich folk who had held their Abbey after them.
Mr. Clunk was much interested. He found the stone
which bore the name of Alfred Garston, younger son
of Sir Samuel Garston, Baronet, R.I.P. Close by another stone was inscribed to Samuel Garston, First
Baronet of Bradstock Abbey. The father had not lived
many weeks after his son's death.

Mr. Clunk tapped his teeth. "Dear, dear. That was
very sad for Lord Croyland," he murmured. "And he,

even he only, is left." Mr. Clunk gave a queer little
chuckle and turned away.

The village of Bradstock does not offer many possibilities of lodging strangers. Mr. Clunk made his way
with easy confidence to the Cock and Pie. It is a
homely inn, of cream cob walls and thatched roof set
back behind a square of green. At that hour of Sunday
afternoon, when public beer is forbidden, it was pro-
foundly still and silent. But on the long seat under its
windows was stretched Tony smoking a pipe and contemplating the unconscious approach of Mr. Clunk
with bitter amusement. It is difficult even for the expert to overlook anyone of Tony's size in a plausible
way. But Mr. Clunk did well.

He tripped to the door, he tapped and stood waiting,
and Tony spoke. "Why not see me?"

Mr. Clunk jumped. "Bless my soul!" he cried.
"Tony! My dear boy, what ever are you doing here?"

"Admiring you. And what have you come for?"

"A cup of tea," said Mr. Clunk, and tapped again.

"Don't do that. Old Collins won't like it. He's having
his afternoon shut eye. And he hates getting teas."

"But how wrong that is!" said Mr. Clunk. "A li-
cence holder is bound to serve reasonable refreshment
at reasonable hours. And he ought to encourage tea
drinking. It is far better for everyone, body and soul.
And a very good profit too."

"Oh gosh," Tony groaned. "You are, you really are!
And why are you? It don't cut any ice."

"I don't follow you, my boy," said Mr. Clunk tolerantly, and tapped more loudly at the door. It was flung
open, a lump of a man scowled at him. "Mr. Wisberry
says you can let me have some tea," Mr. Clunk smiled.
"For both of us if you please." The man vanished with
a growl.

Tony had to laugh. "That's a dirty trick. Now he'll take it out of me. Persistent beggar, aren't you?"

"Oh, really, do you think so?" Mr. Clunk came to the bench and Tony's legs reluctantly moved to let him sit down. "Thank you, my boy, I rather depend on my tea."

"I'm not thinking of your tea," Tony grunted, watching him. "You didn't come down to Bradstock for a cup of tea."

The tea came, banged down on the bare table in front of them by an angry man. "Thank you so much." Mr. Clunk eagerly poured out the black fluid. "How nice and strong. There you are, my boy." He sipped his own and beamed. And the landlord was mollified to ask if the gentleman would like a bit o' lobster.

Tony waved him away. "Now then, Mr. Clunk. What is it you do want? Let's have it out."

"But my dear boy, I want nothing. When I came down here, I had no idea I should meet you."

"Oh, rats."

"Really, Tony, if you won't choose to believe me, why ask? But there's no mystery about my being here. I'm staying at Limbay defending a poor fellow who is accused of theft. You will find the case in the papers. He's in court again to-morrow. I drove out to-day to look at the country."

"And to see Croyland, I suppose."

"I have never seen Lord Croyland in my life," said Mr. Clunk. "I've no intention of trying. But of course that is what has brought you. Dear me, I might have known."

"You might," Tony grinned. "In fact you did. And you came over to say I'd better not."

"No indeed. My dear boy, if you remember our last important interview, you must see that I could not advise you further. You made it plain you did not trust me, Tony. I don't care to deny that I was much hurt. But that is nothing. The point is, I make it a rule to give no advice if I am not trusted."

"Thanks so much. That's just as well. I have seen Croyland."

"Dear me! I confess I am surprised. Well, well, well! In a long experience I have seldom been more surprised."

Tony frowned. An old unpleasant suspicion that Mr. Clunk was too clever for him asserted itself. "Bound to say that, aren't you?" he growled. "You told me I had no sort of case against him."

"Certainly that was my opinion," Mr. Clunk murmured, and tapped his teeth.

"What are you suggesting now?"

"No, no, my boy. I suggest nothing. It's not my business," Mr. Clunk said sadly.

"Well, he did see me. And heard all I'd got to say in order to tell me I had no case and could go to the devil; just like you, Mr. Clunk. Curious, isn't it?"

"My dear boy!" Mr. Clunk was quick to protest. "I could never tell you to go to the devil."

"No. He was more honest. Sorry. And I told him I should fight."

"Really! Well, well, well!" Mr. Clunk sighed.

"Don't like that, do you?" Tony glared at him.

Mr. Clunk took a lump of sugar and sucked. "Dear me, I couldn't say. It's not for me to object. What you think best, my dear boy, what you think right. Do right and fear nothing. There's no other rule in life." He crunched the sugar and took another lump while Tony glowered at him. "Good-bye, my dear boy. Always your friend. I bear no malice, Tony, none. Good-bye. I'll pay for the tea."

"Oh, be damned," said Tony. But Mr. Clunk did not hear that, and in fact was not meant to. It was an expression of bewilderment.

That day Mr. Clunk did no more. Lewis came to the conclusion that he was not feeling well. His prevailing habit is to be conversational. He said during the rest of Sunday nothing which was not necessary; he abstained even from humming. He was wrapped in solemn thought and he went very early to bed. Such retirement, Mrs. Clunk might have explained to Lewis, indicates a felt want of ideas.

But he was in court next morning, brisk and beaming as ever. Neither the solicitor on the other side nor Bell and Gunn made so prompt an appearance. They were indeed something after the hour, and when they came at last Mr. Clunk looked at his watch with ostentation and his *hem* of comment was audible.

The magistrates took their seats, the solicitor whispered to the clerk, the clerk to the magistrates, and again Mr. Clunk's watch came out and he sighed loud and clear.

Billy Bones was put in the dock. The solicitor came back to his place and addressed the bench. Since the last sitting of the court, he had had an opportunity of examining the evidence which could be offered.

"Dear me," said Mr. Clunk.

The solicitor appreciated his friend's anxiety. He was bound to tell the bench that upon full consideration he had come to the conclusion it would not be right to ask the bench to commit the prisoner for trial.

Then Mr. Clunk rose and enjoyed himself. Superintendent Bell did not.

The bench remained calm: pronounced that the charge must be dismissed and did not desire to express any opinion on the conduct of the case.

Mr. Clunk, with a smile and a nod at Bell's stolid face, tripped out of court to find his client. Billy Bones was a happy man. "Good for you, Clunk. Shake. You did that fine. I nearly burst myself watching Bell squirm."

"You're a very lucky man, my friend," Mr. Clunk admonished him. "You must know that. Don't forget it."

"Not half. You've done me proud. I never forget a pal."

"Don't forget yourself," said Mr. Clunk austerely. "I hope I shall never see you again."

"All right, all right," Billy Bones was surprised and grieved. "No offence, Mr. Clunk."

"You silly fellow. I'm not angry with you. It's my business to help silly fellows. But I don't want any more of this case."

"I say, you mean Bell's worrying at it still?"

"I mean that you had better be very quiet, my friend."

"Not half," Billy Bones winked. "It's me for the Continong. I'll take Gracie for a bit of a honeymoon, what?"

Mr. Clunk sighed. "That will do," he admitted with regret. "Go abroad and stay there. Try to be a good fellow, Benson."

"You bet. I've had enough for a bit. I say, do you think there's going to be more trouble?"

"My poor fellow, you know Bell. Does he look satisfied?"

Billy Bones pondered. "I say, Clunk, on the square —are you inside this?"

"I know nothing about it but what you've told me."

"Smell something though, eh?"

"My dear fellow, I can see it wasn't the jewels you were after," said Mr. Clunk.

"Who are you acting for, anyway?"

"Myself," said Mr. Clunk. "I find it a curiously interesting case, my friend."

Again Billy Bones pondered. "I don't know. Look here, Clunk, you've done me well. Can I do you a bit o' good? I reckon you'd like to know what was in the old girl's letters?" Billy looked wary. "Well, if you took it her man Alfred was telling her his brother hated him enough to do him in, you wouldn't be so far out."

"Oh dear, what sad stuff." Mr. Clunk was shocked. "The letters were wanted for blackmail, I suppose."

"What do you think?" Billy Bones grinned. .

"You're a sad fellow," Mr. Clunk sighed. "Try to get away from it all, Benson."

"Bet your life. Right away at jolly old Monte. Cheerio, Clunk. Wish you luck. You ought to have a share of the dibs, I swear you ought." Billy Bones gripped his hand. "Toodle-oo."

On his way through the police officers Mr. Clunk met Inspector Gunn and Superintendent Bell. "Well now!" He stopped. "This is very pleasant. How are you? How are you?"

"None the better for seeing you, Mr. Clunk," Gunn said grinning. "You've had a nice bit of fun with us, haven't you?"

"Really now. You mustn't take it like that," Mr. Clunk protested. "I have my duty to do, just as you have, Inspector. And you know you've given me a great deal of trouble. You shouldn't have handled the case in this way, really you shouldn't. Quite wrong. But we can be good friends now, I hope and trust. I bear no malice, I promise you."

"Thank you kindly," said Gunn, and took Bell away. When they were behind a shut door, "There's gall for you," he exploded. "Bears no malice! That's the limit. Nasty little monkey."

Bell was calmer. "I wouldn't say. I don't know so much. Bag o' tricks, he is. But it's not like Josh Clunk to rile you."

"Isn't it? You surprise me! He told us off in court spiteful enough."

"Oh, in court," Bell said with contempt. "That's all guff. That's nothing. He's always very civil in private. Too civil by half. I don't think he meant to put your back up, Gunn. It looked to me he was throwing a fly."

"How do you mean?"

"Well, say giving us the office we'd got this case by the wrong end. I don't know but what we have." Bell frowned and pondered and gave a short and angry laugh. "I was thinking so myself, old man. What bothers me now is that Josh Clunk wants me to think so. That's a nasty blow."

"Here, go easy," Gunn complained. "Where are we getting to? What do you mean, the wrong end?"

"We went for the man that pinched the jewels. What about going for the man who wanted the love letters?"

"How do you know who he is? Lord, this is a bit too clever. We don't even know anybody did want the letters."

"We don't. But that's the only idea that makes sense of the case. Old Clunk hinted at it when he cross-examined Miss Morrow. He went very gently then. Now he's given us a straight tip. The only reason there can be for anybody wanting the love letters is something to do with Garstons."

"That old case! Twenty years dead!"

Bell nodded. "I know. But Josh Clunk don't bother himself with cases that are dead. Look here—if those letters tell something the Garston family wants kept

dark they might be worth anything you like—to Croyland. He could pay it." Bell lit a pipe. "Remember him
—in the old days, Gunn? Mr. Henry Garston. Hard as
they make 'em, wasn't he? I don't suppose he's got
any softer. I've been thinking about him. He wouldn't
have stuck at a trifle when we knew him."

"The other end of the case is the Garstons?"

Bell nodded. "Looks like it. It did look like it—
till Josh Clunk chipped in with his tip and his all-
friends talk. Now I don't know."

"I wouldn't trust the little monkey if he told me I
had my pants on."

"No, but you might have, all the same. Oh, he's up
to something, I know that. And he thinks it's going to
be worth his while to stand in with us."

"Then you bet your life he's up to something uncommon dirty."

"I'm not betting," said Bell. "But if Clunk's staying on here, I'm staying too. I reckon you'll want me."

And inquiries discovered that Mr. Clunk remained at
the Victoria Hotel.

CHAPTER XIII

IN THE DARK

A LETTER which is posted in Bradstock on Saturday is delivered at Bradstock Abbey on Monday morning. Such is the reckless speed of modern civilization.

It was therefore when her morning tea was brought to her bedroom on Monday that May received her letter from Tony. She thought it an odd letter: an absurd letter; and in conclusion she did not like it.

DEAR MISS DEAN:

I know it looks cheek of me to write to you at all. Don't take it that way. It would be, if I hadn't reasons that matter. The reasons are about as serious as they can be.

I've seen Lord Croyland. That's one. I shan't be seeing him again. I can't come to the Abbey again. But I must see you. I should have to anyway. But after what happened with Croyland I want to see you at once. I have things to say I can't write.

I suppose you'll get this on Monday. Walk over towards Bradstock any time you can. I shall be on the road looking for you. You must come. There's things you've got to know.

Yours sincerely,

TONY WISBERRY.

An absurd person.

She read it again and liked it less. The tone of authority became clearer. A horrid youth.

It is probable that if Tony had not written she must come, she would have come to him. And if she had, he might have turned the stream of things, taken her at least from their course, perhaps others too. Afterwards, as he struggled, he wondered sometimes dismally over what might have been.

She crushed the letter in her hand, then tore it into small pieces and threw it away. She was not going to answer a letter like that.

The day went worse than dismally. Mrs. Garston was at her most exacting and unreasonable, her maid in a malignant temper. They spent the morning nagging at each other and uniting to put May in the wrong.

Mrs. Garston being told, what she had just said, that she was not well enough to go down to lunch, wept and insisted on going, and at table sighed and moaned.

Croyland's usual careful kindness to her failed. Gladys, for the first time in May's knowledge of the house, gave no help, or less than none. She was sulky and sharp of speech when she did speak, making the dismal awkwardness of the party more oppressive.

That meal was hurried to its end. Mrs. Garston was taken complaining upstairs and a long struggle induced her to swallow some of Dr. Eves' sedative. Then for her there was at last quiescence and May stole wearily away to her room and tried in vain to rest. Everything was too horrible.

But the evening brought worse. Mrs. Garston woke late, fretting that she had not been waked, that the medicine made her so heavy, so weak, so depressed. Of course she knew that nobody wanted her, she was only in the way, but they needn't make her feel so always—and the maid came in to dress her and inflame this state of mind.

She would go down to dinner, and greeted Croyland by pathetic surprise that he was still there. Why was he still there? He never stayed over Monday. He never did stay so long. Of course she knew it wasn't to be with her. He needn't say that! She gave a queer high laugh. And then was tearful.

Dinner was served. Croyland made talk of the affairs of Bradstock and May struggled desperately to help him. Gladys was still out of humour. Sneering at them all. But anything was better than silence. Croyland laboured on about the park, the gardens, something to be done to the house. "Oh!" Mrs. Garston gave a cry of pain. "You love Bradstock!" And she laughed and wept.

Croyland's politeness snapped. "That's enough," he growled. He looked over his shoulder at the servants. He leaned across the table. "Control yourself, Mother, can't you?" But Mrs. Garston lay back in her chair and sobbed. "Oh, be quiet, for God's sake."

Imperturbable servants served on and departed.

Croyland started up. "I can't stand any more of this," he glowered over his mother. "You're not fit to be here. Take her away, Miss Dean. Get her to bed. You shouldn't have let her come down."

"Oh, I'll go, I'll go. I know nobody wants me." Mrs. Garston hurried to the door.

"It's no use scolding," May cried. "You've made her like this, Lord Croyland."

When she was gone too, Croyland stood plucking at his mouth.

"Doing anything to-night?" said the scornful voice of Gladys.

He grumbled an oath and strode out.

Gladys poured herself another glass of port. "The dirty dog," she said, and her smile was malignant.

Mrs. Garston gave May the worst hour of all her wearing work at Bradstock. She would have nothing done for her; nothing could be done with her, but endure her complaints and reproaches. She would not go to bed. She knew that was all they wanted, to keep her shut up in her room, but she wouldn't be, she wouldn't, she wouldn't. She wasn't dead yet. Of course they all wanted her dead. She wept. It would be the best thing for her, far best. But she mustn't die. She wouldn't.

"Who's talking about dying?" The maid came in. "You aren't going to die, ma'am. I'll see to that, I'm sure." She flashed a glance at May. "Don't want any nurse, do we?" The maid began to put her to bed against her will.

And so to bed at last she went.

Utterly tired, body and spirit, May dragged back to her room. She could hardly find energy to undress. She lay down feeling as if she had never slept and would never sleep again.

She woke with the room dark and a cry in her ears. Another cry came, a stifled cry and a thud, the sound of a shutting, dragging door. She sprang up and, pulling a wrapper about her, ran out.

The vaulted corridor had no more than a glimmer of moonlight through its lancet windows, a ghostly place. She stood listening. There was movement somewhere. By the archway, or beyond, in the new part of the house. She ran on along the corridor, and in the black darkness of the archway stumbled over something soft and fell on her knees. She found herself beside a woman's body.

Then she screamed, "Help! Help! Help!" and bending over the body in the dark felt at it. "Mrs. Garston?" she gasped, and then more loudly, "Mrs. Garston!" The body did not answer.

May scrambled to her feet, fumbled about the walls for the switch of the corridor lights, could not find it, ran to her room for a torch.

She came out with it, turned it on, and the beam piercing into the gloom of the archway showed Croyland standing there, still in his evening clothes, and at his feet the face of Mrs. Garston livid under the white glare.

"Who's that?" he roared. "Miss Dean? What the devil's happened?"

"How should I know?" May cried. "Hold the torch for me." She knelt down by Mrs. Garston.

Servants were coming along the corridor. "Turn on the light, someone," Croyland called, and the lights went up; but the archway remained dark save for the beam of the torch upon May and the unmoving body.

"It's my mistress," came a cry. "What have you done to her, Nurse?" The maid ran up to them. "What are you doing? How did she come here?"

"Hold your damned tongue," Croyland growled. "Don't you meddle." And the maid gulped and muttered.

May stood up slowly. "I can't do anything," she said. "I'm afraid she's gone."

Croyland bent to look at the livid face and suddenly turned the torch from it.

"You must telephone for the doctor to come," May said.

Croyland made noises.

Behind him spoke the voice of Gladys. For the first time May was aware of her presence. "Phone the doctor," she repeated. "That's my job. What's the message?"

"Say Mrs. Garston's had some sort of shock and he must come at once."

"Right, I'll get him." Gladys swept away.

Croyland cleared his throat. "Mustn't lie here. Get her back to her room, eh?"

"Leave me do it." The maid thrust forward. "I've carried her often. As light as a baby, she is, poor angel."

"Let her alone," Croyland growled. He bent and lifted his mother. "Put the lights on for me, some of you." The gallery beyond the arch was lit but in the archway darkness remained. He strode away with his burden. "Want you, Miss Dean."

"Did you think I shouldn't come?" May said fiercely. The maid pressed on at her side.

So Mrs. Garston was brought back to her room and laid on the bed. The maid ran round Croyland and hung over her. "Ah, the poor dear! She was a good lady, she was." She began to fuss about the body with nervous hands. "She——"

"Don't want you," Croyland growled. "Miss Dean will look after her till the doctor comes."

"Look after her!" the maid snarled. "She has, hasn't she?"

"Get out." Croyland turned on her and she went muttering.

May composed and covered the body, and while she did so was aware of Croyland wandering around the room, looking at things, opening drawers.

A tap came at the door. Gladys appeared. "Dr. Eves is on the way. Anything I can do?"

"Wait downstairs for him, will you?" said Croyland. "Bring him straight up."

"Right," Gladys nodded. "I'll be about." She was in a dressing gown, but as carefully arranged as usual and her cool and competent self. She seemed to have no emotions, but before she went out her bold eyes lingered on May with a queer, searching glance.

May sat down by the bed and Croyland came and stood over her.

"Well, Miss Dean. How did this happen?"

"I don't know in the least. After that scene at dinner she was terribly upset. I was a long time with her. When she was settled in bed I left her and went to sleep. I woke up hearing a cry and some noise and a fall. I ran out and fell over her in the archway. Then I called for help."

"Hmph. What was she doing there?"

"I don't know. How should I know? What did you hear?"

"Heard someone screaming for help."

"That was me, I suppose. You didn't hear anything before?"

"Nothing at all. I was at work." He looked heavily at May. "I suppose she felt ill and was coming to you and had a stroke, what?"

"I don't know," said May. She had reasons for another supposition.

"Hmph. Hear what the doctor says. Eves knows all about her," Croyland grunted, and again he wandered about the room prying into his mother's things. . . .

Dr. Eves came, purple of face and blowing. "Aha," he nodded at Croyland, "you're here with her. Let's see now, Nurse." He was disturbed, he made jerky repeated movements and conversed with himself in sounds of surprise and disappointment, but in his muddling way he was thorough. May noticed that.

He turned to Croyland and shook his head. "Ah'm sorry." His voice was subdued. "It's all over with her, Croyland."

"That's what Miss Dean said. I thought you'd better see her though. Don't mind my troubling you, eh?"

"I told him to telephone for you," May cried.

Dr. Eves looked from one to the other. "Ah'm here," he said. "How did it come on her? How did ye find her?"

"Miss Dean found her. She'll tell you," Croyland said, and again May told.

"Thaat's all ye know of it. Croyland, will you be stepping downstairs? Ah'll have to make an examination." Left alone with May and the dead woman, he stood still meditating. "Aha. Ye left her in bed, the maid and yourself going away together. The next ye know she was lying out there in the corridor. Did she ever get up o' nights before?"

"I never heard her."

"Was she alive when ye came to her?"

"She didn't stir. She didn't seem to be breathing. I felt for her pulse and couldn't find it."

Eves went to the body again and his examination was long. . . . He stood up. "Come ye here," he said, and pointed to small bruises on either side of the throat. "Did ye see that?"

"Yes, I did." May looked at him. "They were red at first. They've darkened since."

"Maybe so. Ye said there was some trouble putting her to bed. Was she handled then?"

"No, not like that. Not there, of course. Her maid almost made her take off her things."

"Ye caan't account for it at all. Then ye'd better maake no talk about it."

"What do you mean?"

"Ah mean just whaat ah say, my girl."

"Are you going to say she died naturally?"

Dr. Eves rubbed his chin. "Ah'm advising ye for your own good. Now, ye're overwrought. Ye'd better be off to bed, my dear. Run along with you and get you rest. Ah'll lock up here."

May stared at him in horror. "You can't hide it! You shan't," she cried.

"Now that's foolish," said Dr. Eves. "Away with

you." He thrust her out gently enough and locked the door on the dead woman and stumped downstairs.

Croyland stood in his study smoking. "Hmph. Here you are at last! What is it, eh, what was it?"

"Baad business, Croyland." Dr. Eves shook his head. "Ah caan't certify. Ah daren't. Ah tell you fraankly, ah don't like the looks of it. She's been mishaandled, the poor woman. There's been violence used to her."

"What the devil do you mean?"

"She's had haands to her throat."

Croyland swallowed. "Good God, man, it can't be," he said thickly. "What are you saying? She was strangled? That's mad."

"Ah'm not saying it. There's a bit of a look of strangulation. But it wouldn't need so much to kill her. She was weak all through, weak. The shock of it would be her death, poor soul."

"Hmph. That's what I thought," Croyland turned to the glass at his elbow and drank. "Shock—some sort of shock. You know what she was. Full of fancies and wild ideas—dreams—imagining things all the time. Something startled her, I suppose—she ran out into the dark—frightened—and then—— That must be it. Just shock."

Dr. Eves shook his head. "Ah daren't do it, Croyland. That's the truth. She died by violence. Ah'll have to say so."

"It's crazy. Who would hurt her here?"

"Thaat's not for me. Ah can't help ye. Ah'm sorry. There's nothing ah can do in this, Croyland. Ah'll just have to give information."

"Police?" Croyland growled.

"Ay, ay, ye'll have the police. There's no stopping it. Ah'm clear, ah can't do other. It's a baad, baad business for you. Ah'll be off now, if ye please."

CHAPTER XIV

ON THE ROAD

AMONG the more genial qualities of Superintendent Bell is an enviable ability to find an old and cosy inn. He can do this in the most unlikely places. He had done it even among the opulence of modernized Limbay. He was in the bar parlour at the third sausage of breakfast when Inspector Gunn arrived.

"All right. Finish it," Gunn answered his questioning eyes. "There's no special hurry."

"You can talk here," Bell said placidly, and went on eating.

"Oh, I know. Well, it's only murder. And we're not more than six hours late on it."

"Too bad." Bell took much marmalade. "Who's murdered?"

"Old Mrs. Garston, that's all."

"The mother!" Bell munched on. "Makes you think, doesn't it?"

"I haven't begun to think myself. I don't know whether I'm on my head or my heels."

"No use getting rattled." Bell poured another cup of coffee. "How was it done?"

"That's one of the little things we don't know. It's supposed to have been done in the Abbey."

"Inside the house? Queer."

"That's the story. We don't know anything first hand. It comes to us like this. Dr. Eves drove over to the coroner early this morning, said he'd tried to tele-

phone him in the night and couldn't get through—
that may be true, but look how it sets us back——"

"Half a minute," said Bell. "Eves. Isn't that the doctor who gave evidence in the Alfred Garston inquest?"

"That's right. He's the Garston family doctor. Lives
near. Well, he told the coroner he was rung up from
the Abbey in the night about one-thirty to go to Mrs.
Garston. When he got there he found her dead. Been
dead an hour or less. Dr. Eves says he believes the cause
of death was shock following violence; he's sure she'd
been violently handled. So he came to the coroner."

"Why didn't he come to the police?" said Bell.

"Yes, there's that. Still, you can't make much of it.
He's quite correct—couldn't give a certificate—informed the coroner at once. But it makes a rotten case
for us. When he saw her, she'd been moved. Now it's
half a dozen hours after. Anything nasty can have been
cleared away. Anyone who is in it can have covered
his tracks "

"What have you done?"

"Sent our own doctor out to examine the body and
some men with him to look things over."

Bell nodded and lit a pipe and stood up. "Well,
George, I was betting you'd have a bit of work to do
with old Josh Clunk staying on. And here we are."

"What, you don't think Clunk was in this?"

"I'm not thinking yet, only wondering. But I do
wonder why Josh Clunk's been so fond of these parts."

They drove away in Gunn's car.

"I don't see how you can work Clunk into it," Gunn
pronounced. "The old lady was killed in the house, as
far as we know. He isn't the sort of fellow to break in:
he isn't the sort of fellow for rough stuff at all."

"No, I don't suppose he did it himself." Bell smiled
grimly at the fancy of Mr. Clunk being violent.

"Meaning he arranged it? But how could he stand to gain by putting Mrs. Garston out of the way?"

"Ah. If we knew who did stand to gain we'd know something, wouldn't we? Look here, Gunn: we began with somebody stealing letters that Alfred Garston wrote; now somebody murders Alfred Garston's mother. Well? Don't that mean somebody wants to get rid of evidence about Alfred Garston?"

Gunn shook his head. "Neat idea. But it won't do, to my mind. The man's been dead twenty years, and never any bother about it till now. Miss Morrow's had the letters all the time. She must know everything in 'em, and she's not been touched."

"I don't set up to see my way through it," Bell said slowly. "Take it again though. The letters are stolen and soon after they're in the hands of the fellow who wanted 'em, Mrs. Garston is murdered. Suppose we say something has turned up to make it mighty important to wipe out what was left on record of Alfred Garston's private life. How about that for a theory?"

"I don't care so much about theories myself," Gunn objected. "I haven't found it's any good expecting things to be reasonable. Some chap pinched the jewel case. Some chap killed the old lady. That's all we really know. Very likely one thing's nothing to do with the other. Say they had a burglar at the Abbey, she heard him and he shut her mouth and bolted. That explains it all."

"Theory too, isn't it?" Bell grinned. "And very nice, I'm sure. I wish you were right. But it's a bit too simple, old man. Why hasn't Croyland rung up the police to say he's been burgled?"

"He may not know it. Fellow bunked before he got anything. House all up on end with the old lady's death."

"All right. Maybe. Try it that way. We'll have to try everything. Do you know what bothers me? Josh Clunk was defending the man who stole the letters and he stayed on down here for the week of the remand, which wasn't business, and as soon as he gets the fellow off, Mrs. Garston is done in. I'd like to know who Josh Clunk is acting for."

"But I say," Gunn was startled, "the last time you talked about Clunk, you said he was trying to stand in with us."

"So he was. All the more reason to wonder what he's up to."

"Where are you getting to?" Gunn protested. "You said he was giving us the tip to look for the man who wanted the letters."

"So he did, so he did," said Bell impatiently. "And what about it? The only man I know that could be interested in Alfred Garston's letters is Croyland. And now the mother of both of 'em has got murdered in Croyland's house with Josh Clunk in the offing. That looks like Josh had a notion things might happen with Croyland behind 'em. But how did he know? And where does Josh come in himself? He don't take up things for his health."

"Oh, search me!" Gunn said. "You're fogging yourself, I should say. Let's work on the facts."

"Plenty of fog about without me. You'll find it all right when you look," Bell smiled. "One of the facts I shall want is where Josh Clunk's got to now."

But about that there was no mystery. Mr. Clunk was in a car which, driven by Lewis, followed them not many minutes behind.

When Mr. Clunk came down to breakfast that morning Lewis remarked that there was a sort of liveliness at the police station. Fellow drove up in a car early:

cars coming and going: and one of them went loaded up with constables. Lewis had never seen so much doing in the Limbay police force.

"Dear me," Mr. Clunk beamed. "And so early in the morning! I wonder what it's all about, Lewis. A carful of constables in uniform! That's very impressive." He tittered. "It looks like a desperate situation somewhere."

"Most likely going to arrest a kid for poaching bunnies," said the sardonic Lewis.

"I'm afraid you're not very respectful, Lewis," Mr. Clunk sighed. "You know, I shouldn't underrate the police. I never found that answer, my boy. And Mr. Bell is still with us, you know. Did you happen to see his friend, Mr. Gunn?"

"Not showing." Lewis gulped his tea.

"I wish you would find out whether Mr. Bell has been called upon," said Mr. Clunk plaintively. "He's at the White Lion, I noticed. I don't want to spoil your breakfast, my boy. But I should rather like to know."

Lewis looked at him without any affection, swallowed egg and bacon in uncomely bulk, and departed.

Mr. Clunk finished his breakfast with much strawberry jam, put a lump of sugar in his mouth and three in his pocket, went out to a chair in front of the hotel, and sat and sucked, contemplating benignly the sunlit sea, and as he sucked he murmured:

> "*Will you meet me in the morning,*
> *On that bright and golden shore?*
> *Will your lamp be trimmed and burning*
> *When He comes to take you o'er?*
> *Yes, I'll meet you in the morning——*"

Lewis appeared briskly and Mr. Clunk sauntered out to meet him. "Gunn's been round to Bell," said Lewis under his breath. "Took him off in a car. Went Bradstock way."

Mr. Clunk's large eyes became more prominent. "Were you going to get our car, my boy?" he asked, and Lewis vanished at speed. Mr. Clunk stood still and tapped his teeth. An unusual keenness sharpened his mild and glossy face. He did not look pleasant.

But that had passed when Lewis came back with the car. He climbed in smiling. "Very good and quick, my boy. And now I think you might go just as fast as you can safely. Safety first, my boy, eh, always safety first." The idea seemed to amuse Mr. Clunk unreasonably.

"What's up now, sir?" said Lewis.

"Dear me, I can't tell at all. I can't imagine. Mr. Bell is so hasty. I'm quite afraid of him, Lewis."

And Lewis, being annoyed, drove on without any regard for safety. Mr. Clunk put one hand to his mouth and with the other held himself in the car.

Gunn and Bell, driving at less illegal speed, were stopped by a man who ran out from a field to shout and hold up his arms. "What's the matter with you?" said Gunn.

"There be a man dead here, mister. I found un."

"What, in that field?"

"That's right. Lying dead as mutton. And a policeman, too."

"My oath!" Gunn muttered, and jumped out. "Where is he?"

Inside the field, two horses stood patiently with a harrow among the young barley. Just beyond them, up against the hedge, lay a policeman and a bicycle.

Bell reached him first. "Shot through the eye," he grunted. "Been dead hours. Do you know him?"

"Of course I know him. It's Brownlie, the man at Cranton, the village near the Abbey, where Eves comes from."

"That's right, sir. He be George Brownlie to Cranton," the countryman said.

"Is he though?" Bell stared. "He was killed some time ago. That means in the night. He'd be out patrolling on his bike." He whistled.

"When did you find him, my lad?" Gunn turned to the countryman.

"Just a bit ago. When I came down with harrow. I was loading a cart o' pigs for market after breakfast. Then I come along to harrow this bit o' barley and there a was lying dead." He sucked his teeth. "And what be I to do with un, if you please?"

"I'll stand by, my lad," said Bell, and turned to Gunn. "You take the car and get on to the next telephone."

"Right. That's the Abbey now. I'll be back with some men in a few minutes." Gunn ran off.

Bell looked at the dead man and scratched his head. The body lay on its back; the tunic was drawn up in crumpled folds from the trousers; the button of the left breast pocket was undone. Bell put his hand inside and found nothing. He tried the other pockets, and put back their trivial contents. Then he strolled into the road and paced about studying the surface.

Lewis sounded his horn, was hooting again more truculently when Mr. Clunk grasped his arm and cried: "Stop, you foolish fellow, stop!" The car slid to rest under Bell's nose.

"Oh, Mr. Clunk, is it?" Bell stared. "Fancy meeting you here."

"Dear me, it's Superintendent Bell," Mr. Clunk beamed. "Can I be of any assistance, my friend?"

"How could you?" said Bell.

"Why really, I don't know," Mr. Clunk tittered. "But you seemed to be rather at a loss. I thought perhaps your car had broken down. You might like a lift."

"Well, it hasn't, thanks," Bell growled.

"Not the car?" said Mr. Clunk sweetly. "Well, well, well. Nothing I can do for you?"

"I wonder if there is. I wonder if you could be of some use," Bell considered him. "Just come and have a look, Mr. Clunk." He took the little man's arm in a professional grasp, which made Mr. Clunk look up at him with mild amusement, and marched into the field.

Then Mr. Clunk's amusement was suddenly lost. Bell saw his big eyes swell, his sleek face distorted with horror. "Christ Jesus have mercy," he said in a queer whining voice, and plucked off his hat with a hand that shook, and stood bowing his head and murmuring scraps of the Bible. Then he drew a long breath and was again erect and turned to Bell. "This is a dreadful thing. Really it is," he said quietly.

"You think so, do you? That was rather my idea." Bell frowned. There was a gleam in Mr. Clunk's prominent eyes which puzzled Bell, a look of hate or ferocity. He seemed to Bell like an angry cat, turning at bay to claw.

But he spoke very placidly. "Yes, indeed. It is the kind of thing which I can never forgive."

Bell gave a contemptuous laugh. "I wasn't thinking of forgiving it myself. It's the sort of thing I've heard you defend sometimes."

"Ah, how wrong of you to say that." Mr. Clunk was hurt. "Really so wrong. Sometimes I must defend the vilest creatures, as a doctor must try to cure those whose diseases are the wages of sin. But do we forgive them? No, indeed. That is not in our hearts. We do——"

"All right. Cut the sermon," said Bell gruffly.

"My dear sir, believe me, this kind of crime revolts me. The poor, poor fellow. Sent to his account, all unready perhaps, shot down, unarmed, unoffending, robbed of his sweet life to make sin easier for a cruel, selfish villain——" He stopped and shook his head.

Bell was looking at him with grim curiosity. "Go on, go on," Bell exhorted. "You know a lot, don't you, Mr. Clunk? Let's have some more."

"Oh, my friend, I know what I see." Mr. Clunk was not embarrassed. "Here is a village policeman shot down on the road as he made his night patrol and hidden behind the hedge. It is perfectly clear he was killed by some scoundrel because he had observed what would have interfered with a crime."

"Thanks. I'd got as far as that myself. And what exactly was the crime?"

"What has been done about here, my friend?" said Mr. Clunk. "You should know more about that than I do."

"Should I?" Bell grinned. "Well, I'll try to, Mr. Clunk, you may take your oath."

"I am sure you will, Superintendent," Mr. Clunk nodded. "Yes, indeed!"

The conversation was interrupted by the arrival of two cars. From the first came Gunn with a sharp-faced, quick-moving man, from the other a couple of stolid constables.

Gunn's companion bent over the body. "Our own surgeon," said Gunn in Bell's ear. "He's finished at the Abbey. It's——" Bell trod on his foot and directed his eyes to the unobtrusive presence of Mr. Clunk.

"And what can we do for you?" Gunn glared.

"Don't you want him, George?" Bell chuckled. "Well, I don't know that I do either. Not yet. How about moving on, Mr. Clunk?"

"Dear me, am I in the way?" Mr. Clunk was pained. "I didn't know. Good-day, then, gentlemen. But do please remember, I should be so grieved if you don't apply to me when you're in any difficulty, I should really. Don't hesitate, pray. It would be no trouble to me at all. Quite a pleasure. Good-day." He tripped out of the field.

"Can you beat it!" Gunn growled. "Perishing cheek! The nasty little insect!"

"Ah." Bell was not irritated. "I wish I knew what his game was, George."

The surgeon rose from the body. "This man was shot at close quarters. Pistol or revolver, of course. No marks of struggle. His tunic was pulled about dragging him here, I should say. Killed not less than six hours ago. I'll get back now, Gunn. You'll send the body to the mortuary with Mrs. Garston's?"

"All right, sir." Gunn nodded and the surgeon strode away. "There we are then." Gunn looked at Bell. "Shot in the small hours—somewhere."

"Out on the road just close by," Bell corrected. "There's a bit of blood about. Better have your chaps note the place. I should say he stopped a car, he had his notebook out, he was getting particulars, and he was killed for it. His notebook's been taken."

"My oath!" Gunn muttered. "Poor chap. Dirty, isn't it?"

"The man in that car was feeling pretty desperate," said Bell. "I wonder what he'd been up to. Hullo! Look at that, George. Josh has only just got going." He pointed to Mr. Clunk's car.

"Nasty little maggot," Gunn growled. "Been hopping about behind the hedge to listen."

"And he's going on towards Bradstock Abbey. I think we'd better get there too, George." They went.

But in fact Mr. Clunk, though he may have heard something, had not been listening. He wandered about the road like Bell, and, like Bell, he saw the drops of blood where the murder had been done.

Then he came back to Lewis. "Well, my boy, we had better be going," he said cheerfully.

"Queer start, sir," Lewis ventured, as they drove on.

Mr. Clunk did not answer and Lewis, glancing sideways, saw on his smooth yellow face a strange expression of pleasure. Lewis, like Bell, was reminded of a cat, but of a cat that after watching and waiting marked its prey at last within reach of a spring.

CHAPTER XV

THE DARK ARCHWAY

THE car which conveyed Bell and Gunn followed the car which conveyed Mr. Clunk on the road to Bradstock Abbey. But they did not overtake him.

Two or three miles were covered before Bell spoke. "What did your doctor say about the old lady, George?"

Gunn roused himself. "Ah, I didn't tell you. I was just going to when——"

"When I trod on your corns. Yes, we don't know so much you want to give it away to Josh Clunk."

"Of course I don't. Sorry. I didn't see the blighter. He is the devil and all, isn't he? Fancy him turning up by that poor chap's body! How did he know? How did he get on to it? He knows a deal too much, old man."

"Yes, he always does," Bell said slowly. "That's his little way. If you ask me, he knows more than he likes about this Garston case. Give us a bit of luck and we might catch Josh Clunk bending at last. But I don't think he knew anything about your man being killed. He just butted into that, and when he saw the body it pretty near turned him up. Queer little cat, he is."

"Why, what did he do?"

"Oh, he prayed and he preached." Bell made a grimace of nausea. "Good Lord, I don't set up to say any man's religion isn't honest. I've seen too much. But Josh Clunk being pious! Well, it isn't that got me, though. He was very queer. First the dead body gave him a turn. Then he kind of got his back up as if he was going to give someone hell— and nasty pleased about it. That's what beats me, George. He never lost his head, either. He knew what he was doing right through. Heard him purring at me, didn't you? And with that spiteful look in his eyes. As good as told me he could put us on to something when he chose. Looks to me he was wanting to do the dirty on somebody and that poor chap's murder showed him how."

"My oath!" Gunn was excited. "Maybe he has an idea of putting the murder on a chap he wants out of the way. How about that?"

"Quite likely, George. Bear it in mind." Bell smiled. "When Josh Clunk starts giving evidence anything may turn up—except the truth. Oh, we'll have a lot to bear in mind before we're through. Now then, let's get back to the old lady. What did the doctor say?"

"What didn't he say!" Gunn groaned. "He makes it murder all right. Cause of death, shock following violent assault. She'd been taken by the throat and half strangled. Marks of hands on her neck. But he thinks she's been doped and that helped. He has to make a post mortem before he can be sure what was used. Might have been chloral or veronal. And of course she was a bad life—turned seventy-five and feeble. Pretty mixed, isn't it? If there was dope, that fixes murder on somebody in the house."

Bell shook his head. "Not for certain. She might have been doped regular to keep her quiet, and yet been throttled by somebody from outside. She may have doped herself. And anyway, with an old woman who used dope there might have been a struggle quite innocent—people only trying to keep her quiet."

"I don't think!" Gunn laughed. "If that's all there is to it, they'd have told Eves, and Eves wouldn't have bucked off to the coroner."

"Funk," said Bell. "Everybody's in a funk. You can see that. Why didn't Eves show up to meet your doctor?"

"It's a fact, he didn't," Gunn nodded.

"Our Dr. Eves is keeping well out of this, isn't he?" Bell smiled.

"Yes, so he is. But what do you make of that?"

"Nothing, George. I don't make anything of anything yet. Here we are. By the way, where's Josh got to? We haven't passed him."

"Oh hell," said Gunn. "Forget him. He wouldn't be here, would he?"

"I wouldn't be surprised if we found him with Croyland," Bell laughed.

But they did not. Mr. Clunk's car was parked at the place appointed for the cars of visitors to the ruins. Mr. Clunk was resuming his study of ecclesiastical antiquities.

Gladys, a correct and solemn Gladys in black and only half a coat of paint, brought them to Croyland's study. He was at work on a mass of papers and smoking. He waved them to chairs and stared at them and made noises. Gunn introduced himself and Bell without a word of their having worked on another case in the Garston family twenty years before. And if Croyland remembered them, he did not say so. He did not say anything. He continued to clear his throat.

"This is a terrible affair, my lord," Gunn began. "I have to tell you the police surgeon's report is that Mrs. Garston was killed by violence."

"Hmph. That's what Eves said," Croyland growled.

"It's my duty to ask you if you can give us any information how it happened."

"Heard a noise in the night. Went upstairs and found her lying in the corridor. Nurse had just got to her. She seemed to be dead."

"What time was that?"

"Don't know. Small hours."

"You hadn't gone to bed?"

"Working in here."

"You hadn't heard any noise before?"

"Heard nothing."

"You see what I mean, my lord?" Gunn asked. "Any reason to think somebody had broken into the house?"

"No sign of it."

"Well, you see what that comes to. Mrs. Garston was killed by one of the people living here."

"If she was killed."

"We have to believe the doctors, my lord." Croyland did not deny it, but he made rumbling noises. "Do you think she died natural?"

"She was old. Bad health a long time," Croyland growled. "Doctors talk about shock. Anything would upset her. Seen it often."

"There's marks of violence on her throat. The surgeon's report is she was half strangled."

"Can't understand that." Croyland stared at him with heavy eyes. "No sense in it. More likely the doctors are wrong. Who could want to hurt her?"

"That's what we've got to ask you, my lord. Would you answer for all the people in the house?"

"How the devil could I?" Croyland growled. "No more than I can answer for the doctors. If you're asking whether I know anybody with a grudge against my mother, I don't. I don't believe there's anyone in the world."

"All the servants above suspicion?"

"The upper servants have all been here for years. I don't know the others. Better ask the housekeeper."

"Thank you, my lord. Anyone else in the house?"

"I was in the house." Croyland glared. "D'you mean me?"

"Beg your pardon, my lord. I meant visitors."

"No visitors. Servants. My secretary, Miss Hurst. My mother's nurse, Miss Dean."

For the first time Bell spoke. "Have they been with you long?"

"Had Miss Hurst a year or more. Miss Dean came a few weeks ago."

"Mrs. Garston's health been getting worse lately?" said Bell.

"Eves said she ought to have a nurse."

"I see. Then we'd better hear what the nurse has to say about it."

"Want her in here?" Croyland frowned.

"Sorry to trouble you," said Bell. "By the way, where did she come from?"

"No idea. My secretary found her."

"Trained nurse, I suppose?"

"You can ask her," Croyland growled.

May stood before them, looking less a nurse than a tired child. She was not, like Gladys, prepared with black. The gray and white of her frock made the pallor of her little face ashen. She tried to stand very straight and in the effort the slim youth of her body and its weariness were manifest. But all that did not interest the comprehensive gaze of Bell. It seemed to him there was something desperate and defiant in the drawn face and the eyes, sunken above dark curves, but bright.

"Miss Dean?" he said coldly. "Sit down, please." And May did not sit. "As you like. We are police officers. I have to tell you your patient, Mrs. Garston, was murdered."

"I know she was!" May cried.

"When did you know?"

"When I saw the marks on her neck."

"Very good. What can you tell us about it?"

"About how she was killed? I can't tell you anything. I don't know. I can tell you how I found her," and she did.

"She was dead when you reached her?"

"I think so. If not, she died almost at once. As soon as I felt for her pulse, it wasn't there, she wasn't breathing."

"How long was it from when you heard the cry to when you reached her?"

"I couldn't possibly say. Not more than a few minutes."

"Was it Mrs. Garston's voice that cried?"

"Oh yes. At least I think so. Oh, I feel sure it was."

"What did she say?"

"I don't know. I was only just waking. I'm not sure. And then the cry seemed stifled."

"It wasn't your name?"

"Oh no. Nothing like my name. She always called me Miss Dean. It wasn't that." She pushed back her hair. "I can't tell you really. It did seem something like a man's name."

"What name?" Bell snapped.

"I don't know, truly."

Croyland cleared his throat. "My name's Henry, if that's what you want."

"Oh no, it wasn't that," May said.

"Thanks," Bell grunted. "Now then. Before all this happened—how did you leave her last night? Anything wrong with her?"

"I left her in bed. She'd been very difficult. Her maid put her to bed. I couldn't do anything with her."

"What do you mean, there'd been a struggle?"

"No, of course not. She wasn't like that. Just refusing to do anything. She was fretful and excited. There'd been a scene at dinner."

"Oh, had there? Who with?"

"With me," Croyland growled. "My mother was in a state of nerves. Broke down and was hysterical. I told her she wasn't fit to be up. That's what Miss Dean's thinking of."

"What was it all about?"

"I haven't any idea," May cried.

And Croyland said quickly. "About nothing."

Bell allowed a satiric expression to appear on his stolid face. "I see. She was upset. The maid put her to bed and the nurse left her and in the night she was killed. That's what we've got. Now I want to see where she was found. Both of you, please."

"What do you want me for?" Croyland jerked back his head.

"Miss Dean was first at the body. You were second. I want you to check each other about what you saw."

Croyland dragged himself on to his feet and strode out.

With his eyes looking every way, Bell followed slowly up the Tudor staircase and along the bright gallery to the darkness of the archway. Croyland stopped so suddenly that the two men jolted him and each other.

"Here, was she?" Bell said. "Queer place. What is it?"

"Corner of the old part of the house," Croyland told him. "Where you've been is Elizabethan. This archway goes through the old wall to the monks' *dortoir*."

"The what?" Bell asked.

"Where the monks used to sleep."

"Oh." Bell walked through to the light of the vaulted

corridor, looked about him and came back to the gloom. "And what would Mrs. Garston have been doing up here?"

"I don't know. Miss Dean's room is beyond in the *dortoir*. She might have been going there."

"I see." Bell turned to May. "Show me Mrs. Garston's room and yours, will you?"

He was taken first to Mrs. Garston's. "The door's locked," May said. "Dr. Eves took the key. The other doctor had it."

"All right. We've got it. Now where's your room?" She took him back through the archway and opened her door. "I see." He did not go in. "She might have been coming to you."

"But she didn't," May cried.

"Ever come to you in the night before?"

"Never. I can't imagine her doing it. She never wanted me."

"Didn't she? Uncomfortable job for you, Nurse." He looked at her. "She didn't like your being here, eh?"

"She didn't like having a nurse," said May.

"I see." Bell came back to the gloom of the archway. "And you found her lying here?"

"I fell over her. I fell on top of her."

"Did you, though?" Bell was interested. "Lying right across the floor, was she?"

"Yes, I suppose so. I don't know quite. Yes, I think so."

"Dark here, isn't it?" Bell was almost affable. He peered about the archway. "Ah, there is a lamp. Could we have it on, my lord!" Croyland moved away and snapped the switch. "Hallo. Not working. Get us a chair, George." He stood on it, took off the bulb, and fetching another from a point in the vaulted corridor put that on. The light came. "Oh, it was just the bulb gone wrong." He turned it over in his hand. "Filament broken." He looked at May. "Did you have the light on here last night?"

"I had a torch. I don't remember. There were lights on when people came."

"I told them to put the lights on," Croyland growled.

"Oh, did you? No light anywhere till then?"

"It was all dark," said May.

"And this light came on with the rest?"

"Whole place lit up," Croyland grunted.

"I don't know." May put her hand to her head. "I don't believe there was ever any light in here." She shuddered.

"Ah well, you can't tell when a filament will go," Bell said, and looked about the archway Its floor was of old oak planks, black and shining; on either side it was panelled from the floor to the spring of the arch above their heads in oak of linen-fold carving, old and dark as the floor. He worked over the floor and walls with careful eyes and hands and found nothing.

"Thank you, my lord." He turned to Croyland. "I'm keeping you too long. Now we'll just have a look round Mrs. Garston's room, and then we'll want to see some of your people: if you'll tell 'em to have a room ready for us."

Croyland cleared his throat. "Give your own orders," he said: "want you to report to me before you go." He lumbered off.

"Thank you, Nurse. That'll do now," Bell dismissed May. "I'll want you later." He watched her hurry back to her room. He rolled the lamp in his hand and looked from it to Gunn. Then he went to the switches in the corridors on either side and put them on. The lights flashed out. "See that, George," he whistled. "She was found dead in the one place where the lamp didn't work."

"What do you make of that?" Gunn frowned.

"Ah. I wish I knew," said Bell, and moved away to Mrs. Garston's room.

CHAPTER XVI

BEFORE LUNCH

MRS. GARSTON's room, with the morning sunshine pouring into it, made an ugly show of things confused and awry.

The police surgeon who drew back the curtains to examine the body had not repaired the disorder of the night but made more, and locking the door again behind him kept all the mess inviolate.

"My oath! You couldn't say whether somebody had been upsetting things o' purpose or they've been careful not to touch anything," Gunn grumbled.

Bell stood in the middle surveying chaos. "Ah, there's a lot you can't say, George," he pronounced.

"Look here though, old man." Gunn approached the table which was normally at the bedside. "Just look at her medicines. My word, there's a blooming shopful. She must have taken a drop of everything she could get."

"I see. Well, you'd better pack up the lot and bring 'em along for the doctor to look at. But if there was dope used, you can bet your life it isn't there. Whoever did this didn't leave things lying about."

"I don't know. Everybody makes a mistake sometimes," said Gunn.

"Don't you believe it." Bell turned away and began to look over Mrs. Garston's possessions. "Keys on the dressing table. That's handy. Bit too handy. Nothing much locked either. Jewel case. Aha. That is locked. Good bit of stuff too. Well, if she had any love letters, they aren't there." He continued his researches." Don't seem to have kept much in the way of papers." He whistled softly. "What do you think about that, George?"

Gunn came to look at the open drawer of a bureau in which was a flat leather case, scraped and at one corner bent. "I don't know." Gunn stared at him.

"Looks like the drawer was shut up in a hurry with that thing tumbled over so it caught. Say a fellow was pinching something else from the drawer and that's just what would happen."

"But nobody could get in here. Eves went off with the key."

"Oh, George!" Bell laughed. "Eves locked the door all right—when the horse was stolen. Plenty o' time to pinch anything before he came along."

"Do you mean somebody came to her room to steal something and did her in?"

"I don't know. Might have been. Or it might have been taken after she was found dead. Because it gave things away."

"Half a minute. They carried her back in here at once. Then Croyland and the nurse were in here with her till Eves came."

"That's the story. Well?"

"You're putting it on Croyland and the nurse?"

"Well?" said Bell again.

Gunn was troubled. "After all, you can't be sure anything has been taken."

"I can't prove it," Bell agreed. "But I know all right. Let's see what was left behind." He took up the leather case and opened it out. It displayed three old photographs, of a child, of a boy, of a young man.

At the man Gunn pointed. "My oath! Alfred Garston," he said.

"That's right. Alfred Garston at three ages. The child —what will he become!" Bell laughed grimly. "Kept by mother. God help us all! Makes you feel a brute, don't it? Poor woman. I wonder how much she ever knew?" He breathed hard. "Ah, well, no use talking like that. Look what it comes to, George. She's murdered and something's taken from the drawer where she kept Alfred's photos: likely it would be letters of his. That links the murder with hushing up something about Alfred. Did you say I was putting it on Croyland and the nurse? Well?"

"Getting a bit thick, isn't it?" Gunn agreed. "Croyland has a nurse brought in that his mother didn't want and his mother's murdered and him and the nurse are in at the death. And over the murder something about his brother which she had is stolen. Don't look too well for Croyland."

"No. And it all happens—— What the devil's that?" Someone knocked at the door. Bell lowered his voice. "It all happens when something else to do with his brother has just been stolen. Bite on that, George. Now then." He strode to the door and opened it. Mrs. Garston's maid stood there. "What do you want?"

She was not prepossessing. Her sallow face was paler than common and more haggard, her brown eyes shrunken into beads. She came very close to him. "I want to speak to you, sir. I want to tell you about last night."

"Much obliged. Who are you?"

"My name's Jones, sir. Mrs. Jones. I'm Mrs. Garston's maid, if you please, sir. I've been with her fifteen years. Ah, she was a dear good mistress to me, so she was. I want to tell you the truth about last night.

Ah, my poor dear! There's no one knows the truth but me."

"Oh, isn't there?" Bell shut the door behind her. "Then you'd better mind what you say."

"You don't have to caution me, sir. I haven't anything to be afraid of, thank God."

"That's good," said Bell. "Well, what is the truth about last night?"

And Mrs. Jones spoke at high speed, in one continuous sentence of fervent emphasis. "It was like this, sir. I came up to make Mistress comfortable for the night, which I always did it myself, for this nurse never did anything for her decent, and she was that frightened of her, she used to cry about it often, poor lamb, and there I found her in a dreadful taking, I can't tell you what Nurse had been doing to her, I'm sure, I never saw the like, and her always the lady with everybody, poor lamb, but this I do know, for I heard it with my own ears, Mistress was saying, 'You want me dead,' she said, yes, sir, as God hears me, that's what she was saying, 'Of course I know you want me dead,' she said, but I didn't think so much of it then, knowing this nurse had a hard way with her and being wishful to quieten the poor dear and have her rest, which she was wanting terrible but now—now!" She broke off panting and her beads of eyes searched Bell to discover if she had made her effect.

"Now you think a lot of it," Bell said stolidly. "Why?" The maid swallowed and began to speak again. "Take your time. Sort of thing women do say when they're hysterical. Why should the nurse want her dead?"

"It's not my place to say, I'm sure." The maid was less fluent. "I don't know why Nurse ever came. It wasn't that Mistress wanted her, nor liked her neither.

Never had a quiet hour, she didn't, after this nurse was about her."

"What did the nurse do?"

The maid hesitated. "I won't say anything I don't know, sir, I'm not that kind. If you ask me, Nurse was always driving her. Always at her."

And again Bell asked, "Why?"

"It's not for me to say. I told you, I don't know why she came. I don't go prying, I'm sure." She tossed her head. "But I've got my duty to Mistress, poor lady. There's some things I couldn't let be hid. I'll have to tell you, sir, after it happened last night, I went up to Nurse's room, just to see if she'd have me to help her with anything. She wasn't there. You never do know where to find her. But she'd been tearing up a letter or something and I couldn't help but see bits of it. Fair turned my heart over. I kept 'em for you. Here, sir. You look at that."

Bell read these scraps of Tony's letter ". . . reasons about as serious as they can be . . . after what happened with Croyland I want to see you at once . . . things to say I can't write. . . ."

His square face showed no sign of interest. "Is that all you found?" She nodded. "Pity. Anything else to bring out?" She shook her head. "Then you can go away and hold your tongue. Hold it tight, or I shall have to be nasty. See?"

"I'm not one to talk." The maid tossed her head and strutted out, pleased with herself but not at ease.

Bell looked at Gunn. "This has been a happy home, George."

"That's a vixen all right," Gunn said.

"I believe you. Poor old lady—between that maid and the minx of a nurse and Croyland—my God! Well, let's get on with it. Perhaps there's some more jolly

folks in the house. But look here. We'll have to watch
out for anyone getting into touch with people outside."

"Might as well ask Nurse Dean who the chap is
that wants to see her about what happened with Croyland."

"I don't think so, George," Bell smiled. "We won't
ask Nurse anything more just yet. Why frighten the
poor girl? If she'd like to pop off and meet the bloke,
that suits us nicely. Just let your men know that anybody who leaves the house is to be shadowed. We'll
run over the household. Croyland's secretary—housekeeper—butler. That'll give us the hang of things."

So they established themselves in the morning room
and sent for Gladys.

The mind of Superintendent Bell catalogued her as
a business woman. It is not a type he is capable of admiring, but he respected her. If a man must have a
woman secretary, which he deplores, it appeared to
him that a man could not do much better than Gladys.
She was quick, she was clear, she had no nonsense about
her.

Gladys did not affect any emotion at Mrs. Garston's
murder. "Pretty ghastly," was her phrase for it. She
couldn't herself imagine anybody killing the old lady.
"Most harmless old thing you ever saw."

Gladys had never heard of Mrs. Garston having any
trouble with the nurse or the maid. Of course there
would be some. She was feeble, and didn't want to be
looked after. Like other old people.

A scene at dinner? Gladys smiled tolerance. Yes, a
bit of a fuss. The old lady got weepy and queer and
Lord Croyland couldn't stand it. Nothing to think
twice about. "An old woman rather nervy and a busy
man—that's all there was to it." Lord Croyland was
always very decent to her.

The maid? Gladys didn't know much about the maid. "Genuine antique. Faithful family retainer. That kind of thing."

"You engaged the nurse yourself, didn't you?" said Bell.

"Not quite. Lord Croyland told me to look out for one. He wanted a nurse enough of a lady to be a companion. So I got on to Miss Dean and he took to her. I knew her at school. She was trained at St. Hugh's. She's had nursing-home experience. Looks a bit young, don't she? But she's done very well."

"Well, what it comes to is, you can't think how it happened?" said Bell.

"I cannot. Mad, it looks like, if you ask me."

And the housekeeper and the butler were also without theories. They showed in a genteel way more horror than Gladys, more regret. But their feelings had not inspired them with suspicion of anyone. They were free from animosity as she. It emerged from their discretion that neither had a love for the maid. Towards May they exhibited the cool neutrality proper between higher servants and a trained nurse, but they had no personal grudge against her. As for Croyland, a question about him warmed them into respectful sympathy. "It's been a dreadful thing for his lordship." That seemed to be their deepest feeling.

Bell dismissed them and blinked at Gunn. "They like him, George," he said solemnly. "Would you believe it? They like him. After that I want my lunch."

That morning Mr. Clunk also conducted a small investigation.

He wandered about the ruins till he came upon a gardener, a wooden-faced stalwart, and then exhibited all his charm to induce conversation. The effort was not well received. But Mr. Clunk's affability ignored the broadest hints that he should take himself off. He tripped among the flowers, chirping about them and the skill of the gardener and the delights of Bradstock Abbey and the good fortune of its owner.

The gardener was pushed beyond the limit of his endurance. He thrust his fork deep in the ground, he straightened his back and scowled at Mr. Clunk. "Here! Ain't you got no decency?" he inquired.

"Dear me, yes, I hope so," said Mr. Clunk eagerly. "What can I do for you?"

"Dancing about like a little old midge in the sunshine and buz-buzzing," the gardener rebuked him. "Think shame of yourself."

"But why should I, my friend? I'm told visitors may come here freely. Lord Croyland very kindly allows ——"

"'Taint what you be allowed to do. 'Tis what's decent for 'e. Didn't you never learn no respect? Us don't want no trippers coming trapesing about to-day."

"But I'm very sorry to offend you. My dear friend, I had no thought of doing anything wrong. What has happened to-day?"

"You trippers do never know nothing surely," the gardener spat. "There's death in the house, that's what. Mistress died in the night." He was gratified by the impression he made.

Mr. Clunk stood very still. His large eyes swelled. "Mrs. Garston," he said in a whisper. He shuddered. He took off his hat and wiped his brow.

"Ah. My lord's mother."

"I didn't know." Mr. Clunk's voice was small and humble. "I hadn't thought of that. That's terrible indeed."

"Ah," the gardener was pleased with him.

"I didn't know," Mr. Clunk repeated. "Was she ill?"

"No, no. 'Tis that makes it so mournful. It come on us terrible sudden. Dr. Eves, he can't tell how she died. There's the police from Limbay up to the house now."

"Dear, dear, this is a dreadful thing for you all," Clunk murmured. "My good fellow, you must have thought me too heartless." He inserted a half crown into the gardener's hand. "Of course you don't want visitors to-day." He shook a sad sympathetic head and stole away.

But his sorrow was not all affected for the gardener. His face remained paler than its wont, and still confessed fear. Out of sight of the gardener he stopped and sighed, "The poor forlorn soul!" and bent his head and murmured texts which passed into a hymn:

> "Deep waters crossed life's pathway,
>   The hedge of thorns was sharp:
> Now these all lie behind me—
>   Oh, for a well-tuned harp!"

Much cheered, but looking dreamy rather than his usual alert self, he wandered to the seat in the niche of the arches of the nave and there sat at his ease. After a while he fumbled in his pocket, found a paper of boiled sweets, selected one and sucked. Under that stimulus his face became again wakeful and confident. He looked about him and his prominent eyes gleamed with that pleasure which seemed to Lewis feline.

He stood up, looked warily all round, and delicately made his way among the shrubs and flowers. A syringa was bent and broken as if someone had blundered into it, a patch of columbines was crushed with a footprint.

Mr. Clunk contemplated these injuries and tapped his teeth. It appeared to him that someone had recently made a short cut from the seat in the niche to the drive.

Quite recently. The broken columbines were not faded. He gazed back at the smooth stone seat and returned to examine it. "Well, well, well," he concluded and tripped away to Lewis and his car.

"We had better go and have some lunch, my boy," he beamed. "Let us go to Bradstock Village."

Lewis leaned towards him and said confidentially, "Bell's come on here. And the local. Still inside."

"So I'm told." Mr. Clunk got in. "Mrs. Garston is dead, you see. She died mysteriously in the night."

"I say!" Lewis was shaken from his sardonic composure. "Do you mean murder?"

"Oh yes, certainly, I should think she was murdered." Mr. Clunk blinked. "Poor soul, I feel quite sure of it."

"My Lord!" said Lewis with respect. "This case is piling up, sir."

"A terrible affair, indeed," Mr. Clunk sighed. "Dear me, I wonder what Superintendent Bell will make of it? But let us be going. I really need my lunch."

CHAPTER XVII

AFTER LUNCH

MAY came down to the call of the luncheon gong and found Gladys alone. "Hullo, baby. Let's go in. The old man's not having any. Off his feed—and making work. He's been hanging on the end of the phone all morning. Poor old thing. He's a terror with a trunk call. I tell you he don't need a phone when his blood is up. They'd get him with the naked ear in America. Come on. You look about all in, baby."

"I'm all right, really," said May, but they went in with Gladys's arm round her.

"By the way, Jackson," Gladys turned to the butler, "Lord Croyland wants you to look after the police officers."

"Thank you, ma'am. It has been attended to."

Under service which ignored any cause for disturbance, under watchful pressure from Gladys, May found herself eating through a meal which was impossible before it began. But it was a point of honour to be normal, to admit no weakness or dread.

"Good for you, baby," Gladys laughed, and pushed back her chair. "No use starving the little system, what?" and again encircling May's waist, took her back into the drawing room. "You've got grit, May, I'll tell the world." Coffee came. "What about a spot of poison? Benedictine for baby? No? All right, all right. Gasper? No, again. Well, cheerio, old thing." She lay back luxuriously and blew smoke through her nose. "Did these bright bobbies put you through it?"

"It was rather ghastly," said May.

Gladys nodded. "Get you on the sore place?"

"Of course they seemed to think it was my fault. I don't blame them. So it was, in a way."

"Oh, come off it! You! You couldn't kill a canary."

May flushed. "Ah, don't talk like that. Of course I never hurt her. You know I didn't, Gladys."

"I'm saying so, dearie." Gladys opened her eyes. "Why fuss?"

"She was my patient. I oughtn't to have let it happen. I ought to have stopped it."

"As how?" Gladys drawled.

"If I'd been sleeping in her room she wouldn't have been killed."

"You never know. She wasn't killed in her room."

"That's what's so queer. I can't think what she was doing in that archway."

"No, that is rum. What do the bobbies think?"

"I don't know. Of course, she might have been coming to me. They're bound to think that. Oh, if I'd only been with her."

"What's the good of saying that? She wouldn't have let you. The old girl hadn't exactly fallen for you, had she?"

"She hated me, I know. Oh, poor thing, it's too horrible."

"Did you tell 'em that?"

"That she didn't like me? Of course I did. That's part of it."

"I say, you have been going it, baby." Gladys lit another cigarette. "Why talk so much?"

"They've got to know everything."

"I should smile. But look here, my child, supposing she was coming to you, who met her on the way?"

"I haven't an idea. Of course I haven't." May wrung her hands. "Gladys, have you?"

"Search me. I can't half believe she was killed."

"Oh, she was! She was!" May cried.

"All right. Then somebody went mad. No sense in it. Just temper. What do our bright bobbies think?"

"I don't know at all."

"Bit thick in the head, aren't they? Bone from the mouth up. They're going to be a damn nuisance, baby. They'll pinch the lot of us before they're through."

"Oh, don't talk like that!"

"I should worry!" Gladys laughed. "Look here, what about somebody from outside the jolly old place? Have these bright boys thought of that?"

"How can I tell?" May cried. "You mean somebody breaking in? But what for? A sort of burglary? Nothing's gone, is there?"

"Bless you, no. Not a sign of a burglar. Of course there wasn't one. That's why I wondered if these bobbies might go and look for him."

"They didn't say anything to me like that." May pushed back her hair. "It couldn't be——" She stopped suddenly. "No, it couldn't."

"Sure thing." Gladys looked at her with interest. "Not a chance. Only wanted to know you'd got that right. Won't do starting false scents. You have to watch your step now, baby. Well, be good." She slid out.

May was left with her mind in a tumult. She had not been able to think calmly of the murder as a problem. The thought that Croyland had killed his mother was with her from the first as a ghastly probability, yet too horrible for belief. Suspicions of the maid had risen in her, been banished as the ugly fancies of dislike and risen again, but not admitted as possible. She told herself that both had loved the poor woman and her unreasonable heart accepted it. For she was so made that her unconscious desire was not to discover the guilty and punish but to find everyone innocent. A purpose outside reason: she had no doubt that the death was murder and the cowardly cruelty of it a wrong which she was bound to fight against with all her strength, a wrong for which there could be no mercy in earth or heaven.

The cool cross-questioning of Gladys set thought and feeling in a whirl. Gladys was always hard, of course, and rather vulgar—but she had never been so horrid. It was all ghastly before but she made it uglier, taking it in that cold way, as a mess to get rid of. And she thought she was being kind, she meant to be kind, with her warnings about what the police would suspect and taking care to say nothing! Oh, but how vile it was!

May was sure that the police suspected her already. They must, of course. They ought to. She couldn't do anything but just face it and tell everything.

Everything! That boy Tony Wisberry! When Gladys talked about somebody getting into the house, did she mean it might have been? Was that a warning to know nothing? Had they found a trace of someone getting in?

Oh, but it was mad! That boy never hurt anyone. And why should he come into the house? He said he wouldn't ever again. He said Lord Croyland had treated him so badly he couldn't come. What did he say?

She ran upstairs to her room. The fragments of the letter were gone. The waste-paper basket was empty. Of course it would have been cleared. But if somebody had looked at the letter, if the police knew he had had a quarrel with Lord Croyland!

Well, but a quarrel with Croyland was no reason

for breaking into the house. Why should he? He wouldn't, of course. One only had to look at him to know that. Such a boy! But the police might think so. If Croyland had papers he wanted and wouldn't give them up—he talked as if there was something like that. Then the police would think he broke in to get them—and Mrs. Garston heard him—and then——

May pulled on her hat and hurried out. He might be on the road where he said—it was a day late—but he might be—he was the sort of man who would come again—or he might be still in the village. She must see him, she must talk to him—ask him——

In the morning room Superintendent Bell pushed away his plate with a sigh of satisfaction.

"They've done us very well, I will say," Inspector Gunn agreed. "That pigeon pie was prime."

Bell took an easy chair and lit his pipe. "Were you going to tell me what you think of things, George?" he inquired. "I'd like to get it in order, myself."

"That's right," Gunn nodded. "It is all sorts of a muddle. Well, you know, what keeps sticking in my gizzard is they're a nasty lot of people. Croyland—the nurse—the maid—that smart secretary. I wouldn't like any of 'em to mind my baby."

"No, George," Bell smiled. "But that's confusing to me. Let's take it another way, do you mind? Begin from the murder. Leaving out the chance of dope, the woman was killed by throttling. That means a bit o' strength, though she was old. I should say neither the nurse nor the maid is up to it. The secretary, p'r'aps—she's a hefty wench. But it's more a man's way of killing than a woman's."

"I thought of that too. Points Croyland's way, don't it? And the nurse said she was calling out a man's name."

"Said she thought so," Bell corrected. "Also said it wasn't Henry, which is Croyland's name. It might have been some pet name his mother used."

"While he was killing her! Lord, it is nasty, isn't it?"

"Go easy. You haven't got him in the dock yet. Keep on the facts. She was found dead up in that archway. I should say she was killed there. If the job had been done somewhere else, why should anyone choose that place to dump the body? But what was she doing up there? She might have been going to the nurse's room—not very likely. She hated the nurse; she'd have rung up her maid if she wanted anything. She might have heard a noise to get her out. That's been done before now. Anyhow—who was it she met in the archway?"

"Might have been more than one of 'em," Gunn answered. "If you ask me, they all know a bit too much."

"Did they get you that way, George?" Bell smiled. "You may be right. I should say they're all wondering how much the others know. Or how much they're going to give away. That don't have to mean they're all in it together. But they've all got notions about it."

"The maid has, hasn't she?" Gunn grinned.

"Putting it on the nurse? Yes, I wasn't falling for that, George. She's yellow with spite: so what she says cuts both ways. But there might be something in it. Half a minute, I'm taking it a man did the job. Well, if there was a man in the archway, it was Croyland or some chap from outside."

Gunn shook his head. "Nobody got in last night. My chaps have been all over the place. Nothing broken. Not a sign."

"Oh, George!" Bell laughed. "Tell me another. There's about a hundred ways of getting into this place. A man wouldn't want to do anything rough. Besides, who told you he wasn't let in?"

"There's that, of course," Gunn said sulkily. "That only brings you back to these people inside."

"It does so. Might fit with the gent who wrote to the nurse, eh? But let's take it in order. Croyland or a man from outside. Either of 'em possibly helped by the women. Now what about motive? Who had any reason to kill the old lady? The nurse—having had a deal of trouble with her and a big blaze-up last night. The maid—for jealousy of the nurse, to get her in a mess— I've known that done—or just in a mad temper. We can't tell any motive Croyland had. But somebody had the motive of wanting what she kept with Alfred's photographs. That would fit Croyland. We know him and her have been quarrelling hard. Or it would fit a chap from outside."

"Look here though—if she was killed to get something in her room, why was she killed up in the arch-way?"

"Oh, that's easy. The chap got in and got away with it, but she woke and went after him, calling out, and he scragged her."

"Theory, isn't it?" Gunn objected. "You don't even know anything was taken."

Bell made an impatient noise. "I know all right, George. You mean I can't prove it. Something about Alfred Garston was taken. Just like something about him was taken from that old girl in Limbay. But this time it cost two lives."

"Two?"

"What do you think your constable was killed for last night? He stopped someone who was buzzing about these roads and couldn't afford to have it known. Why not? You don't have a whole lot of motor thieves in these parts, do you? You get one ready for murder the same night another murder was done. The chap that killed the constable was right in this, you bet your life. That's why it didn't suit him to be put in the note-book."

"My oath! I believe you've got it," Gunn muttered.

"Have I?" Bell made a grimace. "I wish I knew what to do with it. What were you thinking of doing next, George?"

"If that's right," said Gunn reluctantly, "it lets Croyland out."

"Yes, you'd think so," Bell nodded. "Why should he go a jaunt in a car because he killed his mother? But I don't know, George. There's a lot of things I don't know yet. I'd like to know what the devil it is about Alfred Garston that's got so blooming precious now. I'd like to know what's brought Josh Clunk into it and what his little game is." Bell filled another pipe. "And if you'd kindly tell me why the old lady was killed just where a lamp wouldn't light, that'd be something to go on with."

"The lamp? What's the matter with supposing the lamp gave out?" said Gunn. "That's common enough."

"Yes, I have met electric light before. I knew that. But when a common little thing goes and happens just where a lot of uncommon things have happened, I get wondering about it."

Gunn took some time over lighting a cigarette. "If you don't mind my saying so, old man," he hesitated, "you're making too much work over a lot of little things. To my mind we'd do better to take it straight."

"God bless you!" Bell applauded. "Get on with it, George. How do you start?"

"Well, I mean to say, follow up this clue of a chap in a car out for murder. Of course, I've sent out a notice, asking for information of any car seen last night; now we'll work over the whole district with inquiries for strangers with cars staying anywhere about. And I'll go through all the servants here to find out if any of them have noticed a chap round the house."

"The old stuff," Bell grunted. "All right. You have to try it. It never did me any good yet. I always get nothing—or a bit too much. But you may be dealing with a silly ass this time. Only I don't think you are, George. By the way, were you meaning to go through Croyland again?"

"All of 'em. And the nurse. I want to know all about her young man."

"Then I wouldn't ask her. Go easy about what you ask. There isn't much we've got gives us any pull: only that the nurse had a letter from a chap who'd quarrelled with Croyland and that something about Brother Alfred is gone from Mrs. G.'s room. That's all—and precious little. Don't give any of it away."

A constable came in. "That nurse has gone out, sir. Smithers is on to her like you said."

Bell started up. "I was thinking of taking a walk myself, George," he smiled.

Tony Wisberry sat down to his lunch that day in melancholy determination. He could not indeed make up his mind about May. It seemed too probable that she was a girl with nothing to her, a silly, futile girl, since she did not make any answer to the earnest attention of Mr. Wisberry. She might have been prevented from coming to meet him as instructed. But clearly she ought to have written. Difficult to believe she was properly impressed with the importance of Mr. Wisberry. In fact, she didn't care two hoots about him. And that was that. Yet she did seem rather a darling. And she was all on her own with that tricky beast, Croyland. Might be having a hell of a time. Only decent to give her a chance. But his magnanimity did not avert melancholy.

Thus allowing May the benefit of the doubt, he made his plans. In action, if not in judgment, he was, as has been exhibited, a youth who had no difficulty in decision. His determination was to go again after lunch on that road to the Abbey where he had instructed her to appear the day before, and if she failed and no word came from her, to depart from Bradstock that night, as from a woman of no importance.

While settling down to cold pork he was disgusted to see a car stop, from which descended Mr. Clunk.

"Ah, my dear boy!" Mr. Clunk's face shone and his teeth gleamed. "Delighted to find you. May I share your lunch?"

Tony failed in hospitality. "Better ask Collins," he growled. "It's his pig."

"Your good landlord?" Mr. Clunk said. "To be sure." He tapped at the inner door and to the walnut face which came round it he remarked that Mr. Wisberry spoke so well of the pork he must taste it; and could he have a pot of tea?

"Tea?" The walnut face gaped. "Lord love you!"

"Yes, indeed, I hope so," Mr. Clunk beamed. "And the same to you." He came back to the table and made himself a place. "Well, Tony, how have things gone with you?"

"They haven't," Tony growled.

The landlord stumped in and banged down plates and knives and forks. Mr. Clunk began to eat bread and pickles. "You'll carve for 'e, Muster Wisberry?" the landlord asked.

"A little of the crackling, my dear boy," said Mr. Clunk eagerly. "And I shall have my tea, shan't I?"

It came, a large pot, bumped down with a snarl of contempt. Mr. Clunk poured it, dark and syrupy, sugared it richly, stirred and drank. "Ah, delicious," he murmured, and fell to the pork.

"My God!" said Tony with awe.

"I hope you don't take that name in vain, Tony," Mr. Clunk reproved him, eating heartily. "Well now, you were telling me you hadn't made any progress. I suppose you haven't been to the Abbey since I saw you."

"I have not. If that's anything to do with you."

"It is, my dear boy, indeed it is. Because it's quite an important thing for you. I'm very glad to hear it."

"Why?"

Mr. Clunk stopped eating to drink. "You don't know what happened last night, Tony?"

"No, I don't. Do you mean at the Abbey?"

"At the Abbey—and on the road from the Abbey to Limbay. Two horrible crimes. Mrs. Garston was murdered in the house, on the road a poor fellow of a policeman out patrolling was shot dead. That is what I came to tell you, Tony."

"Good God, it's ghastly!"

"The devil is with power," said Mr. Clunk.

"Mrs. Garston—how was she killed?"

"I can't tell you. The doctor who was called to her brought in the police."

"That means some sort of tricky business."

Mr. Clunk considered a pickled onion critically. "I couldn't say at all."

"But the policeman was shot. What's that got to do with her death?"

"My dear boy, I don't pretend to know. You can see what the police will assume—someone broke into the Abbey, murdered Mrs. Garston, and in making his escape shot a policeman who stopped him."

"A burglar?"

Mr. Clunk smiled. "A man who breaks into a house at night is a burglar certainly. It doesn't matter very much what we call him, Tony. The point for us to consider is that the police will at once look for any strangers in the district. They will show a particular interest in a stranger who has been visiting the Abbey. By the way, you haven't your own car, have you?"

"I haven't got a car," Tony growled.

"No, that's excellent," Mr. Clunk beamed.

"You mean they'll suspect me?"

"My dear boy, that's just what I came to put before you. I'm afraid you must be quite prepared for that."

"Do you think I did it?"

"No, indeed. I'm quite sure you didn't," Mr. Clunk smiled.

"Thanks. Why the devil should they think I did?"

"Now, you mustn't get angry," Mr. Clunk soothed him. "What you should have before you is that the police take a very comprehensive view in these matters. They suspect everyone. But I've always found that the police mind is quite a simple mind. My friend Superintendent Bell is taking this case. Now he's very typical. He likes to follow the obvious line. And, you see, you're so obvious, Tony. You came to stay in this little place, you went to see Croyland and quarrelled with him, you continued to stay here. What my friend Bell will get in his head is that you wanted something from Croyland, and as he wouldn't give it you, you broke into his house to take it. I——"

"What on earth should I take?"

"Ah, what indeed? Of course, you couldn't have found anything of use to you. You're not so foolish as to think so." Mr. Clunk beamed at him affection-

ately but found him a little amusing. "And quite incapable of planning a crime. Dear me, yes. But you
can't expect my friend Bell to know that. I want you
to see that he will certainly ask you to account for
yourself and what you've been doing at the Abbey.
When he does, don't be angry, my dear boy, don't be
hasty——"

"Oh, be damned!" Tony cried. He started up so
violently that the table recoiled from him into Mr.
Clunk's stomach, and he marched out at the best of
his long-legged speed.

Mr. Clunk separated himself from the table. "Tut,
tut. That is provoking," he complained. When he
reached the window Tony had already vanished into
the village. Mr. Clunk stood looking out at the emptiness of the green, a grave and pained little man. He
tapped his teeth. "Really quite perplexing," he sighed,
and made his way to the bar where Lewis was happy
with bread and cheese and beer. "Oh, there is no
hurry," said Mr. Clunk plaintively. "No hurry at all.
When you are quite ready." He went back to his tea,
and pensively dipping lumps of sugar in it crunched
them.

"Car's all ready, sir." Lewis appeared. "Where
would you like to go now?"

"We may as well go back by the Abbey," said Mr.
Clunk sadly.

The road, curving round the gulf and creeks of the
harbour, makes some five miles of salt-meadow loneliness between the Abbey and the village. They had
travelled three when Mr. Clunk saw Tony striding out
in front of them. He touched Lewis's arm. "Don't stop,
my boy. But go gently." They passed Tony at a sedate pace, and if he saw who they were he gave no sign.
Nor did Mr. Clunk. His prominent eyes, very wide-

open, watched the road ahead. It was not straight;
here and there beside it were osier beds and pollard
willows, but it had no other cover. From some distance Mr. Clunk saw May hurrying on to the hurrying
Tony. He did not fail to see a man vanish and appear
again behind her, and behind him another man. A
chuckle came from Lewis. "Deuce of a place to be
shadowing anyone, ain't it, sir?"

Mr. Clunk shook his head. "Most inconvenient,
Lewis, most."

They passed May, and his alert eyes recognized her
as the girl he had spoken to at the Abbey. "Oh, very
inconvenient," he sighed.

"She's almighty innocent, or she's having somebody
on proper," he grinned.

"Dear me, yes, I fear so, Lewis," Mr. Clunk agreed
sadly.

They passed the plain-clothes policeman, who gave
an imitation of a loitering rambler; they passed Bell,
who plodded on, ignoring them with stolid determination. Mr. Clunk touched Lewis's arm again. "Stop
by the next willows," he said, and when they stopped
in that shelter he stood up in the car and watched till
May reached Tony and Tony grasped at her hand.
"Well, well, well," he sniffed. "Turn the car, Lewis.
Quickly please. Let us go back."

Thus he returned to them just as their first confused
greetings were broken off by the arrival of Superintendent Bell. "I want a few words with you two please,"
Bell was saying, well aware of the rush of the car behind him. "Just stand fast." He swung round. "Why,
if it isn't Mr. Clunk! Fancy meeting you! Always bob-
bing up, aren't you? And what might you want here,
sir?"

Mr. Clunk descended from the car with slow, prim

motions. "My dear friend, have I disturbed a little trap of yours?" he asked blandly. "You shouldn't use these tricks, you know, really you shouldn't."

"I don't take my instructions from you, Mr. Clunk." Bell glared. "And I'm not going to stand any impertinence."

"Dear me, why use foolish language?" Mr. Clunk complained. "We all know you've been amusing yourself by following this lady in order to come upon her when she met the gentleman. That is, in order to be unfair to both of them. If you wanted to know where she was going, why didn't you ask her? Because you hoped to alarm them both. That is what I call a trick and a trap, Mr. Bell."

"He hasn't alarmed me," Tony growled.

"No, I'm sure he hasn't, Tony," Mr. Clunk smiled. "But that isn't an excuse for playing tricks on a lady."

"I've had all I want of you, Mr. Clunk." Bell grew loud. "You'd better take yourself off. If you're going to interfere with me in the execution of my duty, I know how to deal with you."

"My dear friend, I'm sure you do," Mr. Clunk beamed. "You know me quite well. Now I'm a very old friend of Mr. Wisberry's. I was his mother's solicitor. I don't propose to allow you to play tricks on him or any friend of his. Is that quite clear?"

Bell scowled at him and turned to Tony. "Mr. Joshua Clunk's a friend of yours, is he? Sorry for that."

"He knew my people before I was born," Tony said. "What about it?"

"Did he? And you want to have Mr. Clunk with you as your solicitor when I ask you for information about a murder?"

"Why don't you want his solicitor to be with him?" May cried.

"I'm not talking to you, Miss Dean." Bell glared.

"No indeed. You don't seem to like talking to Miss Dean," Mr. Clunk remarked. "You prefer to lay traps for her."

"If Miss Dean had told me the truth we needn't have had all this nonsense." Bell spoke with compressed rage. "Now then——"

"Oh, that's shameful. I did tell you the truth." May cried. "Everything I knew that you asked. You didn't ask anything at all about Mr. Wisberry, and he was nothing to do with it; and you didn't ask where I was going or tell me not to go out. You've just been hunting me."

Tony's jaw hardened. "Pretty work," he said with an angry eye on Bell. "About time there was a solicitor looking after you, my lad."

Bell stared at him. "You're not doing yourself any good. Nor her either. Now, I came here to ask you two for information about the murder of Mrs. Garston of Bradstock Abbey. You won't answer unless your solicitor's present to stop you saying anything dangerous to you."

"Oh no, no, my friend," Mr. Clunk beamed—"to stop you asking anything dangerous to the course of justice."

"Yes, you would," Bell growled. "All right. Now I know where I am with you." He turned to May. How long had she known Mr. Wisberry? Never seen him till he came to the Abbey? How often had she met him at the Abbey? Only that once? Humph. Why did she come out to meet him? Because he wrote and asked her to? Humph. What for?

"Why does a man ask a girl to meet him?" Tony broke in fiercely. "Don't play the fool."

"I've known a lot of bad reasons," said Bell. "Now, Mr. Wisberry, what were you doing down here?"

"I came down to see Lord Croyland. And I did. Last week. Hasn't he told you?"

Bell answered with another question. "Never been there again?"

"I have not."

"Why did you stay on in this little place?"

"I wanted to see Miss Dean," said Tony. And May flushed.

"I see. That's all now. You'd better stay here a bit longer, Mr. Wisberry. What's your address?"

"Cock and Pie at Bradstock. Don't worry. I'm going to see this through before I go."

"Yes. I think you are," said Bell grimly. "Good-day to you."

Only Mr. Clunk answered him. And Mr. Clunk said, "Oh, good-day, my friend. You see how simple it all is when you deal with it naturally. Such a pity for the police to put themselves in the wrong. But we won't let that rankle, don't be afraid. We're quite ready to help you. You may depend on that."

Bell marched off with a stamping tread to relieve his feelings. He was far from pleased with himself. But what particularly displeased him was the condescension of Mr. Clunk. Being patronized by that little squirt! Bell's heels punished the road.

Mr. Clunk with his smile of many teeth beamed upon May. "Now, my dear, may I drive you back to the Abbey?"

"Thanks very much," said Tony sharply. "I'll walk back with Miss Dean."

Mr. Clunk surveyed them with benignity. "That would do very nicely," he said. "But really now it's rude of me to say so. Good-bye then for the present, my dear. I'm sure we shall meet again. Pray don't let yourself be frightened by anybody." He patted her shoulder. "There's a brave girl." He turned to his car. "Oh, Tony my boy, just a moment." Tony came to him reluctantly. "If our friend Mr. Bell gets hold of you again, don't be angry, my dear boy, don't be hasty; tell him the whole truth."

"What the hell did you think I should tell him?" Tony muttered.

"Really now! That isn't at all nice of you." Mr. Clunk was annoyed. "I resent it, Tony. You ought to understand me. I mean tell him all your story: your father's disappearance—the discovery you found in his papers—your claim upon the Garston firm—everything."

Tony was startled. "About my father—what's that got to do with this? And you tried to make me keep quiet about it. Now you want it all told to the police!"

"My dear boy, it must be told," said Mr. Clunk earnestly. "That's necessary in your own interests. But a duty also, your duty in the interests of others. And we are all bound to assist justice in the punishment of crime."

"I say, don't preach," Tony muttered. He stared at Mr. Clunk, bewildered between irritation and the coming of an amused approval. "This beats me. You did your damnedest to make me bury it. Now you want to dig it all up."

"Just so, Tony." Mr. Clunk lifted his eyes to the heavens and was pathetic. "We see through a glass darkly. But we were meant to use our own poor judgment. I don't think I was wrong then." He came down to earth again and cheered up. "I'm sure I am right now. But you're keeping the lady waiting. Good-bye, my dear boy." He took Tony's hand and pressed it affectionately and climbed into his car.

May had gone on. "Sorry," said Tony, overhauling her.

"Not a bit. I thought he was nice. But what a quaint little man."

"I don't know what I think he is," Tony grinned. "I used to loathe him. He's clever as sin."

"He was awfully clever with that hateful detective. Nice to have him on your side."

"Want somebody on your side?" Tony looked down at her.

May looked straight in front. "I'm perfectly all right."

"Jolly decent of you to come and meet me."

"I suppose you're thinking I might as well have come yesterday—when you said."

"I wasn't. I know it's cheek to ask you."

"It looks as if I was playing, not to come the day you said and then come the next day. I wasn't. I meant not to come at all. I didn't like your letter. You seemed to be ordering me."

"I say, I never meant that. I'm not such an ass. I——"

"It doesn't matter in the least," May informed him. She was still looking resolutely in front of her. "I only wanted you to know I shouldn't have come for that letter."

"No. You'd have stayed away. I see," Tony grinned. "You like to make things quite clear, don't you?"

May looked up into his eyes. "Yes, I do," she said. "I didn't come because of that." She resumed her survey of the road before them. "I only came because

this ghastly thing happened and I thought you ought
to know at once."

"Awfully decent of you," said Tony, and then with
some difficulty, "I say—that means rather a lot—
it's pretty good to me you felt like that—going to be
angry now?"

"Don't be absurd." May's face was pink. "I mean
these detectives are suspecting everybody."

"Meaning me?"

"I don't know. I suppose I've made them worse
about you, being found with you. I'm awfully sorry.
I didn't think of that wretched man following me."

"Silly brute," Tony growled. "Why should you?"

"Of course I should. He suspects me."

"Perishing idiot. That is the absolute limit." Tony
gave forth a loud angry laugh.

"Oh no. I don't wonder at all. It is really my fault
she was murdered. She was my patient. I ought to
have kept her safe."

Tony laughed again, but in a different key. "You
know you're rather like my mother, Miss Dean."

"Please don't talk nonsense," May cried.

"Not a bit. Whenever she heard of anything going
wrong with anybody she cared about, she used to think
it was really her fault."

But May would not take any interest in this foolish
woman. "It's not like that at all," she said sharply.
"I didn't care about Mrs. Garston—it's horrid of me
but I didn't, only as a patient. But if I had slept in
her room last night she wouldn't have been killed."

"One doesn't have a nurse to watch for murderers,"
said Tony. "How was she killed?"

"She was strangled in a corridor in the night."

"Queer sort of murder." Tony frowned. "Looks like
a burglar, doesn't it? She heard something, got up to

see, and the chap stopped her mouth and bolted. That's about it. I say, didn't you know there was another murder down here last night? A policeman shot on the road. That looks like a burglar getting away."

"How dreadful!" May stared at him. "I didn't know. The detectives said nothing about that. How did you know?"

"Clunk told me."

"Mr. Clunk!" She grew very pale. "He knew all about it! What is he doing down here?"

"Now you beat me," Tony grinned. "He's a bag of mystery. He's known me since I was born. I haven't begun to know him. If you'd asked me last week I should have said he was a regular wrong 'un. Now I'm beginning to like him."

"Because he helped us to-day?"

"Yes, partly. And the way he did it. And one thing and another."

"Did he know you were looking for me to-day?"

"I didn't tell him you were coming. Did you?" Tony was amused.

But not May. "Of course not!" she cried, and was the more annoyed at his chuckle.

"Sorry, I never told him you existed."

"What is he doing here then?"

"Well, you know, I don't want to be proud, but I begin to think the little beggar's come after me."

"Did you know he's been at the Abbey?"

"I did not!" Tony cried. "What, seeing Croyland?"

"Oh no. He's not been inside. But he was looking round. I met him one day last week. He said he'd come to see the ruins. Of course, people do."

"Clunk looking at ruins! I do not think."

"But what was he there for?" she checked, and gave Tony a strange searching look.

"I don't know," he said slowly. "You mean what am I here for? That's what I wanted to tell you. That's why I wrote. I——"

"There's no reason why you should tell me," May interrupted. "It's nothing at all to do with me, Mr. Wisberry."

"Sorry, Miss Dean," Tony grinned. "There's a jolly good reason why you should know all about me. If you haven't noticed it, I have."

"I don't know what you mean," said May, and walked faster.

"Well, let's just say I feel you've simply got to."

"Oh"—the word contained much indignation. "Orders! Like your letter. Thank you very much, Mr. Wisberry."

"Orders—if you like. But I didn't give 'em. You've got to know about me. I've got to know about you. It's not my fault, Miss Dean. Just the way things are made."

May did not reply to this theory of the universe. Her hurrying stride suggested that she did not accept it.

But Tony went on talking. She was told of the disappearance of his father twenty years before, of the recent examination of his father's papers and the vanadium steel process there described and introduced twenty years ago by Garstons: of Tony's efforts to force an explanation from Croyland and Croyland's evasions ending in defiance.

"I don't understand." She knit her brows. "It seems so mixed up. It's dreadful for you about your father, of course. But what do you think happened to him? Do you mean Lord Croyland made away with him to steal his invention—murdered him or something horrible?"

"I mean he vanished absolutely. And the people who gained by it were Garstons. That wants a bit of explaining. And Croyland won't explain it."

"You do mean Lord Croyland murdered him," May said. "How ghastly!" She walked on a little way and then stopped and turned to him. "Why did you come here?" she cried. "Why did you stay here? What good could it possibly do?"

"I came to see Croyland, of course." Tony's chin came forward. "I had to. I had to have it out with him."

"But after—why ever didn't you go away?"

"Well—" the chin relaxed its insistence—"I met you, you know. I wanted to meet you again. I found what a beastly place it was. I wanted to get you out of it. I wish to God I had before this happened. I——"

"Oh, stop, stop!" she cried. "This is mad. You had no right—I'm nothing to do with you at all."

"Sorry," Tony said gruffly. "I suppose I've made it worse for you now, being mixed up with me."

"I'm not! For heaven's sake leave me out. Don't you see what these detectives will think—they are thinking so, they can't help it—you stayed to come to the Abbey again, to get something more from Lord Croyland." She looked up at him breathless, fiercely eager.

"What if I did?" Tony frowned. "My Lord! I see, thank you. You mean I was after Croyland's papers. I was the burglar. I murdered his mother. You think that, do you?"

"Of course I don't. I know you couldn't be. Oh—" she stamped her foot—"do you think I'd be here if I believed that?"

"Sorry," said Tony again and with an uncomfortable smile "I seem to be most kinds of a brute with you. Wonder why that is?"

"Don't be so foolish," said May. Her eyes were shining.

"You came out to warn me these beauties were suspecting me. And that's got them on to you too." He looked down at her with a shamefaced affection. "My dear."

"No," said May.

"Yes," said Tony. "Very much yes. And all right. All exceedingly right. Now we know. My ghost! If anyone bothers you, send 'em along to me. This is my show. I say, I wish I could take you right out of that beastly house."

"You are a child," May laughed sadly. "This is all nothing. I don't want anyone to help me. And there can't be any help. I've just got to see it through."

"I know," Tony nodded. "I'm going to see it through too. That's all."

They walked on. There was no more to be said in words. Each head was borne high. At the gate of the Abbey gounds she looked at him, but he made no sign of turning and she let him come with her to the door.

"Send for me if you want me," said Tony.

"Yes," said May, and gave him her hand.

He held it for time that could be felt. "Thanks."

This ceremony was observed by Superintendent Bell and Inspector Gunn from the window of the morning room: from her own window by Gladys.

"My oath," said Gunn.

"Pretty, isn't it, George?" Bell grunted. "Only wants Josh Clunk there saying, 'Bless you, my children.'"

The sagacious face of Gladys was perplexed. She withdrew to her mirror and slowly and with thought repainted her lips.

Gunn and Bell contemplated one another. "Well, what are we going to do about it?" said Gunn.

"That's meant to let us know they don't care a damn for us. Looks like a bluff of Josh Clunk's: just his style, when he's got a shaky case. I thought he was bluffing good and hard this afternoon. But some of this young fellow's story must be true. He did come here before the murder quite open: and Croyland did see him. The next thing is to find out what he came for. Look here, George, I'll go and ask Croyland. You pop over to the pub at Bradstock and ask the young man. Josh Clunk won't be there. He buzzed off the other way."

"All right. But he won't talk without Clunk, will he?"

"I don't know. Struck me he didn't like Mr. Clunk as much as Mr. Clunk liked him. Don't bring in my little turn-up with Clunk. You're on your own. Be civil, George, be hearty. That ought to try him out."

Gunn nodded. "I see. And I'll have a look into his alibi last night. That won't do any harm either."

"Not if you don't sniff too much," Bell said slowly. "Go easy."

"Don't worry, I won't force it," Gunn smiled. "Well, when do we join up again?"

"I'll go back to Limbay when I've finished with Croyland."

"You won't force him," Gunn chuckled, and departed.

Bell was in no way pleased. He knew very well that he had mishandled Tony and May and allowed Mr. Clunk an unwise advantage and that the error came from the weakness for forcing his cases which other enemies besides Mr. Clunk had used. But he did not want Gunn to tell him so. And a deeper discomfort troubled him. The further he went, the less sure he felt of the way. It looked as if it would turn out to be one of those cases in which there was such a tangle of dirty work a man couldn't get anything clear. A result most obnoxious of all to the pride of Superintendent Bell.

His square face was grim and glum as he marched into Croyland's room. Croyland was writing with a glass of whisky beside him. He jerked a nod at a chair. "What have you got to tell me?" he mumbled, and went on writing.

Bell began abruptly. "There's no trace anyone broke into the house last night."

"Hmph. Never supposed there was," Croyland grunted. "Well?"

"I don't connect any of your servants with the murder."

"Thought you wouldn't." Croyland wrote on.

"So we'll have to look for some more information," said Bell.

Croyland cleared his throat. "Can't make evidence, can you?"

"I'm taking it you want the case cleared up." There was a hint of suspicion in Bell's voice.

Croyland finished his writing or his self-control failed. He dropped the pen and flung himself back and stared with sullen eyes. "Told you what I think. It's clear enough. My mother was old and ill. Nothing strange in her sudden death."

"That won't be the verdict. The medical evidence is murder."

Croyland made noises: mumbled something about doctors being damned fools and said, "I can't find a murderer for you."

"Are you giving us all the help you can?" Bell looked hard at him.

"Done what you liked in the place, haven't you?" Croyland growled. "Ask me anything you want and I'll answer."

"Yes, I've been round the house." Bell spoke thought-fully. "I find a man could get in all right without break-ing anything. So——"

Croyland interrupted. "Could he? How?"

"Plenty of ways. Pretty well anywhere if he knew the place."

Croyland drank off his whisky. "Maybe. Don't know much about burglary. Daresay."

"So there might have been someone in last night."

"What about it? I didn't see him."

"Any idea what he could have been after?"

"Damn it, what are burglars after?" Croyland's voice rose in angry contempt.

"You haven't missed anything in your mother's room?"

"She had nothing there but her jewels. They're still there, I suppose. Ask her maid. I haven't heard of anything taken."

"I see. This is what I wanted to ask you, my lord. Do you know of any strangers looking round the place lately."

"No, I shouldn't: only here week-ends. Ask the ser-vants."

"I'm told there's a fellow been staying in Bradstock Village this last week, acting rather queer. Calls himself Wisberry."

Croyland frowned and rumbled. "Wisberry? Ah yes. That fellow. He came to see me. Queer enough. Bee in his bonnet. If he's honest."

"Oh, he came in to see you. What did he say he wanted here?"

"Told a tale about a steel process. Wanted to claim his family invented what we've dropped for years. I have fellows trying that sort of game often enough."

"You turned him down, of course," Bell nodded.

"He might have thought of having a try for your papers."

Croyland was some time considering that. "He might. If he was fool enough. I've no papers any use to him."

"Or he might have put up that tale to get a look round the house. Before trying for something else."

"What?" Croyland said sharply.

"I don't know what there might be here he'd be after."

"Nor do I," Croyland grunted. "Well?"

"Well, that's all now, my lord." Bell rose. "I judge we've some way to go yet."

"And get nowhere." Croyland turned again to his table.

When May came down to dinner that night Gladys met her on the stairs. "Hallo, baby. Who's your young man?" Gladys ogled her.

"What do you mean?" said May.

"Aren't we coy! The boy who saw baby home."

"Oh, that was Mr. Wisberry. The man who came to see Lord Croyland last week. He met me when I was out this afternoon."

"How sweet of him! Did jolly well in the time, what?"

"I don't know."

"What's he up to down here?"

"He's down here to see Lord Croyland."

"What, again?"

"I don't know."

"All right, all right. I don't want him." Gladys laughed unpleasantly. "He seems to have clicked good and hard."

"Don't be disgusting," May cried.

"Got you where he wants you, hasn't he?" said Gladys. Her eyes darkened. "Who is he anyway?"

"Oh, ask him!" said May furiously, and swept on.

CHAPTER XVIII

AFTER TEA

BELL drove back to Limbay and comforted himself with a tea on the ample scale of the White Lion. He was nevertheless at the police station before Gunn and a grim pipe was smoked out before Gunn came.

"Well, George, he's taken you some time," Bell's tone was satiric. "And what did you get out of him?"

Gunn settled down in his chair without hurry. "We got on very nice, thanks. I should judge you went the wrong way to work with him, old man. Bit too much of the high hand, if you know what I mean. These young gents from college won't stand for that. You can't drive 'em. Only get a damn-your-eyes that way. He's a gentleman all right. Don't care if it snows pink, he goes where he wants. Just a boy, of course. But I'll say I took to him. And he didn't mind me, either."

Bell laughed. "Very pleasant all round. Thank you, George, I'll try to do better next time. Well, as he's your blue-eyed darling, I suppose he told you everything?"

"Yes, he told me a bit, old man," said Gunn complacently. "And very rum stuff it is."

"You don't say so!" Bell grunted. "You know, George, in my silly way, I thought it would be, if you got anything."

"All right, all right." Gunn was not disturbed. "Don't start with your back up. That's no way to take it. I tell you, we'll have to do some thinking about this."

"Right you are, George. I'm watching you," Bell chuckled. Gunn pulled out a notebook. "Hallo! Hallo! Took him down, did you? Oh, George! And him such a nice young gentleman."

"You needn't be so smart." Gunn turned the pages. "Just cut out the back chat for a bit. This wants listening to. As soon as I got at him, he opened out proper, told me he didn't want any mysteries about himself—and this is what he said." . . . Put into the order which the mind of Inspector Gunn required, the story of the inheritance of Antony Wisberry was told.

Bell heard to the end in a silence of grim attention. Still silent, he filled his pipe and lit it. Then, "Did you say rum stuff, George?" he inquired. "You were right."

"Gets you guessing, don't it?" said Gunn with satisfaction. "You know what I said to myself as he went on? I was saying, this kind of tale won't do for me. And before he'd finished, it looked so silly queer I couldn't believe he'd made it up. Anybody who was playing tricks would have a better yarn ready."

Bell spread himself and answered deliberately. "I didn't say he made it up, George. I wouldn't be surprised if some of it was true. There might be very queer stuff at the back of this business. Often is, in a nasty murder. But I don't have to believe your Mr. Wisberry is mother's angel boy because he's got hold of a chance to blackmail Garstons'."

"My oath!" Gunn exploded. "You've gone right off the rails. He's no blackmailer. He don't know what it means."

"Keep calm. P'r'aps he don't. But what about Josh Clunk? He was in this from the start. Your Mr. Wisberry says so. Clunk always knew everything—and a bit more. And why is Clunk working in with Mr. Wisberry? Not for his health, George."

"I can't see what Clunk's after," Gunn confessed.
"If you ask me, I don't believe Wisberry knows either.
He was kind of shy when he mentioned Clunk, as if he
wasn't sure how to put it. Look here. Take it Wisberry
went to Clunk, like he says, when he found about the
Garston process in his father's papers, and Clunk
thought he could work that into a nice little thing for
himself. Then you can explain Clunk all right. He wanted to get a good pull on Croyland—Alfred Garston's
letters went and Clunk defends the thief—Mrs. Garston gets murdered, something's gone from Mrs. Garston's room, and Clunk buzzes round the place next
day. If you say Clunk was gathering evidence to
squeeze Croyland good and hard, you've got it all
combed out."

"Thought you didn't like theories, George," Bell
smiled. "Can't do without 'em, can we? That's a good
one. Explains everything—except who killed the old
lady and who killed the constable. And I'd rather like
to know about those little points. But I don't say you're
wrong. I think you're getting very warm. Now I'd like
to put things my own way, if you don't mind. Take it
like this. Your friend Mr. Wisberry goes to Josh Clunk
saying his father discovered some invention Garstons
have been using for twenty years. Soon after a new
young woman gets into the Abbey, this Miss Dean,
coming to nurse Mrs. Garston. A little later Alfred
Garston's love letters are stolen from Miss Morrow.
Wisberry comes down here and goes to the Abbey to
see Croyland. A day or two after Mrs. Garston is murdered and something else about Alfred is taken. And
the next day we find Wisberry and Clunk and Miss
Dean thick as thieves. If that don't mean they're all
in it together, what does it mean?"

Gunn frowned. "You want to say Wisberry did the

murder with that nurse helping him. I'll give you the nurse, I don't feel safe with her myself. But I'm not going to believe Wisberry's done anything dirty."

"Not till you can't help it. All right. You want things so clear, George. I don't suppose each of 'em did the murder. P'r'aps Wisberry didn't. Might be the girl. She could have managed it and handed over the loot to another of 'em—and he shot the constable getting away. I'm not saying they're all equally guilty. When you have three or four in a crime, there's generally one makes the others dance to his tune: some of 'em mayn't even know what he's up to. Might be like that now with Josh Clunk about. But I want 'em all."

"I don't know." Gunn was much troubled. "I've got to own it looks bad. Look here though. You went to ask Croyland about Wisberry. What did he say?"

"Ah. Now you're asking something." Bell knocked out his pipe. "He handed out some rum stuff too, George. It wasn't what he said, it was what he didn't say. He made very small beer of Mr. Wisberry. As far as he went, he bore out what Wisberry told you. Wisberry came to claim rights in an invention Garstons had been using. But Croyland was very anxious to make me believe he didn't care a damn for Wisberry: said if the fellow was honest he was balmy."

"Well, he isn't that," Gunn cried.

"Which?" said Bell, with a grin. "No, I'm not taking much stock in what Croyland put up. I should say Clunk and Wisberry have got on to a bit of dirty work by Garstons. But that don't give 'em leave to murder."

"You think Croyland's keeping something back?"

"Bet your life." Bell was confidently scornful. "He's not a little gentleman, George. I don't think he's be-

having at all nice. For a man that's just had his mother
murdered upstairs, I call him pretty cool. He don't
want any unpleasantness about it. He'd like it brought
in a natural death. If we're going to suspect Wisberry
or the nurse or somebody, well, he won't stop us, but
he stands out. Pretty clear he's in a funk what may
turn up if it gets to a trial, but he means to bluff hard
he knows nothing."

"Well, then——" Gunn stared.

"Well what?"

"That's not far off saying Croyland's our man."

Bell shook his head. "Won't do, George. He might
have killed his mother. But why should he go and kill
the constable? No. That must have been somebody
running away from the Abbey who couldn't afford to
be stopped."

"I see. Yes," Gunn admitted reluctantly. "Somebody
coming towards Limbay though. That cuts out Wisberry. He's staying the other side at Bradstock."

"You've got a point there, George," Bell nodded.
"But Josh Clunk's at Limbay. Take it anyhow you
like, we get back to Clunk. He's the man that put up
the show."

"I don't say you're wrong," Gunn frowned. "But
there's nothing to go into court with."

Bell filled another pipe. "Don't I know it!" he muttered, and began to smoke with some violence.

Gunn watched him sympathetically. "Looks like
a nasty case, don't it?" he said at last. "What did you
think of doing, old man?"

"My Lord, I'd like to get my hands on him," Bell
grunted.

"Ah!" said Gunn.

The door opened. A police sergeant came in and shut
it behind him. "Beg pardon, sir," he said softly. "That

Mr. Clunk's been here some little time. I said you were engaged. He's pressing to see you."

"Got round you, did he?" Gunn sniffed. "Let him wait. I'll ring if I want him." The sergeant withdrew and he turned to Bell with a grin. "Hullo, hullo. This looks like cold feet."

"It does, George. Probably heard you've got at Wisberry and he's afraid Wisberry's told too much. Keep him waiting a bit. Do him good to fret."

But when Mr. Clunk was at last admitted, he came beaming. "How kind of you to let me in, Inspector. I must be disturbing your evening rest. Ah, Superintendent Bell's here too. That's excellent." He drew up a chair and made himself comfortable.

"Well, Mr. Clunk?" Bell's square face set hard. "Come to make a statement?"

"I shouldn't call it that, you know," said Mr. Clunk.

"Confession, eh?"

Mr. Clunk tittered. "My dear friend, you're always so pleasant."

"Thanks. I didn't mean to be funny."

"It's better not, isn't it?" Mr. Clunk sighed. "Really, we ought not to cut jokes. No indeed. This is a very terrible case, my friend. And I'm afraid it's a very difficult one. I have the greatest sympathy with you. One or two little suggestions occurred to me and I felt it was only my duty to give you the advantage of them."

"You're very good," said Bell. "I was thinking of bringing you here, Mr. Clunk. There is some information I want from you. Your young friend Mr. Wisberry has been talking."

"I'm so glad," Mr. Clunk smiled. "I advised him to tell you all about his affairs."

Bell was startled. "Oh, did you! Changed your

mind then. When I was there, you told him not to say a word without a solicitor."

"Quite so," Mr. Clunk beamed. "That was simply for your good, my friend. It was necessary to restrain you. You were attempting to frighten these two young people. That won't do. I never allow that practice. It's most improper—and very bad for the police. My dear friend—don't you see?—if you had gone on bullying my young friends you would have made them sullen and defiant and confused the whole affair. Believe me, your success in this case depends upon their being quite open and candid with you. As soon as you had retired, I advised Tony that when he was asked properly, he should tell the police everything about his position. Now, I hope you've made it possible, eh?" He chuckled and rubbed his hands.

"You're playing a tricky game," Bell scowled. "You own up to it, you arranged with this young fellow what he should tell us."

"Dear me, this is rather paltry," Mr. Clunk sighed. "My conduct is quite correct, it always is. You will make nothing of a quarrel with me, you know that, my friend."

"Expect me to kiss you when you interfere with my inquiries?" Bell was loud: but it did not conceal that he found the confidence, the serenity of Mr. Clunk baffling. "What I don't know is why you're here now."

"Now, really, really!" Mr. Clunk was hurt. "I came to offer any assistance in my power. It is my duty as a citizen, and as a solicitor—and indeed as a friend, for I feel that my dear friend Tony Wisberry is in a manner involved."

"So do I," said Bell. "Very much involved. And my dear friend Mr. Joshua Clunk."

Mr. Clunk giggled. "Oh, I? Well, certainly, as his

friend and adviser and the solicitor of his family, I am familiar with his affairs. But dear me, what a lot of time we're wasting. Forgive my saying so, I don't think you quite realize the importance of time in this case. Suppose you ask me about any point you think I can clear up for you. And then perhaps I might give you some little ideas of my own."

"That's right," Gunn broke in. "That's the best way. There is a bit we'd like to know from you, Mr. Clunk. I'll run over Wisberry's statement and you can check it."

Mr. Clunk made a very good listener. At the end he nodded and beamed. "Yes, that's very clear and complete. I've nothing to correct. You appreciate it was quite a surprise to me when Tony found this process among his father's papers. A ve-ry great surprise."

"Was it?" said Bell. "You thought it was important? But Wisberry's story is you told him to do nothing about it."

"He is quite right. I advised him that on such evidence he had no chance of making good any claim against Garstons. I am sure any competent solicitor would have given the same advice. And the event has justified me. Tony has told you Lord Croyland's reply to him—the process was discovered in Garstons' own laboratories. No doubt Lord Croyland is prepared to prove that."

"So there won't be an action," Bell grinned. "Pity. Makes it look rather like an attempt at blackmail that didn't come off."

Mr. Clunk was not to be irritated. "You shouldn't say things like that. Really you shouldn't. It makes you seem so foolish. If Lord Croyland felt able to take it as blackmail he would prosecute. We should be happy to meet him."

Bell thought that over. "Croyland told me that if Wisberry's honest, he has a bee in his bonnet."

"Lord Croyland was practically compelled to tell you so, wasn't he?" said Mr. Clunk, and his voice squeaked.

Bell frowned and did business with his pipe and Gunn cut in. "You stick to it, Mr. Clunk, this is a genuine claim?"

"My dear sir! Absolutely. That's beyond dispute. The papers can be produced. And, you will agree, Tony has done nothing secretly." Mr. Clunk giggled. "Quite otherwise, dear boy."

"Yes, he's made himself pretty conspicuous," Bell agreed. "You haven't exactly been lying low either. And just as soon as you two get busy down here, crimes begin to happen. You said you had some suggestions to make. What's your little idea about that?"

"Now this is taking the case rationally." Mr. Clunk rubbed his hands. "But you're not quite accurate, my dear friend. The first crime was committed before either of us came here. If you recall, it was that which brought me to Limbay—the theft of Miss Morrow's jewel case with Alfred Garston's letters. I am free to admit that before that occurred Tony had written about his claim to Lord Croyland. But I give you my own opinion, I do not think the theft of the letters was the consequence of the claim." He stopped and tapped his teeth. "I have considered that very carefully. No, I do not think so, my friend."

The two stared at him, Gunn frankly puzzled, Bell with concentrated interest. "Oh, the jewels were pinched for the sake of the letters, were they? Well, I always thought you knew more about that business than we did."

Mr. Clunk did not deny it. What he said was: "My

dear friend, I put it quite plainly at the police court the object of that theft must have been the letters. You should have taken that up, really you should."

"What was in them?" said Bell sharply.

"I have never seen them," Mr. Clunk answered. "I do not know who arranged the theft. I do not know who has them. I never heard of Alfred Garston till that case." And suddenly he turned towards Gunn and his large eyes became more prominent. "My dear sir, you must have had great experience of these county affairs. Were you here when Alfred Garston met his death?"

"I was. We were both on it," said Gunn.

"Oh, really," Mr. Clunk blinked. "Superintendent Bell too! I didn't know Scotland Yard was interested in that affair. Just an accidental death, wasn't it?"

"That's all," said Bell curtly. "Drowned out sailing."

"Ah yes, so I was told," Mr. Clunk murmured. "Drowned in the harbour. Just so." He seemed to lose the thread of his thoughts. "Well, what I was going to ask was simply this: you gentlemen knew the sort of man Alfred Garston was and his manner of life— what sort of compromising matter could be found in his letters?"

Neither of the two was in a hurry to answer that. Mr. Clunk filled in the delay—or emphasized it—by feeling in his pockets, finding a bag of sweets and offering it to them. It was rejected. "The lady told you there was nothing in the letters," Bell said.

"Quite so, yes." Mr. Clunk took a sweet and sucked complacently. "Nevertheless they were stolen."

"We're wandering," Bell frowned. "I'd like to keep to you and Wisberry, please. About this invention. Do you believe Garstons got it from Wisberry's father?"

"That is our case," Mr. Clunk beamed.

"How would they get hold of it?"

"Oh, my dear friend." Mr. Clunk's protest was reproachful. "You expect too much. I don't undertake to explain everything at this stage. I really can't say how they got hold of it—any more than I can say what became of Tony's father."

"Wisberry's father," Bell repeated. "Thanks, I was coming to that. Wisberry's story is that his father disappeared when he was a baby. Just vanished. But the only evidence for that is you told him so."

"Dear me, no." Mr. Clunk was pained. "You should give me credit for ordinary intelligence, really you should. If you look up the records of the spring of 1908, you will find that the disappearance of Antony Wisberry Senior was reported to the police. I still have official letters about it. Very official letters." He made a grimace. "But I am free to confess I do not blame the police force for failing to solve the mystery. I failed."

"Let's have this clear," said Bell slowly. "The statement is, Wisberry Senior made this invention and then he vanished. The suggestion is, he was put out of the way by Garstons in order to steal the invention."

"No, my friend," Mr. Clunk smiled. "I did not make any suggestion. If you ask me whether I believe yours, I have to say I do not know. It is not definite: a firm cannot commit murder. Also it is a conjecture: there is no evidence. I prefer to rely on what I know. I have made my statement. I add that the moment of the elder Wisberry's disappearance, April 1908, was also the moment of the death of Alfred Garston."

"You mean the two things are connected?" Bell cried.

"Again a conjecture, my friend." Mr. Clunk shook his head. "Again, I do not know. You were satisfied that there was no mystery about the death of Alfred Garston."

He produced a silence. "Alfred was drowned out sailing in the harbour," said Bell stolidly. "The evidence satisfied me."

"And we went into it pretty thorough," said Gunn.

Mr. Clunk contemplated their embarrassment with benignity. "You had, no doubt, reasons for going into it thoroughly." His voice was suave.

"I generally have reasons for what I do," said Bell. "You can take it we came across nothing about inventions or any man mixed up with Alfred Garston."

"My dear friend, of course I accept that," said Mr. Clunk, and again he smiled. He fumbled in a pocket and brought out his bag of sweets and offered them. "No? Really? I find them so stimulating. Sugar! One of God's best gifts, pure sugar." He sucked with gusto. "Nevertheless, my friend, the evidence does suggest to me that in the personality of Alfred Garston we shall find the explanation of this strange case. You'll forgive me, but I always thought you made a mistake in treating the robbery from Miss Morrow as an ordinary jewel theft. I'm sure you won't mind my saying so, Mr. Bell, but if I had been in charge of the case, the first question I should have asked myself is simply this —what could letters of Alfred Garston be wanted for?"

"And the lady told you the answer—for nothing."

"Yes, a dear good lady," Mr. Clunk tittered. "I'm quite sure she meant well. But I didn't feel it necessary to believe her. You see, there must have been something in those letters which could be dangerous to people connected with Alfred Garston."

"You mean something about this Wisberry claim?"

"Dear me, no, I should think that most unlikely," said Mr. Clunk. "Directly referring to the Wisberrys—

I should think that practically impossible. No, I meant something about Alfred Garston, or his family, or his death, which it was most important to keep secret."

"I see. Your suggestion is, Croyland wanted to get hold of the letters."

"Oh, my dear friend, you are so hasty," Mr. Clunk sighed. "That is certainly one possibility."

"Croyland was afraid of something coming out about Alfred Garston," said Bell, "so he had the letters stolen to keep it quiet. And then he remembered his mother knew something, so he had her murdered. That's the idea, eh?"

Mr. Clunk looked at him with plaintive surprise. "Why will you rush on so? It is unwise, really it is. That Lord Croyland may have thought it necessary to obtain possession of the letters is clearly a possibility. But beyond that I should quite decline to go at present. For there is at least one other possibility. The letters may have been stolen by someone who wished to use them to put pressure on Lord Croyland. Without prejudice, I may tell you I rather favour that opinion." He put his fingers together and looked at them. "Yes, as at present advised, I should prefer to act on those lines."

"You think Croyland's been blackmailed about Alfred," Bell summed up curtly. "That's what's back of everything."

⟩ "I should infer an attempt has been made," Mr. Clunk corrected him, "and that it is an element in the case—oh, certainly an element. My dear friend, are you in any way acquainted with Mr. Gordon Harwood?"

Gunn looked at Bell with a blank face. Bell stiffened. "I do happen to have heard of him," he said, heavily sarcastic.

"Quite so, yes, quite so," Mr. Clunk giggled. "I suppose Lord Croyland didn't happen to mention him?"

"He did not."

"That was rather a pity," Mr. Clink beamed. "Yes, indeed. Quite an unhappy oversight. Did you see Lord Croyland's secretary?"

"Miss Hurst? Yes. She didn't say anything about Harwood either."

"No, I was afraid she would forget," Mr. Clunk purred. "That was one of my reasons for coming to you. You know I shouldn't be surprised to hear that she is quite familiar with him."

"What exactly are you giving us?" Bell snapped. "Something you'd swear to, or suspicions?"

"Oh, my dear friend, I have been most careful to distinguish between what I know and what I consider probable. Pray note that. Now I know Mr. Gordon Harwood has been staying for some little time at the Grand Hotel, Spraymouth. I know that he came to see Lord Croyland last week. I know that Miss Hurst drove in the Spraymouth direction the same afternoon. I allow myself to infer that Mr. Harwood is not a stranger to her."

Bell sat silent staring at him. From the bewilderment of Gunn came a grumble. "Who is this chap Harwood anyway?"

Mr. Clunk smiled and appealed to Bell. "Now how would you put it, my friend?" But Bell shook an impatient head. "Well, Mr. Gunn, Mr. Gordon Harwood lends money, quite a lot of money, but I don't think he would lend to you. Mr. Gordon Harwood is an agent, yes, an agent," he giggled, "but I should be sorry if he were yours. He is quite in the front rank of his profession, which is blackmail. But I'm afraid Mr. Bell has never yet been able to—eh?"

"My oath!" Gunn cried. "And that smart minx the secretary is in with him!"

"Ah, my dear sir, we mustn't judge modern women as we did those of our own youth. We shouldn't be prejudiced by their manners or their adornments. These things are within the liberty of choice of each generation. The heart may be true enough, I always say——"

"All right. Don't say it now," Bell broke in. "You've given me plenty to think about without a sermon. I've got to say I'm obliged to you, Mr. Clunk——"

"Now that is most pleasant," Mr. Clunk cried. "That is what I hoped for. Really, I am most anxious to work with you in this case."

"Yes, I believe you are." Bell's grim stolidity did not relax. "And I don't mind telling you that's what bothers me. It's not much in your line, is it? I want to know why you're taking such an almighty interest in this case. You must have done a lot of work on it—and before the big things happened. Where do you come in? If you want it straight, what do you stand to gain?"

Mr. Clunk drew himself up. "My dear friend, I am not offended. I am not hurt. I see it is very natural you should feel so. You have not knowledge. My interest in this case began a very long time ago. Tony Wisberry's mother was my dear friend, my very dear friend. It is the greatest sorrow of my life that she was not granted long years of happy marriage. There is no better blessing in God's gift. She was robbed of it. I did all that I could to discover by what means and I failed. I do not often fail. That has been a bitter memory: a regret that smarts. It is my duty to her, it is my duty to God, to use all my powers to bring the truth to light." He stood up. "God bless your endeavours, my dear friend, God speed you." He tripped out.

"My oath!" Gunn said with relish. "He is a rum little cuss."

"Is he, George?" Bell frowned. "I don't know. I was beginning to believe in him—I did believe in him —till he let off that gush." He glowered at the floor. "Josh Clunk and love and God," he grumbled. "Kind o' stinks, to me." Some moments were consumed in disgusted meditation on the odorous problem of Mr. Clunk. Then his thoughts went another way. "But damn it, we've got to get busy!" He started up. "If Harwood was still at Spraymouth last night, that's another one connected up with the murder. And a man with a motive to go for Mrs. Garston's papers."

"That's right," Gunn nodded "Taking it that Clunk's given us the goods. A man with a pal inside the house too. That secretary vamp."

Bell was already at the telephone calling up the Spraymouth Grand Hotel. It was reluctant to answer him. It yielded to bullying authority. Bell rang off and looked at Gunn with grim satisfaction. "Yes, George, Josh Clunk's given us something nasty. I wonder why. Harwood has been there. More than a week. With a car. And he went off this morning. Quick after early breakfast. Had a telephone message. You'd better send a good man over there to see what can be got about him and his car last night. And I want to know where that telephone call came from. Get on to it, will you? We'll have to go over and see Croyland again. Before I go I'll tell the Yard they've got to find Gordon Harwood and hold him."

Again he took up the telephone and Gunn bustled out.

About the same time Mr. Clunk was also asking for a trunk call to London.

He came back to his hotel in a plaintive mood which

surprised Lewis. He sat and sighed till Lewis asked him if anything was wrong. "Not wrong, my boy," Mr. Clunk mourned, "only not right. I see my way quite clearly. I have told these good fellows how to act. But I can't feel sure of them. Not very clever fellows, Lewis. I'm sadly afraid they will blunder again. That might be ruinous. Well, well, well, we are in God's hands. But we shall have to make our own arrangements. I think we had better have another man down, Lewis. Someone who could do rough work, eh?"

"Scott's up to anything," said Lewis.

"Quite. Yes, quite. A very reliable fellow," Mr. Clunk beamed. And he rang up Scott.

CHAPTER XIX

LORD CROYLAND IS OUT

IT WAS already dark when Bell and Gunn set out again for the Abbey, a clear night with clouds moving across the stars. They made good speed on the empty road, slowed into the darkness of the trees of the Abbey, and their headlights discovered its gray mass.

The butler received them with aggrieved surprise: did not conceal satisfaction in announcing that his lordship was out. He was told it wouldn't do, but insisted that his lordship was out, had gone out into the grounds after dinner—if the gentlemen wished to wait, a gracious hand gave permission.

"Does he often walk in the grounds at night?" said Bell, and was told that his lordship did at times. "All right. We'll have a walk too." He turned away and took Gunn's arm. "Just a bit odd, George," he muttered. The band of light from the hall was shut off by the closing door. They stood and looked through the dark and listened to its rustling murmur. "Not a sign of him. Where's he gone? And why's he gone?"

"You can't make anything of this," Gunn protested. "Lots o' chaps like a stroll in the evening."

Bell did not argue, but looked along the paved walk by the house and drew him away into the garden. There too no one was to be seen, no footfall sounded. They moved quietly down across the lawns and one arm pressed the other and they stopped. "Coming up from the ruins, eh?" Bell whispered.

A small red glow approached, they smelt tobacco, a big form came into sight.

"Good-evening, my lord," said Bell.

"Who are you?" Croyland's voice was fierce.

"Superintendent Bell and Inspector Gunn. Sorry to disturb you."

"What the devil do you want now?"

"Well, shall we talk about it here?"

"I don't mind."

"This will do. If we shan't be disturbed."

"No one disturbs us," Croyland growled. "I'll give you five minutes. You'll have to understand, my man, I can't have you breaking in on me whenever you choose."

"It's your own fault we're here now, my lord. Much better to be frank with us. You leave us to get our information otherwise. You'll have to take the consequences."

"Damn it, are you threatening me?" Croyland said thickly. "If you are, you can go to the devil."

"That sort of thing's no good. I've got to ask you why you didn't tell me Gordon Harwood had been here."

o Croyland made noises. "Hmph. That fellow. Didn't think of it. Nothing to do with this business. Nothing to do with anything."

"Do you know what Harwood's reputation is?"

Croyland laughed. "Stinks, I suppose, doesn't it?"

"But you saw him all the same?"

"I did. Wanted to know what he was up to."

"And what was it?"

Croyland cleared his throat. "Sort of blackmail. Told me he was going to put up a fellow as my brother's son. Wanted me to pay to keep it quiet. I told him to go to the devil."

"I see. There isn't a son, I suppose?"

"Never heard of it. Don't believe a word of it. You know as much about my brother as I do. More, eh? Any reason to think he had a son?"

"I have not," said Bell.

"No," Croyland rumbled. "Blackmailing trick. Cleverly managed. Couldn't prosecute. Nothing to take hold of."

"You might have told us though."

"Why? What's it got to do with you?"

"It might have something to do with your mother's murder."

"Don't see it."

"I've met a good deal of blackmail, my lord, and my experience is there's generally a something to it. Not what the chap threatens, most likely, but just something he feels sure the other fellow wants to keep quiet. Now, I put it to you, is there anything Harwood could be nasty about?"

"Damn it, no," Croyland growled. "I've got nothing to be afraid of."

"Then we have to take it he thinks there is," said Bell. "Else he'd never have tried it on."

"What do you mean?"

"You remember Miss Morrow's letters from your brother were stolen. Your mother may have had some letters too. If an attempt was made to steal them last night, that might be how your mother met her death."

Croyland mumbled and grunted. "Have you got information Harwood was here last night?"

"Not yet," said Bell.

"Hmph. Heard anything about the man that shot the policeman?"

"Not so far."

"Doesn't amount to anything then. No evidence at

all. I don't believe my mother had any letters of my brother's."

Bell was silent for a moment. "That seems a bit odd," he said slowly. "A mother generally keeps some of a son's letters. And a son that's dead—well!"

"I don't know of any," Croyland growled. "That's all I can tell you."

"So you feel no suspicion of Harwood?"

"Suspect nobody." Croyland cleared his throat. "No ground. Told you so."

"I wonder why he stayed on in these parts after you turned him down." Bell asked of the surrounding night. "Must have had something in his mind." He turned to Croyland. "I suppose it never occurred to you some of your people might be standing in with him."

"It didn't," Croyland grunted, and then with a sudden ferocity, "Who do you mean? What are you after now?"

"Somebody who knows your affairs from inside."

Croyland made noises. "Nothing to know. Told you that a dozen times. I've had enough of this. If you have any evidence bring it out. No more time to waste on fancies."

"Thank you. That's all now," said Bell.

Croyland grunted something profane and strode away.

For a moment Bell stood looking down towards the rustling bushes about the ruins. "Ah, well, come on, George," he sighed. "Let's get back."

The car swung out to the road again and Gunn became conversational. "Well, we haven't made much of that, old man. I can't half make him out. All he cares for is to hush it up. But he must know it's going to make a noise with the doctor swearing to murder. The only way I see to take that is that he had a hand in it and he's in an almighty funk. But then you'd think he'd jump at a chance to put it on Harwood. And he won't hear of that."

"He's afraid to have Harwood talk, that's plain enough," said Bell.

"Well, all right. But then he said he told Harwood to go to the devil. That don't look like being afraid of him."

"We don't know if he did, though," Bell objected.

"Ah, but that won't do, old man. Supposing he didn't. Supposing he made terms with Harwood, then Harwood had no reason to try for any more papers, and that cuts Harwood out of the business last night."

"Yes, you've got a point there, George," Bell admitted. "I like that. Remember who put us on to Harwood. It was Josh Clunk. Just like him to come trailing a red herring."

"It's not that quite," said Gunn. "All he said was, the chap was down here seeing Croyland—and that's true and we wouldn't have got it but for Clunk—and if you ask me, our knowing it gave Croyland a knock."

"It did so. A nasty knock. Yes, you're in good form to-night, George. There must be something in the Harwood business that Croyland funks."

"And yet he turned him down," Gunn insisted. "No, I can't half make it out."

"Something that Josh Clunk has a sniff of too," Bell went on. "He wants to get us on to it. I don't like that. Croyland bluffed it last week. Now his mother's been murdered he's afraid of it. What the devil was it?"

"That tale about Alfred leaving a son—that won't do," said Gunn. "He never had a legitimate son. Son cropping up after twenty years too—rats."

"Oh no. Nothing in that. Croyland wouldn't funk it, either: wouldn't have mentioned it if he did. I daresay Harwood may have come with that tale, but you bet your life he's got on to something else. He don't start a game unless he knows where a man's weak. And now Croyland's in a sweat, we should find out too. Since his mother was killed. It beats me, George."

"Ah," Gunn gave him sympathy, and the car made a mile in silence.

"If I knew why Croyland went out to-night I'd know something," Bell announced.

Gunn was not impressed. "You do go for trifles, old man," he said tolerantly. "But I've got to own I don't care for Croyland's ways. He's tricky, to my mind."

"I don't bet against it, George," said Bell.

CHAPTER XX

EMBARRASSMENT OF SUPERINTENDENT BELL

IN THE morning Bell brought a gloomy face to the police station. Sleeping on things, he complained, did not straighten them out. Had Gunn any news? Gunn had not. Bell settled down with his pipe and was philosophical.

He didn't know that he wanted anything more. The trouble with the blamed case was that they had a deal too much. He always found that the worst kind. The case that gave you nothing at all wanted a bit of patience and a lot of work but it was easy going compared to one with a whole lot of queer things about. Starting with nothing, you could keep your head clear and lay out what you had to try for. But when you began with a big mix-up of stuff all pointing different ways, no knowing which to take, you lost yourself trying one thing and another. "Talk about being embarrassed by riches, don't they? That's us, George. We're millionaires in this case. Got so much dirty work stinking at us."

"That's right," Gunn nodded. "What did you think of getting on to first?"

"I'm going to get on to Old Man Clunk," said Bell. "He's been a lot too busy to please me. I'm fed up with Josh Clunk working my cases for me. I'll have him watched. I phoned for young Underwood last night."

"All right." Gunn was not impressed. "Your people haven't picked up Harwood yet?"

Bell shook his head. "Haven't heard. By the way, anything in the papers? I saw the *Record*. Just said Mrs. G. had been found dead and the police had been called in. No harm in that."

"That's all there is. The papers aren't splashing it so far. May have some men down to-day."

"You bet you will. Inquiries are being made, is the answer. That's all. Hullo, here's our doctor."

He came in briskly. "Morning, morning. Well, gentlemen, I've got a little more to tell you. Cause of death is asphyxia, and shock produced by strangulation: pressure of hands on the throat. But probably the violence would not have been sufficient to cause death, even in a woman of her age, if she'd been in a normal condition. She'd been taking a drug, which induced a congested state of lungs: a narcotic of the chloral group. The sedative sent by Dr. Eves did not contain that. Quite a correct prescription. But among the bottles you sent me was a half-empty bottle of Algicure."

"What's that?" said Gunn.

"Beastly name. Sham Greek-Latin. Beastly stuff. Patent medicine. Ought to be on the poison list. It's chloral disguised. No doubt that's what was administered to the poor woman. Accounts for the state of the lungs. It would account for the nervous condition which Eves said he found. That's all the medical evidence. You'll let me know when you're ready for the inquest. Good-morning."

"My oath!" Gunn stared at Bell.

"Brisk, isn't he, George?" Bell let out a doleful chuckle. "Brief, bright, and brotherly. And I don't mind owning I could have done without him. We've had more than we want already. No need to give us a drop o' dope too. I was letting myself take it for a straight murder by violence. That's about all I did believe. Now I don't know anything."

"I'm not so sure," said Gunn. "This puts it on somebody in the house."

"If you like. We only had three of 'em inside we were worrying about: Croyland—the secretary—the nurse. The dope would go with any of 'em. Or anyone else you fancy. Or it needn't mean anything at all."

"I don't see that," Gunn objected. "Because she was actually killed by throttling, that don't make it nothing to drug her beforehand. My idea is she was given this dope to keep her quiet while somebody burgled her room. And the poor old girl woke up all the same and got done in. Or you can take it the dope was meant to finish her and she didn't get enough so they polished her off by hand."

"Yes, you can take it lots of ways," Bell nodded. "That's the worst of it, George. But let's sort some of 'em out. We found the bottle in her room, not hidden. We found it half empty. That means either she was taking the stuff regular or else somebody stuck the bottle there so we should think she was."

"Well, all right. But any of these beauties might have got her to take it in the ordinary way."

"They might. I should say that's how it was worked. Getting her into a dope habit, so they could pile up the dose when required and anyway she wouldn't last long. Well, George, the first thing to try is your chemists down here. Has any of 'em been selling this muck Algicure to anybody from Bradstock Abbey? Put one of your men on to that."

Gunn rang and gave his orders. "Got to try it, of course," he said. "But it's an off chance to my mind. If it was Croyland or that minx the secretary, they'd bring the stuff down from London. It looks a bit like Nurse's touch. Just the sort of thing she might have been put in to do. And all the funny stuff's been happening since she came."

"Yes, George. That's one of the things I'm thinking," said Bell grimly.

"She wouldn't buy her drugs down here though."

"She shouldn't," Bell admitted. "You think everybody slips up some time. Well, it's about time they began. We could do with it."

The telephone rang. Gunn snapped an answer, then changed his tone and murmured grateful approval, listening eagerly. "Many thanks. Just what I wanted. Good-bye." He turned to Bell. "That's the post office. They've traced that call to the Grand at Spraymouth early the morning after the murder. It came from the Abbey. So somebody there gave Harwood the tip he'd better be off. Somebody has slipped up, old man."

"Only we don't know who it is," said Bell. "We are getting a lot of stuff, aren't we?" There was a noise in the outer office. "Hallo! What's going to happen now? Mrs. Garston come back to say she isn't dead?"

A sergeant came in with much care in opening and shutting the door and stood with his back against it. "It's that Miss Morrow, sir. Seems rather losing hold of herself, as you might say. Quite upset. Asking to see you, very wild."

"Come on," said Bell quickly. "Let's have her while she's worked up."

The bulk of Miss Morrow came in violently. She clutched a newspaper. "Is that true, Inspector?" she cried. "Tell me, is that true?" She thrust the crumpled paper upon Gunn and with a trembling hand pointed to a place in it.

"The report of Mrs. Garston's death?" said Gunn. "Yes, that's quite accurate."

"She's been murdered!" Gunn did not answer. "It means that, you know it does. He's murdered her."

"Who might you be referring to, ma'am?" said Gunn, primly correct.

"Who? Why, Henry, of course! Lord Croyland. He did it, I know he did."

"Know?" Gunn repeated. "That's an awkward thing to say, isn't it? The only way you could know who killed Mrs. Garston is seeing it done."

"Indeed it isn't!" she cried. "I know he killed her. I'm perfectly certain."

"You understand you're taking a heavy responsibility," Bell frowned at her. "This is trying to get a man hanged for murder, and the murder of his own mother. We shall have to go into it thoroughly. Unless you have good evidence, you've done very wrong and you'll suffer for it."

"Suffer!" She laughed hysterically. "As if I hadn't suffered! And so did she, poor darling. Oh, he's a wicked man. But I never dreamed it would come to this."

"Can you control yourself?" Bell said without sympathy. "It's no use abusing Lord Croyland. We must have things clear if you want us to believe you. How have you suffered? What's been done to you?"

"He murdered Alfred," she wept.

"What?" Gunn roared. "Lord Croyland murdered Alfred Garston?"

"Of course he did," she sobbed. "I always knew— we both knew—oh, it's been ghastly. What ages!" She shuddered and shook. "But I never thought it would end like this."

"Do you understand what you're saying?" Bell said. "You know Lord Croyland committed a murder twenty years ago and you've never told the police till now. That's a criminal offence. That makes you guilty too."

"Me?" She stared at him, her swollen, reddened face showing no sign of fear but indignation and bewilderment. "Oh, how stupid you are!" She beat upon her knee in futile passion. "It's all so hopeless with men like you. I couldn't say anything. We settled that ever so long ago. Of course we couldn't. It would simply have killed her. And it wouldn't have brought Alfred back to us. It wouldn't have done any good at all. And the horrible disgrace of it!"

"You say both you and Mrs. Garston knew Alfred was murdered by Lord Croyland," Bell said slowly. "How did you know?"

"He told me himself," she cried.

"What! Alfred told you he'd been murdered? Did he! How did he manage that?"

"Why will you be so stupid!" She wrung her hands. "It's simply impossible to make you understand anything. I had his letters, of course. He told me everything—oh, my poor boy!" Weeping again overcame her.

"In his letters," said Bell more gently. "Now do try to think what you say, Miss Morrow. You wouldn't have any letters from him after his death, would you?"

"Of course I didn't," she sobbed. "Oh, how silly. It was before he was killed."

"Before he was killed, he wrote that Croyland had killed him. Is that right?"

"No, no, no, not that he had. How could he? You are so stupid. He wrote to me about Lord Croyland hating him and wanting him dead, and if ever anything happened to him, I could be sure it was Lord Croyland's fault. Dreadful letters. My poor boy. He knew —he knew——"

"I see. And those were the letters in the jewel case which was stolen?"

Miss Morrow nodded and gulped and again wept.

"I wish you'd told us what was in those letters before."

"How could I?" she sobbed. "We always said no one must ever know."

"Mrs. Garston had letters of the same kind?"

"Yes, yes. Just the same."

"I see. Now why should you think Lord Croyland murdered her? She's been living with him for twenty years quite safe."

"Oh yes, it's been dreadful."

"I daresay. Still, nothing happened to her. Why should he murder her now?"

"He murdered Alfred," said Miss Morrow fiercely.

"No other reason?"

"What does it matter about reasons? He did! Can't you see he did?"

"You mustn't talk like that." Bell shook his head. "We shall have to make our inquiries. You mustn't let anyone else hear a word. You see, if you let it out you'll be telling Lord Croyland he's suspected. That won't do. Do you understand?"

Miss Morrow nodded. "Yes, yes, of course. He mustn't know the police know. He'd kill me."

In that satisfactory frame of mind she was put into a cab.

"My oath!" said Gunn. "I don't know but what she's right, old man. Croyland might kill her if he heard what she'd given us. Tightened it up good, hasn't she? You asked her what reason Croyland had for killing his mother now. That's an easy one. He knew somebody had got hold of these letters. He wanted to make sure his mother and her letters were put out of the way."

"Yes, you can take it like that, George," Bell answered slowly. "The trouble is, what started the business? Why did somebody go digging up Alfred twenty years after he was dead?"

"I see how that could happen all right. Miss Morrow and Mrs. Garston may have been talking. You can bet they did talk sometimes. Say the secretary picked it up. She gave this blackmailing chap Harwood the office. He went for Miss Morrow's letters and got 'em. He put Croyland in a funk—and there you are."

"That's quite neat," Bell admitted. "But where am I, George? You mean Croyland did the murder and Harwood was just playing about?"

"You could cut Harwood right out if you like," Gunn explained. "Using this idea the women talked, Croyland got worried, got desperate, and went for one lot of letters first, then the other—and killed his mother by the way."

"And that's quite neat too, George," Bell smiled. "You're in form to-day. But I can't do without Harwood myself. He has been down here. He has been up to something about Croyland. By himself or with that secretary. My Lord! She could have killed the old lady herself. She's hefty enough. We could cut out Croyland, if you like." He meditated sardonically. "But did you say Miss Morrow had tightened the case up? Seems to me she's loosened it quite a lot. What she says you can use against anybody you've ever heard of. It comes to this. She's given us the reason why her letters were stolen: an accusation in 'em of Croyland by Alfred. Everybody's acting against Croyland —Harwood and the secretary, Wisberry and the nurse, and my dear old Josh Clunk—and of course Croyland would like to squash the whole thing. So where are we?"

"You're being too clever to my mind." Gunn shook his head. "I should say, after this, it lies between Croyland and Harwood, with Croyland a strong favourite. Hallo!" The telephone rang. He answered it and listened. "Right. Nothing more doing there, then. You'd better come back." He turned to Bell. "That's my man at Spraymouth. He says Harwood wasn't out the night of the murder. He dined in the hotel. There's no late trains this way. His car was locked up. Pretty good alibi. That does cut Harwood out." He grinned broadly. "And leaves Croyland in, old man."

"All right. I don't mind," Bell grunted. "My Lord, it's a comfort to get something clear. Harwood didn't kill her himself. That don't let the secretary out. Quite otherwise. We still want a little heart-to-heart talk with Mr. Harwood. But look here, George. Take this another way round. Why did Alfred go writing to the women that Croyland wanted him dead? We know a bit about Alfred Garston, we went into him pretty thorough, and we never came across anything between him and his brother."

Gunn shook his head. "No. Alfred was all kinds of a bad egg but there wasn't any suspicion of a row in the family. What we did think was that Croyland— Henry Garston he was then, wasn't he?—that Henry had done his damnedest for the fellow. There was never any idea of any foul play about the death. A chance it might have been suicide, Alfred guessing he was up against it for that girl's murder. About a million to one it was accident. Besides, Croyland had no motive for killing him. Alfred was the younger one. Croyland had the firm and everything in his hands—why should he want Alfred dead?"

"I can think of a reason," Bell said slowly. "To save the family name. He probably knew Alfred would be in the dock for murder. It stopped a nasty business for the family, Alfred going out when he did. But still— pretty steep to suppose Croyland would take the risk of doing a murder himself for that."

"I don't believe it, old man. Not for a moment."

"No, I don't think I believe it," Bell agreed. "Besides, it don't explain anything. If Croyland did kill him on that account, it would all happen quick. But here was Alfred writing letters to the women saying Croyland wanted him dead. That means a bit o' time. I should say it was just one of Alfred's monkey tricks. We know he was a mean, dirty beggar. Just the sort to get the women on his side by pretending he was a poor, injured innocent and his brother a brute."

"You've got it, I should say," Gunn nodded.

"Yes, that's about it. But then—don't you see?— we're up against this. Why should Croyland funk that sort of stuff now? The women may have been giving him private hell for years. But there couldn't be anything else to it. As blackmail, it's rotten. Couldn't be used, only in the family, and they knew already."

"Well, I wouldn't say," Gunn hesitated. "Not so nice for Croyland to have it put about he killed his brother. Once that sort of talk gets going it worries men mad: even when they know it's all bunk. You must have seen that in your time, old man."

"I have," said Bell slowly. "And it makes a very awkward case to handle. But I don't think we've got one of that sort here. Croyland don't look mad to me, not by a jugful. He's playing a deep game, whatever it is. And if Harwood reckoned to make him bleed by a yarn that he murdered his brother, I should say Harwood reckoned him up wrong. And that's not usual with Mr. Harwood." He gazed at Gunn. "Do you know what I've begun to think, George? I'm wondering if Alfred might have put something more in those letters than talk about Croyland wishing him dead."

"Miss Morrow was telling the truth all right," Gunn said.

"Oh yes, absolutely. But maybe not all the truth."

"If there'd been anything else nasty about Croyland, you bet she'd have told us."

"She would," Bell agreed. "If she got the hang of it. Well, maybe there wasn't anything. But suppose there might have been."

"I say, I say," Gunn protested. "This is a bit too clever to make sense. Don't seem to me to get anywhere."

"I know it don't," Bell said gloomily. "What sticks in my head is, Harwood must have had something big to work on, something that really hit Croyland where he lived. Looks like Harwood couldn't prove it, he was trying for proofs, but he'd got on it."

"What could there be? Remember what Croyland said it was—about Alfred having a son. That's all bunk."

"Of course it is. If Croyland cared a damn, he wouldn't have told us. But you can take your oath there's a something."

Gunn stared at him. "This isn't like you, old man. If it was anyone else, I'd say it was being run away with by your own idea."

Bell smiled. "Not my idea, George—Josh Clunk's. Didn't you notice he's always had his nose down after those letters? He put us on to Harwood. He didn't come into this business to work up a yarn Croyland killed his brother. He knows there's something else. I wouldn't be surprised if he knows what it is. Remember him burbling about the personality of Alfred Garston?"

"Then what do you suppose Clunk's up to?" Gunn

cried. "How is it going to help him to get Harwood pinched?"

"Cover him up, wouldn't it?" said Bell. "We get busy making a case against Harwood and Old Man Clunk slips out." He snorted. "I don't think!"

"Well but——" Gunn began, and a plain-clothes constable came in. "What is it?"

"About that medicine, sir. Warrens' have sold several bottles to Mrs. Garston's maid. Paid herself. Didn't have it on the Abbey account."

"All right," Gunn dismissed him. "The maid then, old man," he whistled. "The maid, with her down on the nurse. Looks ugly."

"And that's another of 'em," Bell grinned. "Quite embarrassing, isn't it, George?"

"I own I don't see my way," Gunn lamented.

"See your way!" said Bell grimly. "You want a lot. I know what I'm going to do. We ought to hear about Harwood soon. If he don't turn up in his regular ways in town, we'll know he's the man we want. If he does, our people will get him quick. Then I'll put him through it. And as soon as young Underwood gets here I'll stick him on to Josh Clunk's tail. If Josh isn't up to something on his little own I miss my guess."

In a little while Sergeant Underwood arrived and was given his instructions, and under another name and without a mustache took a humble room at the Victoria.

Before lunch the Chief of the Criminal Investigation Department rang up Bell. Mr. Gordon Harwood had been found at Brighton: he had his usual room at his usual hotel: no attempt at secrecy. He was told that the officers investigating the murder of Mrs. Garston at Bradstock Abbey in Sandshire wanted to ask him some questions. He replied that it was damned nonsense, for he knew nothing about Mrs. Garston and had never seen her. He was told that it would be necessary to take him to Limbay to give him an opportunity of explaining himself. His answer was that they would get themselves into an infernal mess meddling with him.

The Chief of the Criminal Investigation Department gave judgment that Mr. Harwood was rattled and bluffing but confident. He advised Bell to go slow. He did not want another charge which would have to be dropped.

"I'll watch it, sir," said Bell ruefully.

"All right. You'll get him this afternoon. I should say you're on to something. But God knows what. Take your time. Good-bye."

Bell turned to Gunn. "The Chief thinks there's a something, George. And a good judge too. Now what about a bit o' lunch."

But before this, rather before Sergeant Underwood reported himself at the police station, though they had come by the same train, a short, thick-set young man approached the Victoria Hotel. He had an unobtrusive care in keeping out of people's way rather at variance with the pugnacity of his heavy face.

Mr. Clunk was taking the sun on the hotel steps. He strolled away along the promenade into the gardens, and there choosing an empty seat sat down. The young man joined him. "Very good and quick of you, Scott," Mr. Clunk beamed. "Have you any money?"

"Drew twenty pound, sir."

"I'm afraid that won't be enough." Mr. Clunk began to feel in his pocketbook. "You have to get a motor bicycle. If you can hire, that will do, but it must be a good one. You know all about that, don't you?"

The bulldog face grinned. "I think so."

"Yes, Lewis said you did." Mr. Clunk gave him notes. "Now what you have to do is quite easy. Buy a map and you'll find on it Bradstock Abbey. Take your bicycle and go out there. You're a tourist going to look at the ruins. You'll meet Lewis. You have to stay out there all night and notice anybody who comes, but most particularly anybody who goes. What we're most interested in is Lord Croyland, a large gentleman, big head, no neck, stooping shoulders. There"—he passed Scott a portrait cut from a paper. "If he leaves, you follow him wherever he goes. Telephone me as you can. But on no account lose him. Quite a simple job, you see."

"Right, sir. Do I stay out there for ever?"

"Oh no, no. You take the night. Lewis will relieve you in the morning. I don't think this will go on very long. Now have a really good meal and get anything you want for the night and run along. Good-bye, my dear boy."

Mr. Clunk tripped away.

As he sat down to lunch, a little later than others, he remarked that Miss Morrow was not there. That did not surprise him. But he sighed. "Poor dear lady. Too cruel! Really too cruel." He reflected on the shock which the news must have given Miss Morrow. It did not spoil his lunch. He was almost the last in the room, eating a second helping of rice pudding.

As he drank his coffee rather belated among the aspidistras in the lonely lounge, he became aware of a man in its darkest corner: a man who read a paper. The ineligibility of that seat for reading was obvious to Mr. Clunk. He dipped lumps of sugar in his coffee and sucked.

After a while he went out swiftly and tripped away to the post office and went in and spent some time writing a telegram. While thus engaged he saw a man look in and pass on. He put the telegram in his pocket and went out and took a cab to the railway station. Another cab followed him close. He made inquiries about trains and went back to the hotel on foot. He had seen the shaven face of Sergeant Underwood emerge from the cab. It was the face which had looked into the post office.

Mr. Clunk was annoyed. "Tut, tut, tut, a foolish fellow, a very, very foolish fellow," he complained to providence. "That really makes one so uneasy." He sighed heavily. "Ah well, we must do as we can."

He comforted himself with a hymn:

> "There's no time for idle scorning,
>   While the days are going by;
>   Let your face be like the morning
>   While the days are going by!"

CHAPTER XXI

INVESTIGATIONS AT THE ABBEY

CONSIDERING their plans over a steak, Bell and Gunn agreed that a little more work at Bradstock Abbey might provide knowledge useful generally and for the handling of Mr. Harwood in particular. The effect of new facts had to be tried—what the maid would be moved to say about Algicure might be illuminating. The detention of Mr. Harwood—the suggestion that somebody at Limbay knew more about him than anyone had said might have interesting reactions with Croyland or with Gladys.

Gunn undertook this investigation and Bell remained in Limbay to receive Mr. Harwood.

Life in the Abbey through these days seemed to May a cruel ridiculous unreality, such as life is when passing under or waking from an anæsthetic. All the more unreal, because it was so little changed. The exacting bodily presence of Mrs. Garston had vanished, but the dread which she had infused in May, the fear of her and for her, endured. The affairs of the household were ordered with the old smooth precision, the equanimity of those efficient servants undisturbed by shock or grief. For them, nothing had happened. Croyland and Gladys neither sought May nor avoided her and when they met at table talked carefully of things indifferent, as in the days before, when Mrs. Garston sat there looking misery. Nothing was changed. She being dead yet lived with them. . . .

After lunch May was going up to her room, and in the archway from the new part of the house to the old, that archway where she had found Mrs. Garston's body, came upon the maid. She was given so hard a stare that she stopped. "Do you want anything?" she said sharply.

"Want anything? Of you, Nurse?" The tone was insolence. "No, I'm sure." The maid stood still and waited for her to go.

This was the first time May had found anyone watching her. The old suspicion that she was always being watched in the horrible house surged over her. She felt like going mad. It was urgently necessary to get out and away, and to be sure she had meant to go out.

She put on her things in a hurry and was running downstairs when she met Gladys. "Hallo, baby! Off to your young man again? Well, if you can't be good, be careful."

With rage and pink cheeks but a slow step of disdainful composure, May went out. She had, of course, no idea of meeting Mr. Wisberry. How stupid Gladys was when she was spiteful—and how contemptible. As if one could possibly feel in that way! Of course she never thought of meeting him. It wouldn't be the least use. He couldn't do anything that would help. She simply wanted to be alone and away from everybody. And it would only bother him, poor boy: make him worry about her, get him into more trouble with those hateful police. Besides, it was perfectly certain he wouldn't be anywhere. Why should he?

She made her way through the park to the Bradstock road.

A statelier dignity clothed her slim form. If people thought she was afraid to be seen with him, or ashamed, or anything, clearly she must show that she didn't care at all. They could all come and look, Gladys and the policemen and everybody. She was not to be frightened. There was nothing to hide.

Ah! He felt like that too. She gave a little laugh of happy courage. He certainly wasn't hiding himself. Rather difficult for him to hide! What a big fellow! But he wasn't trying by any means.

Tony had the aged car of the Cock and Pie: it was stopped on the summit of one of the hillocks of the road, and from that eminence he watched for her. He waved his hat, he came to her in swinging strides.

"I say!" he took hold of her shy hand and did not say it. She had to look up at him, quite a way up to his face—comical face—big chin and hard but so kind. She smiled at it and felt like crying. So it was necessary to look away.

"Awfully decent of you to come," said Tony in a hurry. "I was coming for you really, but I thought p'raps you'd rather I didn't, so I left it to you for a bit." He still had hold of her hand. "If you hadn't, I should have come along. See?"

"I see."

"Knew I'd be here, didn't you?"

"Well, I came." May looked up at him again and for that was allowed to recover her hand.

"Good girl. I've got to see you every day, you know. Promise."

"How can I? Why?"

"Just because," said Tony, "if I don't I shall come and break in. Get that."

"Oh, don't be absurd."

"I won't. But you're my job."

"Indeed I'm nothing of the sort," she cried.

"Better get used to the idea," Tony smiled.

"I don't want any help," she said fiercely. "I won't

have you think so. You shan't waste your time over me."

"No, dear," said Tony with satisfaction. "I shan't. Well, how's things going?"

She gave him a look of angry surprise. "What do you mean? What things?"

"Things in general. Our jolly old bobbies and their little games."

"Is that what you came for? How can I possibly tell? I don't know in the least what they're doing. I haven't seen any of them."

"Not bothering you. That's good. All gone away from the Abbey?"

"Oh yes. You needn't worry about that." Her voice was cold and contemptuous but her eyes watched him anxiously. "Whatever they're doing, they're not here."

"Well, that's a relief anyway."

"Is it? Oh, we're quite happy. You wouldn't think anything had happened at all."

"Sorry." Tony frowned. "It is ghastly for you, I know."

"Oh, not at all. And there's no reason in the world why you should stay any longer."

Tony pointed a finger at her. "That's one fine, large reason, my child," he laughed. "Great big reason, aren't you?"

"Don't talk as if I were a baby!" She remembered at the word that it was Gladys's name for her and blushed. "You make me furious."

"Your mistake," said Tony placidly. "I'm feeling you're quite grown up, May. All of a woman. I'm a bit of a man, if you don't mind thinking of that."

"But I do! I don't want to!" she cried, and looked at him in bewildered anxiety. "How can you talk like this? It's all wrong. It isn't real, you know it isn't.

There's just this dreadful thing around us all the time. We're caught in it, you're sorry for me and you want to be kind. That's all that really is."

"My ghost! Don't you believe it. There's just you and me and nothing else that really matters to either of us. The mess at the Abbey—the only thing about that you've got to think of is we're in it together."

"You're not. You're not. You're nothing to do with it."

"In it just as deep as you," Tony repeated. "My good girl, these priceless bobbies are on to me all right. If there wasn't any May in the world I should have to stay and see it through."

She looked at him with large eyes. "Oh, but that's my fault," she said unsteadily.

"What, again?" Tony laughed.

"They think I'm something to do with you, so they suspect you too. I ought never to have spoken to you."

"Yes, all your fault," Tony chuckled. "I say, you are like my mother. Anything that went wrong with people she liked was always her fault."

"You told me that before." May was contemptuous.

"Yes, it does keep coming up. You're very like her. But let's be reasonable by all means," he grinned. "Everything is really my fault. The bobbies only worry you because it bothers 'em I should know somebody in the house. I'm the man they're after. I don't blame 'em."

"Don't be so horrible."

"We've got to see it their way. A chap who has a rummy claim on Croyland might break into the house to get his papers and then—the rest just happened."

"They don't think it was you. They couldn't."

"Well, I should say that's one of the things they've pretty well got to think. And we've got to make up our minds to see it through. That's the way to take it, my child. Frightened?"

"Yes," she said vehemently. "Oh, it isn't true?"

"My ghost! No," Tony frowned. "You didn't ever think I did it. You don't have to be told."

She looked at him and her blue eyes darkened. She shook her head. But her dread was plain enough.

Tony put his arm round her. "Fear's a damned liar," he said. "This is going to work out all right, my dear." He felt her against him and his arm hardened. "Very dear. Do you know?"

May said nothing but she came to him yielding and was still. When Tony kissed her, her lips were cold. . . .

After a while, "Little girl," said Tony, and held her more gently and caressed her with diffident hands. . . .

She looked up at him. "What are we going to do?" she asked.

"Marry," Tony smiled. "That's the idea. Can you bear it?"

She put her hands against him with a gesture of holding him off. "It's a thousand miles away."

"Or next week."

"This is just playing. Like a dream."

"Nice dream," said Tony. "Coming all true."

"We're not free," she cried, "we're not free. Anything may happen."

"But it won't," said Tony, and drew her to him again for kissing.

"No—well—let me go then." He had his way and she hers. "I must go. I want to think." She stood away and looked at him and her eyes were dark and troubled.

"All right. To-morrow," said Tony, not pleased but gracious. "Good times to-morrow. Promise."

"To-morrow," she repeated with a little pitiful laugh.

He watched her go well pleased at himself and life. She went with her mind in tumult. She believed him completely: she was as sure as of her own life that he could never hurt anybody, never do anything cruel or mean. She felt him just what she wanted a man to be, strong and gentle and true and rather a child. But he was a child! He didn't seem to think. He hadn't done anything wrong, so everything must come right. As if the world was like that! He just laughed and talked about seeing it through—and all the while he knew those detectives were working to prove him a murderer and they had a sort of evidence. And he was only going to wait and stand up and say he wasn't, though he really knew people must suspect him. Such a child!

She must think for both of them. Unless the real truth was found out, it would be terrible for him. Even if he wasn't accused, there would be dreadful things said. See it through! They would never be free of it unless they could prove how it really happened, why it was done, who did it. No other way to be happy, to be safe. They couldn't ever—without the truth. How could it have happened?

She lived over again the moments of her waking and the stumble on the dead woman's body in the dark. No fresh memory came: it was all cruelly vivid and familiar; no new thought, only the old, first, baffling questions: How did the woman come there in the old archway? Why was it there she was killed?

While May thus stated the problem Inspector Gunn was making his investigations at the Abbey.

The butler received him as if he were a common, insignificant incident. He established himself in the morning room and said that there were one or two people he wanted to have a word with. He would begin with Mrs. Garston's maid.

While he was waiting for her, Gladys came in. "Hallo! I didn't know you'd blown in again. Anything I can do for you?"

"Well, there might be. Later on, miss, if you don't mind. I'll let you know."

"Righto. I shall be about. Any news?"

"Not what you'd call news. I wouldn't say but there might be developments before long."

Gladys laughed. "That's the stuff to give the troops, what?" She winked and swung out.

She produced in the simple mind of Inspector Gunn the conviction that he did not like her; and also a suspicion that she was not as free from anxiety as she wished him to believe.

The maid stood before him tense, fighting excitement, and under his slow inspection broke out. What did he want her for? Was there something he wanted to ask her? Gunn told her to sit down. But that did not check her flow of words. "I'm sure anything I can tell you, you've only got to ask me, I can't hardly bear it, my poor dear lying murdered and nothing done about it, it's too cruel——"

"Now don't talk what you don't know," Gunn said. "There's a good deal been done, Mrs. Jones. And one of the things we've found out is that your mistress was drugged when she was killed. Do you know anything about that?"

The flood was checked. "Ah, poor dear!" Mrs. Jones rolled her eyes. "Who says she was drugged?"

"That's the doctor's statement."

"Then it's that nurse!" Mrs. Jones cried, and her yellow face was paler. "The wicked creature! Didn't I tell you she was always vicious with my poor lamb?"

"You say the nurse drugged her. You didn't think of that before."

"I don't ever say no more than I know." Mrs. Jones tossed her head. "I wouldn't do such a thing, I'm sure."

"The doctor says it was done with a medicine called Algicure. There was a bottle of that in Mrs. Garston's room. You've been buying Algicure in Limbay. The chemist will swear to you. Now be careful. Can you explain that?"

Mrs. Jones licked her lips. "What chemist?" she said.

"I've got the chemist all right. Warren & Son. You bought more than one bottle."

"Which I use it myself, Inspector, suffering with my poor nerves like I do. Sometimes I go about with my head aching fit to split, I don't rightly know what I'm doing, I couldn't never have kep' up and done my duty by my poor dear without my medicine. And it's a very good medicine, I'm sure, I've took it for years, which the chemist recommended me to it himself and now to turn round and say it's drugs, I don't know what he means by it." She wept.

"Your story is you bought the stuff for yourself. Why did Mrs. Garston take it?"

"I'm sure I don't know. I don't know as she did," Mrs. Jones sobbed.

"That won't do. You were her maid. There was a bottle half empty by her bed."

"I don't know anything about it. I never had anything to do with her medicines. She had ever so many. That was the nurse's business. That nurse, she wouldn't let me give her anything, poor dear. I wish she'd never had anything worse than mine, which it's a very good, nice medicine, and I never took any harm from it."

"Very well. I don't think much of your story. I'll have to warn you, you'll be asked about it at the inquest. That'll do now."

"It's cruel, that's what it is," Mrs. Jones sobbed.

"There was never anyone but me cared for her at all. And to blame it on me, oh, it's wicked." She wept herself out of the room.

Gunn thought her over with the help of a cigarette and decided that she was a nasty fool and rang the bell for Gladys.

She kept him waiting some time; she came in with a languid and careless manner and sat herself down. "Well, here we are," she yawned. "What's doing?"

"I thought you might be able to give me a bit of information, Miss Hurst." Gunn gazed at her solemnly. It seemed to him the lines on her well-painted face were rather deep. "Just carry your mind back to the morning after the murder."

"Righto. One steady rush. What about it?"

"I suppose there was a good deal of telephoning?"

"Quite a bit. Lord Croyland was putting people off all over England."

"You'd be at the telephone?"

"Off and on. Getting numbers for him."

"Did you get a number at Spraymouth?"

"Where's that? If he asked me, I daresay I did. Don't remember. Spraymouth. What is it?"

"Seaside place, fifteen mile away. Never heard of it?"

"Not that I know of." She put up her eyebrows. "What's the idea? I shouldn't have thought Croyland had anything doing there. But he was on the phone most of the day."

"Mr. Gordon Harwood was staying at Spraymouth."

"Was he?"—an amused sneer. "Pal of yours?"

"You've met him," Gunn frowned.

"Have I? My error. Didn't know I'd had the pleas-hah. Who is the blighter? Oh, I remember. Fellow that came to see Croyland. I had the honour of showing him in, so I did."

"First time you'd ever seen him?"

"First and only." The eyebrows went up again. "I say, what's all this about?"

"The morning after the murder, Mr. Gordon Harwood had a telephone message from this house. I want to know what it was."

Gladys shrugged. "Then you don't want me. I can't tell you."

"You didn't send it?"

"Not me. I don't know the beggar."

"Any idea who did?"

"Oh, snakes! Anybody might use the phone."

"That's all you're going to say?" Gunn frowned. "No explanation?"

"Not this child. Barking up the wrong tree, old man. What's the matter with your pal, Gordon Harwood?"

"You'd better think about that." Gunn glowered at her. "You can go now."

"Thank you so much," she laughed. She stood up with an elaborate arranging of herself. "Sorry, old thing. You look like making another bloomer." She undulated out.

She left in Gunn's mind the certainty that it was she who had warned Harwood to be off and that she was now alarmed for herself. But he worked his simple mind in vain to discover some way of dealing with her.

"My oath! Pack of beauties. Ought to hang the lot," he grumbled. "Oh well! Got to go through 'em all." He sent the butler to say that he wanted to see Lord Croyland.

Croyland came striding in and banged the door and stood over him. "What the devil do you want now?"

"You don't have to take me like that, my lord." Gunn got on his feet. "You ought to be helpful. And begging your pardon, it would be more decent if you was civil to men that's working to get justice for your dead mother."

Croyland made noises. "Want me to be civil? Don't play the fool then. You're not working, you're making an infernal mess for yourselves. Can't be plagued with nonsense day and night."

"I know my duty, my lord. And I'm going to do it. I've come to tell you we've got that man Harwood."

"What?" Croyland flushed dark. "Do you mean you're charging him with the murder?"

"We're not charging anybody—yet. We're bringing Harwood down to give an account of his actions. Any objection?"

Croyland cleared his throat. "Not my business to object. Do as you like. If you want to know, I think it's damned folly."

"Much obliged. Well, we'll find out what Harwood thinks. This is what I have to ask you, my lord. Who is it in your house that's in collusion with Harwood?"

Croyland stared at him and rumbled. "Humph. Don't believe a word of it."

"That's a pity. Early in the morning after the murder Harwood was rung up from here. As soon as he got that message he left Spraymouth. What was it? Who sent it? That's what I want to know."

Croyland made noises. "Somebody here telephoned Harwood after the murder?" he repeated. His heavy head sank deeper on his shoulders and he stooped the more.

"Yes, who would that be?"

"Damn it, man, I don't know," Croyland growled. "The whole thing is an infernal, mad mess. I can't help you. Lies all round." He drew back. He muttered incoherently. "Pack of fools. Damned fools. Don't know what you're doing." He swung round and blundered out.

"My oath!" Gunn communed with himself. "He's got the wind up proper. And what's that mean? They've all got the wind up." He drove his slow mind on to the increasing difficulties.

To this painful labour, the butler came. "Would you like tea now, sir?"

"I would," said Gunn earnestly. "Thank 'e."

"Thank you, sir." The butler withdrew.

His lofty calm much impressed Gunn. It was a kind of comfort to discover that the Abbey contained someone without fear of what had happened or what was going to happen. That was the line to work on. Get at somebody who didn't care a straw about Harwood or Croyland. The butler would be no good, though: wouldn't know enough. The nurse, of course. Worth hearing what she'd got to say about Miss Hurst. Ought to hear her ideas about the maid too.

The butler came back with tea.

"Giving you a lot of trouble," said Gunn affably.

"Not at all, sir."

"Sad times for you here."

"Very sad, sir."

"Everybody's upset, eh?"

"It has been depressing, sir."

"Noticed anybody in particular?"

"I really couldn't say, sir." The butler stepped back. "Will there be anything else?"

"Yes, I want to speak to Miss Dean, if she's about. You know who I mean, Mrs. Garston's nurse."

"Oh certainly, sir," the butler said quickly.

"Ah." Gunn nodded. "Had rather a bad time, hasn't she?"

"I'm afraid it has been unpleasant, sir." The butler was at last tempted to speech. "I hope she's not felt it too much. Always most careful and considerate."

"Well liked, is she?"

"Very nice lady, if I may say so," the butler pronounced.

"Oh, it's just as well to say these little things, you know. Some aren't."

"No, sir." The butler was not to be tempted further.

"Well, I'd like to see her."

"Thank you, sir."

The butler retired and after some long time returned to say that Miss Dean was out. She had gone out after lunch and not yet come back.

"I'll wait a bit," said Gunn. "Let me know when she comes in."

But May had come back—come back urgently labouring at her problem: why was the murder done in the archway? Her memory had the scene cruelly clear: the black darkness beyond the glimmering corridor, her stumble over the body, the touch of her hands upon it, the stab of knowledge it was Mrs. Garston and dead. Her own cries sounded again in her ears. She saw the flash of her torch pierce into the darkness to show the livid face and Croyland standing beside it. Again the lights came on in the corridors on either side and still in the archway it was dark.

Why was it dark there? She had never seen it like that before or since. There must be a lamp in the archway, or she would have noticed some time. And as Bell had asked before her, she asked herself why it would not come on that night.

The archway! What was there queer in the archway? Something that had to be hidden there that night of the murder?—something more than the body? Or was it darkened for the murder to be done? But what brought Mrs. Garston there? Why should she be taken there, to be killed or in death?

What was there in the archway? Scores of times she must have passed through and never seen anything strange about it—a gloomy, creepy place, but not worse than other old corners of the horrible house—just a tunnel of an archway with panelling up the walls. Never anything strange there. Yes! Mrs. Garston's maid. That very day she had been there, loitering, watching, spying. What could there be in the archway?

May ran upstairs. The archway waited for her, a patch of gloom at the end of the corridor. She switched the lights on and the lamp in it lit with the others. So that had been changed. Of course it had. She would have noticed else. She went into the archway and looked about her. The old oak floor, polished dark with ages of use, was solid as stone. She looked at the walls. There too the panelling shone black. She felt along it, tapped it here and there, and it answered with dull solidity. It was all alike, carved in linen fold with bands of deep bosses dividing the broad panels.

Her fingers ran over it, searching vaguely for something strange, anything—a mark of violence, a secret hiding place. There were marks enough, bruises of centuries, cracks, worm holes. She could find none new or sinister, no trace of anything hidden. She handled the bosses between the panels. At last one turned in her hand. She went on turning it slowly and felt something move with it in the wall. She pushed and pulled in vain. The panelling stood stolid. She tried one boss after another in that line till she found a second which would turn. Then as she pulled at both the whole panel came away, turning as a heavy door higher than her head, and hit the lamp and set it swinging wildly. In the tossing light she saw a black gulf beneath her.

Then she was thrust forward and the door pressed upon her and swept her away and she fell down and down into the dark, heard a faint clang above her, felt pain crush through her head and felt no more.

CHAPTER XXII

FURTHER INVESTIGATIONS

IN THIS, if in this alone, resembling Mr. Clunk, Inspector Gunn liked a large and leisurely tea.

He had it, he rounded it off in comfort with some cigarettes, and the Abbey clock struck six. He rose and stretched himself. Conscience said that he ought to be getting on; waking intelligence remarked that the nurse was taking her time. But when he rang for the butler, he was told that Miss Dean had not come in. "Late, isn't she?" The butler agreed that it was unusual. She was always in to tea. But she had certainly gone out: he had seen her himself: and certainly she had not come back: no one had seen her and she was not in the house.

The reluctant mind of Gunn was roused to suspicion. He had settled it that the nurse, if only the nurse, was all right, confirmed in this useful belief by her association with Tony, for whom he had acquired a liking. But if the girl had bolted just when things began to turn up it looked nasty. Gone out after lunch—that was just what she had done before when Bell followed her and she met Tony. Might have gone to meet him again—and having no policeman to bother 'em got on so nicely they forgot all about the time. Gunn's amiable heart wouldn't blame them. Pretty girl—manly young fellow—didn't ought to be too careful. But he couldn't let it go at that. Got to make sure she hadn't nipped off. Better run over and look up Wisberry.

He did so and found Tony on the beach at Bradstock

in talk with fishermen as they made ready for the night's work. Tony was not pleased at being asked if he knew anything about Miss Dean. Frank wrath gave way to franker amazement and anxiety when he heard the reason.

"But damn it, man, I left her less than a mile from the house, hours ago, four o'clock or so. She must have got back. Nothing could have happened to her."

"Are you sure she meant to go back?"

"Absolutely. Why, I watched her almost up to the place. Besides, what else could she do?"

"Ah. That's more than I know."

"You mean she's run away? That's rot. It's a hell of a house to be in, of course. But she wasn't funking it. Not a bit. She was dead set on seeing this through. You can take that from me. I know she was going back. She was going to meet me again to-morrow."

"Well, I'll have to find out what's happened to her," said Gunn. "Can't have her vanishing like this."

"What do you think's happened?"

"I've got to own it looks queer, Mr. Wisberry."

"Damned queer," Tony growled.

"I'll ask you to come along and show me where you saw her last."

"Righto. Let's go on."

They drove back along the coast road to the hillock where Tony had stopped his car. "We talked just here. I watched her from here as she went back till she was out of sight. It's getting dark now, but you can see how far that would be."

"Pretty well up to the grounds," Gunn nodded. "Anybody else about?"

"Not a soul."

"She ought to have been in the house a few minutes after you saw her. That'd be four o'clock or so?"

"Just about. Couldn't swear to five minutes."

"Near enough." Gunn let the car run on slowly while they scanned the road and the pasture on either side. They came to the house.

"Let me do the talking please, Mr. Wisberry," said Gunn. But when the door was opened the butler began.

"Miss Dean has not returned, sir."

"Just come upstairs." Gunn led the way to the morning room. "This is a strange business. I have imformation Miss Dean was seen just before four o'clock walking straight to the house. You say she never came in."

"I beg your pardon, sir, I said no one saw her. I've made every inquiry. It's quite possible she came in without being seen. But I'm sure she's not here now. I've been everywhere myself."

"Well, what do you suppose has become of her?"

"She may have gone out again," said the butler.

"Also without being seen!" Tony cried.

"Just so, sir," the butler agreed calmly. "There's no certainty she'd be seen coming in or going out."

"I'll make sure if she's in now anyway," Gunn frowned. "I'm going to search the house. You'll come with me, my lad." He turned to Tony. "Mr. Wisberry, you be walking round outside, and if anyone tries to make off, just hold 'em up and call for me." He marched the butler off. "I want to go everywhere and see everyone, understand? I don't like the looks of things. We'll begin with her room."

"Very good, sir. I have already been there," said the butler. "It will take a considerable time to go all over the house."

"It will. And we aren't going to miss anything," Gunn answered grimly.

But he did. As was natural, he missed the one thing which could have shown him where May had gone. He passed through the archway of the murder with no more than a careful glance at its emptiness. The long search found no trace of her anywhere. He made nothing by questioning of the servants but confirmation of the butler—no one had seen her.

All spoke of her simply enough and with decent surprise, except the maid. Her yellow face confessed pleasure. "I've seen nothing of her." She tossed her head. "I suppose she's made off. Don't wonder she wants to get away if she can."

"Why?" said Gunn sharply.

"Suit her much better, I should say," she laughed.

"Ah. That's your idea. All right." Under Gunn's hard stare she lost her assurance.

He kept till the last the two of whom he hoped most. Gladys was in her secretary's room, not at work but smoking in an easy chair with her feet on another. "What's the great idea?" She put back her head and smiled and crossed her displayed legs.

"I'm searching the house for Miss Dean."

"Jumpin' Jews! What's the girl been and done?"

"It's not what she's done, it's what's been done with her." Gunn walked round the room.

"I haven't got her." The bold eyes followed him with amusement. "Like to search me?"

Gunn stopped. "Thanks. I'd like to have your idea about it. She's vanished."

"Done a bunk? I suppose she's gone off with her best boy then."

"Meaning Mr. Wisberry? Well, she hasn't."

"Oh, you've got him. She's off on her own. Wow, wow. Looks queer, doesn't it?" Gladys whistled. "Baby face not such a baby as she looked. Thought she'd better go while the going was good. You must have been getting a bit too near to be comfortable."

"Any reason to say so?" Gunn snapped.

Gladys laughed. "No use being cross with me, old bean, I'm not in on this show."

Gunn marched off to Croyland and was received with snarling fury. "Sorry to disturb you, my lord. I'm looking for Miss Dean."

"Then why in hell do you come here?"

"Because she's vanished. And she must be somewhere, dead or alive."

Croyland's mouth moved and he swallowed. "Dead? How the devil should she be dead?"

"I don't know she is. I don't know where she is. Either she's gone off or she's been made away with."

"Can't be dead," Croyland growled and rumbled. "Must have run away."

"Why should she run away?"

"Damn it all, I don't know. Gone mad, I should think. Everybody's mad. Oh, hell, get out. Girl's not in here, is she? Go to the devil."

"No, she isn't here. She's got to be found. I'm going to search your grounds, my lord."

"Search hell, I don't care. Don't bother me. I've had enough. My God, I've had enough."

Gunn went out and turned to the butler. "Has he been like that often?"

"His lordship has been much distressed," said the butler.

"Distressed! My oath! Well, we've got to have a search party, my lad. Find a man or two with some lanterns." He hurried away to Tony. "She's not inside anywhere. She seems to have left all her things in her room. Of course she couldn't take much if she was rushing off without a car handy."

"She can't have gone," Tony muttered. "Where should she go?"

"She might have wanted to see somebody besides you, Mr. Wisberry."

"That's a lie," Tony cried.

"Go easy. I don't mean anything improper. Somebody about this business. I was thinking of Clunk."

"She wouldn't. She hardly knows him."

"Ah." Gunn was not so sure. "Well, I'm going to search the grounds—just in case, see?"

It was almost dark. Slowly by lantern light they worked over the garden, the ruins, the stretch of the park between the house and the road—a search difficult and inadequate but sufficient to convince Gunn that if May's body lay there it lay well hidden.

"We can't do any more here to-night, Mr. Wisberry," he decided. "Looks more and more likely she's gone off somewhere. I shall go back to Limbay."

"You're thinking of Clunk?" said Tony wearily. "I can't see why she should go to Clunk. I hope to God she has. I'll come in to Limbay with you, if you don't mind."

"Ah. Want to see him yourself. All right. Half a minute. I just want to ring up my people."

He told his Limbay sergeant that he wanted one of the men who had seen Miss Dean, the nurse at the Abbey, to find out if she had been noticed going to Mr. Clunk.

"Right, sir. Mr. Clunk's just been here, talking to Superintendent Bell."

"Has he! Well, make that inquiry. The London man that's watching Clunk will know. And if she hasn't been to Clunk, try the railway station. I'll be with you in ten minutes."

He drove off with Tony. "Queer business, Mr. Wisberry."

"Queer!" Tony gave a miserable laugh. "I feel as if I couldn't think. This beastly gang at the Abbey—they'd made it pretty much like hell for her. Do you suppose they've murdered her?"

"I wouldn't say that. There's some queer fish at the Abbey, to be sure. But they're not all crooked. Don't you see, she came back in broad daylight, if she did come, while I was in the house myself. Well, to murder her and get the body right away and hidden—all in daylight, everyone about—it couldn't be done."

"I hope to God you're right," Tony groaned.

"I'm right about that," said Gunn. "Mr. Wisberry, I've been straight with you, haven't I? I believe you're straight. Now, as man to man, what do you think of Clunk?"

"I don't know," Tony said miserably. "If you'd asked me some time ago, I'd have said he was too tricky to live. Lately I've been thinking he's really all right. When this business all blew up, he told me to tell the police every blessed thing about myself. That don't look like tricks. But what he's really got in his head, I never can feel sure. I'll swear to one thing—Miss Dean didn't know him from Adam till she met him with me."

"Ah! He did take care to meet her though," said Gunn.

"What on earth can you make of that?" Tony cried.

"I haven't made anything," said Gunn. "Well, here we are."

The car drew up at the police station.

CHAPTER XXIII

DISAPPOINTMENT OF MR. CLUNK

Superintendent Bell prepared himself for Mr. Gordon Harwood with a determination to chasten his natural method of driving a suspect hard. The warning from above, that hurry into another failure was not desired, found a tender conscience. He knew enough of Mr. Harwood's career to provide the further warning that fear would not be easily inspired. Mr. Harwood had always shown a very sure sense of the limits of the power of the law.

This determination to restraint was much tried. Mr. Harwood developed bold powers of exasperation. To Bell's mild opening that he had been asked to come to Limbay to give the police some assistance, he replied that he had not been asked but brought by force, and he took it as illegal and an outrage. If he had been arrested, they ought to have told him what the charge was. If he had not, they had no right to meddle with him. Thus Bell was involved in a wrangle about the powers of the police to detain and demand explanations which, futile in itself, made clear the confident ability of Mr. Harwood to defy inquiry.

"You've been brought here in your own interest," said Bell patiently. "We've found suspicious circumstances in connection with your actions and the death of Mrs. Garston of Bradstock Abbey. I'm giving you the opportunity to explain them."

"Suffering snakes!" Harwood laughed contempt.

"What are you giving me? My good fool, somebody's sold you a pup. Who is Mrs. Garston? Don't know the dear lady."

"You know her son," said Bell. "My information is, you went to Bradstock Abbey and made a claim on Lord Croyland to part of his property." Harwood did not answer. "Well, what about it?"

"Go on talking, old bean," Harwood grinned. "I like to hear you."

"You deny that?"

"Deny it? Great Jimmy, what do you take me for? I'm not balmy. I couldn't claim his property."

"There's ways of doing these little things. You know all about that. Your way was to tell Croyland you'd found the son and heir of his dead brother."

"The Lord Croyland's handed that out, has he?" Harwood said slowly. "I wonder why."

"You did tell him so?"

"Where are we going, Gus?" Harwood grinned. "You started off on Mamma's death. What's that got to do with the Lord Croyland's chat about his brother leaving a son?"

"If you were trying to blackmail Croyland——"

"Stop the bus. Am I charged with blackmail?"

"There's no charge yet. I told you so."

"You're playing dirty, aren't you?" Harwood glowered. "You get me here pretending to inquire into some death, and what you're really after is to fake up evidence against a private claim on Croyland. Go to hell and toast yourself."

"There is a claim, is there?" Bell sneered. "Where is this son, Harwood? When do you produce him?"

"Nothing doing, Gus," Harwood laughed. "You've shown your hand, thanks. Get it into your thick head I'm not such a fool as you. Here you are pretending to be a policeman and acting for Croyland. Well, if there was a claim against him should I be such an ass as to tell you how it would be worked?"

"Dangerous game, blackmail, Harwood."

"Don't try it then. Silly game, accusing a man of blackmail when you haven't any evidence. Look here, my bonny boy, you're the blackmailer in this piece."

"What do you mean?"

"You're trying to bluff me into giving things away by threatening me with a charge. Well, I call you. Make your charge."

Bell covered the repulse by his most important manner. "No explanation of the claim," he said solemnly. "Very well. You don't understand your own interest."

"Oh, come off it," Harwood jeered.

"I haven't done with you. Croyland turned you down. But you stayed on at Spraymouth. Why didn't you go away?"

"Why the devil should I? Spraymouth's a bright little place. I liked my pub there."

"You didn't go over to the Abbey again?"

"Hallo, hallo! What else has the Lord Croyland been handing you?"

"I'm not relying on any statement of Croyland's. What about your accomplice in the Abbey?"

"My who?" Harwood was amused. "I say, you have got a nasty mind, Gus. Accomplice! I've no use for 'em, thank you."

"Somebody put into a man's house to spy for you is what I call an accomplice," said Bell. "What do you call it?"

"I call it telling the tale," Harwood grinned. "Who are you making my accomplice?"

"Did you happen to know that Mrs. Garston was murdered?" said Bell sharply.

"Was she? That is nasty." But Harwood was not frightened. "Now why didn't you tell me that when you began? You're playing a lot of tricks."

"You didn't need me to tell you," Bell frowned.

"Put that straight." Harwood leaned forward and his coarse face hardened in resolute defiance. "Are you charging me with murder?"

"I'm asking you why you stayed at Spraymouth till she was murdered and left the morning after."

"I stayed because I liked the place and went away because I had to get back to business."

"When did you know she was murdered?"

"I don't know it now," Harwood snarled.

"Early in the morning after the murder your accomplice in the Abbey telephoned to you at Spraymouth. Then you made off quick."

Harwood's fat lips parted, his breathing made a noise. "Accomplice? Rot," he said. "Who phoned me?"

"You know. You know what the message was. I'm waiting for your explanation, Harwood."

"You can wait," said Harwood sullenly. "I don't explain my business to a man that's acting for Croyland."

With a struggle Bell kept himself to a dry, official manner. "Can't explain it? Very well. That leaves you in a very serious position. You'd better think it over. You'll have time."

Harwood swore at him: "You fool, do you think you're going to keep me here? You can't do it. You can't hold me unless you make a charge. And you daren't."

"I know what I can do, thank you." Bell took the chance to be unpleasant gratefully. "You'll be detained while we investigate your suspicious conduct. You've only yourself to thank."

Harwood raged and wrangled. Bell had at last the

satisfaction of using the strong hand on him. He was beaten into sullen silence and taken away.

Then came the station sergeant and said, "It's that Mr. Clunk, sir. Been here some time. But I didn't like to disturb you."

"Quite right," Bell chuckled. "Do him good. I'll have him now though." The last moments had restored confidence. If the insolent Harwood could be frightened something might be done with the evasive Mr. Clunk.

Mr. Clunk tripped in humming:

> *"There's work in my vineyard*
> *There's plenty to do,*
> *For the harvest is great*
> *And the labourers few.*

"Ah, my dear friend." He held out his plump hand. "How do you do? We ought to be impatient, you know, really we ought."

"Oh, I am," Bell grinned. "Come to give me another tip, Mr. Clunk? Let's have it."

Mr. Clunk put his head on one side. "That's not very amusing," he complained. "And really this isn't the time to be facetious. Don't you perceive, my friend? Time is practically everything. What have you done?"

"Doing as well as can be expected, thanks."

"Dear, dear," said Mr. Clunk. "Is that all?"

"And what did you expect, Mr. Clunk?"

"I hoped for a great deal," Mr. Clunk sighed. "A great deal more than I expected. But I did really expect you would have examined Gordon Harwood by this time."

"That's what you wanted to know. Well, I don't mind. You can take it I've got Harwood all right."

"I'm so glad. What for?"

Bell stared. "How do you mean, what for? He's detained for inquiries."

"Tut, tut, tut, of course he is. Really, you know, this is childish. Haven't you made your inquiries?"

"You're very anxious, Mr. Clunk."

"Indeed I am. Exceedingly anxious. We ought to be. My dear friend, can't you perceive the situation is very, very grave?"

"Who for?"

"Do apply your mind," Mr. Clunk cried. "You have two most shocking murders committed. The ruthless and very able person who did that is still at liberty——"

"Oh, is he?" Bell interrupted. "It wasn't Harwood then. Thanks."

"My good sir, did I ever say it was Harwood?" Mr. Clunk was impatient.

"No, you didn't." Bell watched him keenly. "Who do you say it was? I suppose you know."

"If I did know, I should tell you," said Mr. Clunk slowly. "Be sure of that, my friend. Be very sure. I am helping you by every means in my power."

"Are you? What are you here for now then?"

"Dear me, we are so slow, aren't we?" said Mr. Clunk. "Of course I came to learn what you had made of Harwood. I suppose the answer is nothing—simply nothing."

"Oh no, it isn't. Quite a lot. I've pretty well verified your information, Mr. Clunk. He was at Spraymouth and he was working with someone inside the house. I'm much obliged to you."

"Dear, dear, of course he was." Mr. Clunk was impatient. "Is that all?"

"Don't be in a hurry. It looks to me Harwood knows more about the Garston murder than he ought to."

"Quite possibly." Mr. Clunk was not interested.

"But you say he didn't do it."

"I never thought that at all likely," said Mr. Clunk.
"Then why did you put me on to Harwood?" Bell
cried triumphantly. Mr. Clunk blinked at him. "That's
stumped you, hasn't it?"

"Dear me, it's so foolish." Mr. Clunk was plaintive.
"Can't you grasp the case at all? The central point is,
what did Harwood find out that set him upon Lord
Croyland? That is what we want. Of course he went to
the Abbey to blackmail. In all probability the threat he
used was not the real danger. It very seldom is in a
blackmail case. The operator threatens some action
which he believes his victim dare not face because of
other facts which must be kept secret. Surely you know
that."

"You don't need to tell me how blackmail's worked,"
Bell growled. "I daresay you know all about it. So do
I." With indignation he felt the similarity of Mr.
Clunk's exposition to his own lecture to Gunn, heard
himself saying, "There's always a something."

"My good friend, why not use your knowledge?" Mr.
Clunk mourned. "The main problem is plain before you
—what is it Harwood knows? Did you find that out?"

"He says he didn't come to blackmail," Bell grunted.

"Really, this is provoking," Mr. Clunk cried. "My
good friend, you submitted to be told that! You let such
a fellow baffle you with such a story! Dear, dear, dear, I
didn't expect very much, but I am sadly disappointed.
Grievously disappointed." He shook his head in spasms
of irritation. "Impotence, absolute impotence, in the
one clear opportunity! Well, well, well! It's all in God's
hands. But the methods! Dear me, I suppose they're
arranged to try our faith." He sighed bewilderment at
the divine tactics and, too melancholy to bid good-bye,
faded out of the room.

Then Bell recovered sufficiently to swear at him: an

explosion the more vigorous from a smarting suspicion that the little brute was right—the failure to get at Harwood's secret was missing the best clue.

Uneasy brooding over that was disturbed by the irruption of Gunn and Tony. "Well, old man—here's another nasty job—that nurse Miss Dean has vanished. Absolutely." Between them they told the breathless story. . . .

"Let me get this," Bell frowned. "You hadn't seen her, George. Just when you were going to see her and ask her a few questions, she was reported missing. And wherever she is, she isn't at the Abbey." He turned a glassy stare on Tony. "And what do you make of that, Mr. Wisberry?"

"I can't really believe it," said Tony. "But there it is. We can't find her."

"Not even her body," said Bell. "That is odd, isn't it?"

"Don't be a brute," Tony growled.

"Go easy, old man," Gunn protested. "No call to talk like that."

"Sorry to hurt your feelings." Bell was not sympathetic. "Seems pretty clear to me. You needn't look for her body at the Abbey. Either she ran away or she's been got away. I wish you'd let me know a bit earlier, Mr. Wisberry. I'd have asked your friend, Clunk. I thought he was a bit above himself."

"Clunk's been here?" Gunn cried.

"He has, George. Going very strong. Mr. Clunk don't like the way we're handling the case. Isn't that a pity? However—let's see if we can handle Mr. Clunk. Pardon me, George." He rang the bell and gave orders that a man should go after Mr. Clunk and bring him back.

"Why should she go to Clunk?" Tony protested. "She hardly knows him."

"Doesn't she? That is a pity. I should say he knows her."

Tony glowered at him. "Half a minute, old man," Gunn protested. He winked. "We'll hear all right if she has been to Clunk."

Bell frowned the hint away. "I don't expect Clunk's got her at his hotel, George. He isn't working this alone."

Their conversation was interrupted by Sergeant Underwood, breathless and red. "He's off, sir! Gone off in his car. Him and his man."

"My oath!" Gunn gasped.

"Just step outside, Mr. Wisberry," said Bell sharply. "Oh, if you please!" He thrust Tony through the door. "Now then, Underwood, quick."

"Clunk had a telephone call, sir. Spent a long time in the box. I should say he rang up somebody else. Came out, talked to this man he has with him. I couldn't get that. The man hustled off. Clunk ran upstairs and came down with their coats. Told the hotel people he had to run up to London but he'd keep his rooms and be back in a day or two. The man brought their car round and Clunk said to him to do his best, he wanted to be in London as soon after the train as possible, he hoped the office would have something for them. And off they went."

Bell took up the telephone and put a call through to Scotland Yard and asked for a man to be set to watch Mr. Clunk's office and follow him if he appeared. The telephone was put down with a bang. Bell frowned at Gunn. "If he said he was going there, I suppose he's off somewhere else. But we've got to try everything. What's his car, Underwood?"

"Blaker six, sir. Saloon. Dark blue. I got the number."

"Right. I'm taking your car, George. Good-bye. Keep

your eye on the Abbey. God knows what'll be the next break. Come on, Underwood."

Tony ran out after them. "You're following Clunk? Then I'm coming too."

"Are you?" Bell stopped and looked him over. "All right. You can. I daresay I'll want you in the end." He took the driver's seat and Underwood came beside him.

Thus the chase of Mr. Clunk began.

CHAPTER XXIV

MR. CLUNK'S FLIGHT

MR. CLUNK sat down in the lounge of the Victoria and moved his chair to and fro and fidgeted in it, an angry and nervous little man. A glimpse of the faithful Underwood taking up once more a post of observation brought from him a peevish sound, a fleeting smile. He had just begun to soothe his anxieties with a glass of warm milk when they told him he was wanted on the telephone.

Mr. Clunk tripped to the booth. "Scott speaking, sir," the telephone said. "From the railway station. Lord Croyland's just come here. Sent his car back. Taken ticket for London. Last train just going."

Mr. Clunk's large eyes swelled as he listened. He began to answer while Scott was still speaking. "Go with him, Scott. Wherever he goes. I'll warn our people to meet the train in London, Morris or another. Look out for him. If Croyland goes somewhere else, telephone the office. I'm going up. Do your best, my boy." He rang off and asked for a trunk call to London and waited, tapping his teeth. "Is that Jenks? Good. I want you to go to the office at once, my boy, and wait till I come. Scott may ring up during the night. Before you go warn Morris to meet the night train from Limbay and look out for Scott. If you can't get Morris send someone else. The instructions are to work with Scott so that I am informed what the man does. Scott is following. Repeat that, please. Quite right. Good-bye, my boy."

He tripped away to the smoking room and from its dismal depths his eyes summoned Lewis. He took that young man's reluctant arm. "I hope you haven't been drinking, Lewis," he said anxiously.

"Haven't had time," Lewis grumbled. "Just one little one."

"That's well. You will have to drive to London to-night. Bring the car round at once."

"London!" Lewis groaned. "I'll have to fill up first."

"Not yourself, my boy," Mr. Clunk tittered. "Run along, then. Be as quick as you can. I'll get your coat."

Mr. Clunk made haste to his room. When he came down again with their coats and a case of his own he saw the faithful Underwood reading a timetable in the hall. All a smile, he turned to the office. He had been called to London suddenly, he might be away a day or two but he wanted to keep his rooms. That would be all right? They had his London address if anyone should inquire for him. He lingered, making amiable conversation, till the glum face of Lewis came to his elbow. "All ready, my boy? Good." He saluted the girl in the office and helped Lewis into his coat "Now let's be off. I want to be in London as soon as that last train. A pity we missed it. Do your best, my boy. The office may have something for us." He gave a last look round the hall where the earnest Underwood was studying the barometer and hurried out.

They settled into the car. "I suppose you know that young tec heard every blessed word," said Lewis morosely.

"Dear me, yes. I should think so. I hope so." Mr. Clunk was plaintive. "A stupid business. A poor foolish fellow. But we must try to use him."

They slid away from the hotel. "We aren't going to London then?" Lewis inquired.

"But of course, my dear boy." Mr. Clunk was pained. "As quick as ever you can." The irritation of Lewis relieved itself on the car. They sped through Limbay like a projectile.

Thus began the flight of Mr. Clunk.

The night train from Sandshire, being run to carry the mails, makes no attempt at speed while it moves, stops often and long. If there are no delays in this stately progress its happy passengers arrive in London at four in the morning.

It was only three when Lewis stopped the car at that old house which is the office of Clunk & Clunk. One window in it showed a light. "That's excellent." Mr. Clunk struggled to his feet. "Thank you, my boy. Very well done."

"Wanting the car again, sir?"

"We might, you know," said Mr. Clunk happily. "We might very soon." Lewis groaned. "But come in, come in. We'll make Jenks give us a cup of tea." He looked along the silent street and opened the door.

Jenks met them in the hall. "I've got Morris waiting at the station, sir. I was here before eleven. Nothing's come through."

"Ah, that's excellent." Mr. Clunk rubbed his hands.

Jenks coughed. "I ought to tell you, sir. I'm pretty sure there's a man watching the office. Been about quite a while."

"Yes. I thought there was," Mr. Clunk beamed. "That's very satisfactory. Now make us some tea as quick as ever you can, there's a good boy. I'll just put on a clean collar." He ran upstairs.

Jenks and Lewis stared at each other. "What's the game?" said Jenks.

"Damned if I know," Lewis groaned. "Something unusual dirty. The little blighter won't say a word.

And I've had to drive him a hundred and fifty mile through the night. More to come, he says. Anybody can have my job for twopence. He's got no bowels. Just a nasty bit o' wire."

"Live wire," said Jenks, and fled to make the tea.

Mr. Clunk, in a clean collar and washed and shaved, was drinking it when the telephone rang. "Scott speaking, sir. From Waterloo Station. He's come right through. In the refreshment room now. Morris is in there with him."

"Well done, my boy. Very well done. Ring up again as soon as you know his next move." Mr. Clunk took a lump of sugar, dipped it in the tea and crunched. "Refreshing himself at Waterloo Station, Lewis," he smiled.

"Who is?" Lewis snapped.

"Really, my dear boy!" Mr. Clunk took another piece of sugar. "Lord Croyland, of course."

"Him." Lewis was puzzled. "Come by train, did he?"

"Yes, though it's such a bad train. That's significant, isn't it? And now he seems to be waiting for another train. That's very significant, isn't it?"

The telephone rang again. "Scott speaking. He's just taken a cab. Told the man London Bridge Station. Morris is following."

"You had better go too. I'll be there as soon as I can. Come along, Lewis. Quickly." Mr. Clunk ran downstairs. By the car he stopped and stood buttoning his coat. A man crossed the street close by. "Now, my boy, it's London Bridge Station," said Mr. Clunk. "London Bridge. As quick as you can safely." And he began to hum something about "Scatter seeds of kindness— scatter seeds of kindness—for your reaping by and by."

The car shot away. "Going there?" Lewis grunted.

"But of course I am," Mr. Clunk reproved him. "I hope when I get there I shall have done with you. You'd

better have some sleep and take the car back to Limbay.
I expect I shall be there again very soon."

When they stopped at the station, a man came out of
the booking office. "He's here, sir. Took his ticket to
Folkestone. Morris is in the next compartment. Plenty
o' time. Train don't go till five-thirty."

"That's very nice," said Mr. Clunk. "Good-bye,
Lewis. Sleep well, my boy. I shall want you, Scott." He
tripped into the booking office and with a good deal of
conversation took two first-class tickets to Folkestone.
"Now, my boy, you'd better get in with Morris, unless
you think Lord Croyland has noticed you."

"Not him, sir. He's never had a look at me. Besides,
he's like a man half drunk. Don't seem to rightly know
what he's doing. Kind of dazed."

"Is he indeed?" said Mr. Clunk, and the look on his
yellow face was not amiable. "Well, watch him carefully. I think he'll go through to Folkestone. But if he
doesn't, let me know at once. I shall be right at the back
of the train. Run along now."

In the last coach of the train he chose his place,
bought several packets of butterscotch from an auto-
matic machine, and stood at the door of his compartment sucking with gusto while daylight dimmed the
station lamps.

Doors slammed along the train, porters shouted. Mr.
Clunk looked at his watch and frowned and gazed plaintively up the platform and sighed and climbed into his
carriage and shut the door and leaned out of the window.
Bell and Tony came running hard, saw his shining face,
and made a dash for it as the train began to move. Mr.
Clunk opened the door and was fussy helping them in.
"That's it, that's it! Do be careful, Tony. It's so dangerous—ah! that's well." He sank back in his seat flutter-
ing. "I'm so glad!" He beamed clean-shaven and glossy

at their dirty, unshorn faces. He patted Bell's arm. "My dear friend, this is very intelligent of you. You did gather my little hints then? How clever! I was really beginning to be nervous."

"Were you!" Bell eyed him grimly. "Fancy that! And where might you be going in such a hurry?"

"Well, I think I'm going to Folkestone. It's not quite certain. I feel sure myself."

"Folkestone, eh?" Bell was amused. "Nice place, Mr. Clunk. But a bit too near the Continent."

"That did cross my mind," said Mr. Clunk pensively. "But I don't think so. No, really, I'm almost certain it won't be that."

"So do I," Bell chuckled. "You'll stay in England all right, Mr. Clunk."

"Me?" Mr. Clunk sat up. "My good friend, were you talking about my intentions? Dear, dear, this is too foolish. Surely you don't suppose I have been trying to run away from you?"

"Well, it does look just a trifle like it," Bell grinned.

"Tut, tut, tut. It looks nothing of the sort." Mr. Clunk was annoyed. "You silly fellow, how can you say so? You only contrived to get here because I was particularly careful to let your men know where I was going. Surely you have noticed that?"

"If you mean I had you watched, I did, and it was just as well." Bell frowned. "If you aren't trying to run away, what are you trying to do?"

"What I am doing, my friend, is what you ought to have done," said Mr. Clunk tartly. "I am following Lord Croyland."

"Croyland!" Tony roared. "You're after him?"

"My dear boy, I am practically with him. He's in the train in front of us. Now pray don't be excited. He is being very carefully observed."

"You mean to say Croyland left Bradstock last night?" Bell said slowly.

"Dear me, this is too childish!" Mr. Clunk complained. "You didn't know it! Of course not. How can you expect to know anything if you won't take the simplest, obvious measures? I had to arrange for keeping Lord Croyland under observation myself. My good friend, I don't mind doing your work for you, but when you can't even understand the easy opportunities I provide for you, you're very tiresome, you really are."

"I don't want any lectures from you, Mr. Clunk," Bell growled. "If you knew Croyland was bolting, why didn't you tell us?"

Mr. Clunk stared mild dislike. "I do think you are the most ungrateful man I ever worked with," he said slowly. "I have brought you here on Croyland's track, which you could never have found for yourself till too late. And you have the impudence to complain!"

"How do you mean, too late?" Bell cried. "What's he trying to do, fly the country?"

"Oh dear me, I told you that was most unlikely." Mr. Clunk could hardly bear it. "My good friend, do try to apply your mind to the case. I pointed out to you long ago the central point is, what had Harwood discovered which is dangerous to Croyland? You failed, you failed most deplorably, to extract that from Harwood. I hope we are going to find it at Folkestone. If you leave the matter to me, I am confident that we shall find it."

"And what do you want to do?" Bell growled.

"I want to find out where Lord Croyland is going and to whom he is going. And he must not be frightened first, or he'll not go."

"You want to follow him yourself. All right. I don't

mind that. I follow you, Mr. Clunk. And when he's marked down I come in."

Mr. Clunk looked at him and from him to Tony, with some complacency. "By all means. Both of you. I shall be very glad. I think it will be desirable to have some force. That is one reason why I was anxious to bring you with me."

"You believe Croyland's going to see some chap who's got a pull on him. Is that the idea?"

"Do employ your mind," said Mr. Clunk plaintively. "Lord Croyland chose to make for Folkestone by a slow night train to London and then this very slow train on. It would have been easier and pleasanter to go straight there by car. Therefore we must assume that he could not afford to let his chauffeur know where he was going. I infer that he is going to see someone whose connection with him it is important to keep secret. So I intend to find it out."

Bell nodded. "All right. That sounds straight." He meditated. "You know I've only your word for it he's on this train."

"My dear friend," said Mr. Clunk acidly, "you might have noticed by now that my word is the only thing you have found reliable in this case."

"Oh God, stop wrangling!" Tony broke out. "Clunk, do you know what happened at the Abbey yesterday?"

Mr. Clunk turned to him a startled face. "My dear boy, you alarm me. What could happen?"

"Miss Dean's vanished," Tony groaned. "Vanished absolutely. In the afternoon. I left her going to the house. No one's seen her since."

"Yes, what do you know about that, Mr. Clunk?" Bell chimed in eagerly.

He was ignored. "My dear boy," Mr. Clunk put his hand on Tony's, "I'm so sorry. My dear boy! These fellows," a nod indicated Bell, "they've done nothing? They've made nothing of it?"

Tony shook his head. "That other chap, Gunn, says he was in the house himself when she ought to have got there. He came to me asking about her. He's had the house searched, grounds searched, everything. She's just gone."

Mr. Clunk swung in his seat and stared at Bell with bulging eyes. "Is that all?" he asked. "Is anyone else gone?"

"They were all there last night," said Bell sullenly.

Mr. Clunk made a little ugly giggle of contempt. "You believed Croyland was there, my friend."

"Do you think it was him?" Tony cried. "Do you think he killed her? There's the harbour——"

"The harbour!" Mr. Clunk echoed him in a voice of fear. "No, I won't believe that. I won't! Hope in God yet, my boy."

"What's the hope?" Tony groaned.

"If we can make Croyland speak—if we can get at his motives——" Mr. Clunk said slowly, and paused, tapping his teeth. "Yes, that is the best chance, Tony. Be patient yet."

"Patient!" Tony groaned.

The jog trot of the wheels made the only sound in the carriage, beating out a deadly slow rhythm.

Mr. Clunk felt his pockets, found a packet of butter-scotch, broke it, began to suck, and offered a piece to Tony. It was rejected violently. Bell also declined it. Mr. Clunk gave forth a little deprecating noise and sucked on.

CHAPTER XXV

DECISIVE ACTION BY TONY

EVEN that train comes at last to Folkestone. Mr. Clunk started up. "Now please be patient. Don't show yourselves." He put his own small person across the window and watched till he saw the big form of Croyland come hurrying down the platform, two men carefully aloof behind him. "Ah, that's well." Mr. Clunk opened the door. "Now, my friends. Not too quick. Follow me at a distance." As they got out Croyland vanished.

Scott was waiting outside the station. "He's taken a cab, sir. Told the man to drive out to Hythe and he'd tell him where to stop. Morris is following in another cab. I've got one for you."

"Excellent, my boy." Mr. Clunk beckoned to Bell and Tony. "Come along, come along." He bustled them into the cab.

Scott turned to the driver. "Saw the gentleman with me took a cab just now? Know it again, won't you? Get on after it quick as you can: going out Hythe way." He packed himself in with the others.

"My young friend Mr. Scott, gentlemen," Mr. Clunk beamed. "We owe him a great deal. He's had a very trying night."

Scott grinned through his bristling beard. "I should say you've had some too, Mr. Bell." He twisted in his seat and his tired eyes puckered to watch the cab ahead. They swung round into the straight of the Sandgate road. "Come on, step on the gas, son," he exhorted the driver. "Ah. There we are. That's Morris's outfit all right." It led them down the hill, through Sandgate, and on by the sea.

Mr. Clunk looked out over the glitter of foam and green water and sniffed the breeze from it. "Delicious," he murmured. "I'm so glad of the sea, aren't you?" But no one attended to him. "What a refreshing day!"

The sea vanished behind a belt of vacant ground; on the other side were the fences and hedges of houses. Scott moved. "Hallo. Slowing." He talked to the driver. "Don't pass him. Go easy. Stop." He turned to Mr. Clunk. "Morris getting out, sir."

"Run along after him," said Mr. Clunk. He gave the driver a pound note and told him to wait. "Now, my friends, the quicker the better."

Bell and Tony strode on, Mr. Clunk trotting beside them, and Croyland's cab passed them going back. Scott had turned up a road which curved and climbed. In a little way they came on him and Morris lighting cigarettes. "There we are, sir," Scott said. "In that house over there. Gone right in as if he owned it."

It was a low gray house, a petty imitation of an Elizabethan manor. Through a double hedge of euonymus they passed among flowering shrubs to a garden of crazy paving with plants set in it, suggesting, as a small reproduction may, the wild garden of Bradstock Abbey. But none of them noticed that suggestion. They made haste to the house. Mr. Clunk rang the bell and was answered by a startled maid. "Take us to Lord Croyland at once, please," he panted.

"There's no lord here," she said. "I don't know what you mean."

"Oh yes, you do," Bell pushed forward. "The gentleman that's just come in. Where is he?"

"I suppose he'll be with Master," she faltered. "Will you wait, please?"

"No, I won't. I'm a police officer. Superintendent Bell. Show me the room. Go on."

She went upstairs slowly. She knocked at a door and was told to go to the devil. Bell flung it open and saw a bedroom. Croyland was there, and with him a man in a dressing gown half turned from a table by the fire which held a breakfast tray.

"Dear me," Mr. Clunk giggled, "Mr. Alfred Garston, I presume."

"What?" Bell roared. He strode across the room. "My God!" He looked from one man to the other. The likeness was plain enough. The man in the dressing gown matched Croyland in the broad bulk of his shoulders and his heavy head. Its big features were of the same mould. They had not Croyland's sullen gloom, but something of his look of power, looser, more vicious, set in a sneer. Bell studied him. "So you weren't dead," he said. "That's good."

"Out of a lunatic asylum, aren't you?" the man laughed. "What do you suppose you want in my house? My name's Gray, Herbert Gray."

"Dear me, no," said Mr. Clunk. "This is quite futile. Mr. Alfred Garston, let me introduce Mr. Wisberry. You'll remember Mr. Wisberry." He stood aside and indicated Tony.

Alfred Garston got on his feet with a jerk. He stared at Tony and his big face reddened and he made mouths and swallowed.

"I was sure you'd remember," Mr. Clunk purred. "So kind of Lord Croyland to give us the opportunity."

Alfred looked at his brother. "A put-up job, is it?" he said. "You've made the mistake of your lives." He sat down again and his hand went into a drawer of the table. "You dirty dog, Henry," he cried. The hand came out with a pistol. Mr. Clunk gave forth a squeal of terror and flung his little weight at the rising arm, but the shot was fired into Croyland's body and he staggered and went down and lay groaning.

Mr. Clunk hung squeaking to the pistol arm and a second shot went wide as Bell took the man by throat and wrist. But again he fired. Tony caught at a chair and heaved it up and brought it crashing down on his head. He was limp in the grasping hands, he fell away from them with a thud and a clatter into his fire.

"Here, get him out of that," Bell panted, and Tony and he dragged the heavy body from the scattered flame. "Killer, isn't he? Lord, his head's a muck of blood. That's where he hit the grate. But this——" He whistled. "You got him proper. Looks to me you may have done him in."

"Really now?" said Mr. Clunk eagerly. "My dear boy! Ah, we ought not to ask for such things. But you know we really must think that was the will of the good providence."

Bell gazed at him with a sort of awe. "I've seen some hard-boiled in my time," he muttered. "But you—— Here, what about Croyland? I must have a look at him. Clunk, find the telephone and ring up the police. Tell 'em Superintendent Bell wants 'em here quick with a doctor." He knelt down and spoke to Croyland gently enough, but the only answer was moaning and writhing.

Mr. Clunk stood watching, held in a horrified fascination. After a moment he came to himself. "I'll telephone, yes," he said quickly. "With pleasure. I shall be glad to." He pattered away from the blood, his handkerchief to his mouth. . . .

Tony came down to him in the hall where he stood

listening to the telephone, watched by frightened servants. "Yes, quite right," he spoke with bland condescension. "Come quickly now. Good-bye." He turned. "Ah, my dear boy!" He reached for Tony's hand. "What a brave strong fellow you are! That was really splendid."

"Croyland's unconscious," Tony growled. "The other fellow's dead."

Mr. Clunk nodded. "Quite so, yes. I was sure of it. Well, well, well!" He patted himself and rubbed his hands.

"Damn it, don't purr like that," Tony broke out. "You were going to make Croyland speak, weren't you? Splendid, isn't it? Providential!"

"Oh hush, my boy." Mr. Clunk was shocked. "Don't talk so. You're thinking of the young lady, of course. That's quite right of you. But we mustn't be ungrateful, we mustn't expect everything to be done for us. We have to use our own powers." He took up the telephone again. "I want a trunk call, please. For Superintendent Bell of Scotland Yard to the police station at Limbay in Sandshire. I don't know the number. Get them as quick as you can. Thank you. . . . Is that the Limbay police? Message from Superintendent Bell. Is Inspector Gunn there? At Bradstock Abbey? Very good. Send him a message at once to search the ruins carefully and watch the secretary. That's right. Good-bye."

"You believe that girl has killed her?" Tony muttered.

"Dear me, no. I don't let myself believe anything," said Mr. Clunk. "But I think that young person might be helpful. I should dislike to lose her."

"Oh, what's the good of talking here?" Tony cried.

"None at all," said Mr. Clunk cheerfully. "Not the least," and tripped upstairs again. "My dear friend," he looked round the door of the bedroom, "the police are on the way. You won't want us any more just now. We're going back to Bradstock at once. The young lady, you know."

"Here! Half a minute," Bell called, but Mr. Clunk ran away.

The faithful Scott was with Morris staring at the house. "Now, Scott, go in to Superintendent Bell and ask if there's anything you can do. I've finished with you. I'll leave you one cab. Come along, Morris." To the other cab he ran. "Take us to the best garage in Folkestone. I want a good car for a long run. As quick as you can."

They were driving by the sea again when Mr. Clunk through the sucking of butterscotch began to giggle.

"What's funny?" Tony growled.

"Well, you know, I was thinking of the trunk call to Bradstock," Mr. Clunk tittered. "It will be put down to Alfred Garston's account, you see. That seemed to me rather amusing."

Tony glowered at him in a sort of stupefied disgust.

Mr. Clunk, having consumed his butterscotch, began to hum:

> "If a smile we can renew
> As our journey we pursue
> Oh, the good we all may do
> While the days are going by."

CHAPTER XXVI

THE SEAT IN THE RUINS

BRADSTOCK HARBOUR was a lake of gold under the western sun when the car drew up at the door of the Abbey.

Gunn came out to meet them. "Found her?" Tony cried hoarsely. "Found anything?"

"Not a trace." Gunn shook his head. "Can't make out what's become of her."

"Well, well, well." Mr. Clunk came lightly down from the car. "Let's talk it over, my friend."

"Talk!" Tony groaned.

Gunn led them to that morning room of many conferences. "If you've got anything to say, I'll be glad, I'm sure. I've been over the ruins with a magnifying glass. Nothing, absolutely nothing. I've put that vamp, the secretary, through it again. She just laughs at me."

"Dear, dear," Mr. Clunk sighed. "I'm afraid she's a bad creature, Mr. Gunn. I should rather like to talk to her myself."

"You're welcome," said Gunn heartily. "Look here though, I've had Bell on the phone for half an hour. It beats me, but you seem to have seen your way through this case from the start, Mr. Clunk. And still I——"

"Oh dear, no," Mr. Clunk protested. "Really not. Only little by little. Precept upon precept, line upon line, you know. Always trying. Just like that."

"Well you got there anyway. Alfred Garston again after all these years! It's a perishing marvel. But look here—I can see him killing his mother so she shouldn't give him away and shooting the constable who knew him. That's all right. If you said him and Croyland put the nurse out of the way to stop her mouth, I could understand it, though deuce knows what they've done with her. But why did you put me on to the secretary? The idea is, she's Harwood's woman, isn't she, put in to help him blackmail Croyland over Alfred? That's all right. She looks it. But then why should she meddle with the nurse? I can't see any sense in it."

"Well, well, well," said Mr. Clunk patiently. "Just let me try to make sense of her. Have her brought here, my friend."

She came in with her usual undulating show of herself, her usual bold stare. "Oh dear me," Mr. Clunk sighed. "Is this the lady? Miss Hurst, my name is Clunk, Joshua Clunk. I am Miss Dean's solicitor. Inspector Gunn has very kindly agreed to give you an opportunity of explaining the disappearance of Miss Dean."

Gladys laughed. "I like that. Say another piece."

"I think I will." Mr. Clunk purred satisfaction. "You don't know quite enough. This is your uncomfortable position, Miss Hurst. Your friend Mr. Gordon Harwood is detained under suspicion of blackmail and murder. You know that, of course. It is very awkward for you. But you've been so foolish, you've made it much worse. You shouldn't have tried to divert suspicion to someone else. That couldn't have done you any good. We knew far too much. You were stupid enough to think if you made Miss Dean vanish, the police would believe she was the murderer. But that won't happen." He looked at Gunn.

"It will not," said Gunn with vigour. "We know all about the murders."

Gladys looked from one man to the other. She could

not grow pale, but her face was drawn and her big bosom heaved.

"What will happen," Mr. Clunk went on happily, "what will happen is that you will find yourself charged with another crime—the murder of Miss Dean."

Gladys laughed. "Found the body, old man?"

"Thank you. I see you know where she is," said Mr. Clunk.

"Come off it!" Gladys sneered. "You can't scare me into talking, because I've nothing to say. I know nothing about her."

Mr. Clunk sat back. "You'll have this lady looked after, won't you, Mr. Gunn?" he said placidly. "That's all now."

"You bet I will." Gunn gave her to a constable at the door. "Looks bad, Mr. Clunk."

"A hard creature," Mr. Clunk sighed. "Very hard. How ugly that is. And in a woman, oh dear, dear! Well, let us get on, my friends, let us get on." He started up.

"Get on where?" Gunn cried.

"The poor, dear child," Mr. Clunk lamented. "It's evident that creature has thrust her somewhere. It must have been somewhere near." He tapped his teeth. "The ruins, I think, yes, certainly the ruins. Come along."

"I haven't half been over 'em already," Gunn grumbled as he followed. "But it's odd, you know. It came to my mind when you phoned, there might be something about the ruins. Bell and me came over one night to see Croyland, and he was by himself and he came up from that way kind of startled."

"Did he indeed?" Mr. Clunk said. "Yes, I think there's something about the ruins. I have long thought so. The morning after Mrs. Garston's murder I saw that somebody had plunged through the flowers in the

ruins. That seemed to me very curious." He tripped on.
"It was just here. Yes. Just here." He stood still and
looked about him till his gaze lingered on that smooth
slab in the niche of the wall of the nave. "Let us try.
Now, Tony, you're a strong fellow. Would you help
him, Mr. Gunn? Just see if that stone can be moved.
Try it every way. Lifting, sliding, and so on." He knelt
down and his little plump yellow hands pawed at the
wall beneath.

"Gives a bit," Tony panted. "Won't lift. Won't slide.
As if something's holding it. Nothing on top. Try it
this way." They pulled it towards them, feet against
the wall, backs straining, but it held fast. Mr. Clunk
had come upon a loose stone in the wall below. He
clawed it out and the hole it left was bigger than the
stone. He put his hand in, found an iron ring, and tugged
in vain. He twisted it this way and that and it went
hard and metal squeaked.

Gunn and Tony sat down in the flowers with the slab
upon them. "Ah, that's splendid," said Mr. Clunk.

"My oath!" Gunn groaned.

"Shove it this way," Tony gasped, and they freed
themselves.

"You hurt, Mr. Wisberry?" Gunn rubbed his knees.
"Came sudden, didn't it?"

"Oh, I just turned this ring," said Mr. Clunk. He
was peering down into the dark cavity which the slab
had covered. He ran away.

Tony scrambled to his feet and came to the hole.
"What's he found?" Gunn said.

"It's so damned dark," Tony muttered. "May!"
His voice rose hoarsely. "May!" They could not hear
any answer.

Gunn came to him. "Rum place. Look here, there's
long bolts fixed. They'd work into staples on the under

side of the stone. And that ring he found moves 'em. And very neat too. Firm as houses till you find the dodge. See?"

"Of course I see," Tony growled. He was leaning down into the hole. The light which came into it showed only a shaft like a well about twice as deep as his own height. That was empty.

"What's the good of it though?" said Gunn. "These old monks had some queer dodges. Just a hiding place, or kind o' strong room or something?"

Tony swung himself over the edge and dropped down and groped about. "Here's a passage or something," he called. "Come on, got any matches?"

The voice of Mr. Clunk was heard. "Tony, my boy, Tony, one minute." He came to the hole with a stable lantern. "Here, I have a light and a torch too. Oh dear me, can I get down there?" He sat nervously on the wall.

"Let yourself drop. I'll catch you," Tony cried.

"Dear, dear, this is very unpleasant," Mr. Clunk gasped. But he put his legs over and, clinging with one hand, edged himself over. "Oh Tony!" He squeaked and dropped.

Tony caught him, set him on his feet, and took the lantern.

"It's all very well, you know," Gunn called, "but you won't get out of there without a ladder." He whistled for his men.

"Yes, there should really be a ladder," said Mr. Clunk, "I'm afraid Lord Croyland has removed it. That is why he came here at night."

"Damn the ladder," Tony muttered. "Come on, Clunk." The lantern light showed a low arched passage. Mr. Clunk sent the beam of his torch into it. It became higher soon and led on, curving. They flashed the light to either side as they went, but there was no sign of any other way or any hiding place in the stone walls.

"Deuce of a lot of it," Tony muttered. "Must run up towards the house."

"Oh yes, quite," Mr. Clunk panted. "It would. Ah, what's that?" They stopped. It was the sound of footsteps, but footsteps behind them.

Gunn appeared, striking matches. "Hello, young fellows. This isn't half a queer place. Found anything?"

"Not yet, no," Mr. Clunk said.

"Shut up," Tony growled. "What's that?"

They heard a faint moaning cry, then laughter, strange wretched laughter.

"My oath!" Gunn muttered.

"May!" Tony shouted. "May! I'm here, May! It's Tony."

"Ah, come, come, come!" she cried.

He ran on. He found her trying to raise herself and moaning as she tried. "My dear." He knelt by her and gathered her into his arms. "Oh my dear."

She clung to him sobbing, laughing, feeling at him. "It's you, it's you."

"My own darling! Have you been here all the time?"

"When is it? I don't know. I came back from you and I found the door and somebody pushed me down here. When is it now?"

"It's the day after. Are you much hurt?"

"Only a day! Oh, it's been so long. I fainted, I think. Wasn't that silly? Then I tried to make them hear and they wouldn't. It was so ghastly, Tony. Take me somewhere, dear. Take me right away. I can't bear it."

"Yes, that's best, yes," Mr. Clunk bustled on. "Now let us see what we can do."

"Can you walk, miss?" said Gunn.

"Not very well. My leg is hurt. It's the ankle, I

think. I fell, you know." She looked up at Tony and clung to him.

"Bit of a job getting her up out of that well place." Gunn scratched his head.

"Can do," said Tony.

"No, no. I don't think we need bother." Mr. Clunk tripped back. "There are quite good stairs here. Now, my dear, if you don't mind Tony carrying you. He'll do it very gently. Now, now, let me show the light. That's the way. Here's the door, with a queer, big old latch. Just a minute." He fumbled with it, the door swung, and they came out into the gloomy archway of Mrs. Garston's murder. "That's all right, you see." Mr. Clunk patted her cheek affectionately. "Now where are we?"

"Oh, take me away." She shuddered and hid her face in Tony's shoulder. "Tony, take me away from here, please."

"Rather," said Tony.

"My poor child." Mr. Clunk stroked her. "Of course he shall. At once. Just make them give her a little something, Tony, and take her right away to Limbay. The car's waiting, you know. She must have a doctor. I suppose there's a nursing home, Mr. Gunn. Send one of your men to show Tony the way. She really shouldn't stay in this house another moment. It's been too cruel to her. My dear child!" He kissed her tumbled hair. "All's well now. All's well."

Tony marched off with her, Gunn at his heels.

Mr. Clunk began to pry about the door and the archway, and as he moved and peered he sang to himself:

> "There's a treasure is waiting for me
> In a mansion of gold I shall be
> On the shores of the silvery sea
>   Hallelujah!"

Gunn came back to him. "Poor kid, she's pretty well all in. Don't wonder either. Do you know why it gave her such a turn finding herself here again? This is where she found Mrs. Garston murdered."

"Is it really?" said Mr. Clunk without surprise. "I see. Yes. Quite. This is the way Alfred came in, so that no one should know he was coming to Croyland. And he met his mother. A wicked fellow." Mr. Clunk swung the big door and it hit the lamp.

"Lord! Look at that!" said Gunn.

"Yes? The lamp, my friend? What then?"

"Why, when we got here the filament in that lamp there was broken. We couldn't make out why it should get broken over killing her."

Mr. Clunk blinked at him. "You found the lamp broken. Just that one lamp. And that suggested nothing to you! Well, well, well. We won't tell anyone, my dear friend." He shut the door.

"Look at it now." Gunn ran his hand over the panelling. "Why should we think anything opened there?"

"To be sure!" Mr. Clunk beamed upon him. "Why should you think?"

But Gunn was satisfied. His simple mind passed on. "Filthy dirty business about this girl, isn't it? But as far as I see we can't do anything. She don't know who pushed her down. It was that vamp the secretary all right, I don't doubt it, but we've no evidence."

"No, I fear not," Mr. Clunk sighed. "One would so like to punish her, wouldn't one? One does want to punish these hard people. But we mustn't be discontented. We've really done rather well, yes, ra-ather well." He turned away humming:

> "There's work for me and a work for you,
> Something for each of us still to do."

As they went downstairs Gladys came to the door of her room and looked round the shoulder of the policeman on guard.

"Hallo, Grandpa!" she called. "So baby wasn't killed. What a blow!"

"Dear me, I suppose it is, Miss Hurst," said Mr. Clunk. "It ought to be a warning. Do you think it will be?"

"Not much, old dear," she laughed. "You'll just go on mucking things."

Mr. Clunk stood and contemplated her. "Oh, I hope so," he beamed. "I think so." He tripped away. "I shouldn't hurry to let her go, my friend," he purred. "I should be just as unpleasant as possible."

"Not half," Gunn winked.

CHAPTER XXVII

MR. CLUNK AT HOME

Mr. Clunk sat in his drawing room drinking tea. The hour was two o'clock. The massive midday meal provided by Mrs. Clunk was inside him, the tea was strong. His glossy face shone with deep content. He bit a piece of sugar in half, walked to the window and gave one half to each of the two canaries, chirruped to them, caressed the row of scented geraniums underneath them, came back to his easy chair, arranged his little legs on a hassock and a peppermint lozenge in his mouth. Mrs. Clunk, kissing the top of his head, rustled to the harmonium. After a little while she also sang. Mr. Clunk, gurgling peppermint, joined in:

> "*If we knew those baby fingers,*
>   *Pressed against the windowpane,*
> *Would be cold and stiff to-morrow,*
>   *Never trouble us again,*
> *Would the bright eyes of our darling*
>   *Catch the frown upon our brow?*
> *Would the print of baby fingers*
>   *Vex us then as they do now?*"

To this domestic felicity was introduced Superintendent Bell. He stopped short, he seemed uncomfortable, whether at the pathos of the lyric, or the mingled scent of peppermint and oak-leaf geraniums.

Mr. Clunk started up. "My dear friend, how nice of you! Maria dearie, you've often heard me speak of Superintendent Bell."

"Yes, dearie." Mrs. Clunk came beside him. "Of course I have. Joshua's always saying he'd like me to meet you, Mr. Bell. How good of you to come! Well now, do sit down. And you'll have a little refreshment, won't you? Let me have some fresh tea made, it'll only be a minute. Or a glass of port wine would you like and some cake? Or a little whisky perhaps? I don't know if you'd care for some of my home-made lemonade?"

"You're very kind," Bell said as soon as he could get a word in. "Nothing, thank you."

"Now, now," Mr. Clunk shook his finger archly. "We can't have that, you know. The whisky, dearie, and some soda."

Mrs. Clunk rustled out. It was the maid who brought the whisky.

"Well, I didn't want to drive your good lady away," said Bell with relief.

"My dear friend, Mrs. Clunk doesn't like to hear business talk. She says it bothers her, dear soul. She likes me to tell her the points afterwards, if they're interesting. She's the best of counsellors."

"I should think so," Bell agreed. "Well, here's to you, Mr. Clunk. I don't mind owning you've done us proud in this business."

"Really now!" Mr. Clunk tittered. "Not at all. You're too kind. It's been a great pleasure to me, my friend. One of the greatest pleasures of my life."

Bell contemplated him. "I suppose it has," he said with appreciation. "Pretty good work. Well, you know, we've got things more or less straightened out now, but I thought I'd like to run over it with you."

"Just so. That's very desirable," Mr. Clunk nodded. "What is the last news of Croyland?"

"The doctors say they're going to pull him through. But we shan't get anything out of him this long while."

"I am afraid it is going to be very difficult to deal with Lord Croyland in a criminal prosecution," Mr. Clunk sighed.

"Can't touch him," Bell grunted. "Can't prove a thing against him."

"Probably not. No. When he is well enough, I propose to cause him a good deal of annoyance," said Mr. Clunk. "I must have payment for that process. Tony says he will take nothing. But I always stand for justice. We will concede that Lord Croyland has been placed in a difficult position: a very terrible position. We are not to suffer for that. He's been a hard proud man." Mr. Clunk put his finger tips together and gazed at them. "Well, well, well. Let us take it from the beginning. Tony's father, poor fellow. He discovered this steel process. There is no doubt now that he got into touch with our friend Alfred Garston. Ah, if I had only had evidence of that at the time!" He sighed. "Well, we mustn't repine. No doubt poor Wisberry thought that he was doing the best for himself in approaching the big firm privately through Alfred. So Alfred was able to introduce the process as his own invention. We need not say Croyland was a party to the fraud."

"Croyland's straight in business," said Bell. "Everybody says that. So was his father. Alfred's the wrong 'un in that family. What they call a detrimental. In the mud at school and college. His old father had a fierce time with him. I shouldn't wonder if he pinched this invention to make a show he was doing some good, so the old man would go easy with him."

"That is quite probable, my friend. Well then, Wisberry would naturally press for some results and Alfred's position grew difficult. I understand that Alfred had other troubles, eh?"

"He had. There was a girl down in the New Forest. He'd lived with her under another name and she was found shot. I expect she got pressing, like poor Wisberry. I was on that case—Gunn and me. We did a lot of work, and just when we were ready to put Mr. Alfred in the dock—*phut!* Alfred was found drowned."

"Very clever, wasn't it?" said Mr. Clunk. "Very ingenious. Poor Wisberry went off on his spring holiday to meet Alfred and Alfred met him and killed him. I should think it very likely that Alfred invited him to Bradstock. And showed him that secret passage. Then, having killed Wisberry and changed clothes with the body, Alfred put it in the harbour. I'm afraid he must have battered the face too. He could hardly rely on the action of the water. A nasty fellow. A very nasty fellow. But I rather think at this point we must impute some guilty knowledge to Croyland. Let us be just, my friend. Probably Alfred represented to him that he was in danger of being arrested for murder. I do not think Lord Croyland a man likely to sacrifice himself to save his brother. But he seems to have affections of a kind. He has a regard for the reputation of his family and his firm. There was the old father still alive, the affectionate mother. For his own sake Croyland would no doubt prefer to prevent his brother's conviction for murder. And Alfred had managed the affair so skillfully that what Croyland had to do involved no risk at all—only to identify Wisberry's much damaged body as Alfred's. If the fraud should be discovered, he could plead that he had made a mistake, a mistake easily possible when a body has been long in the water. I'm afraid we can't prove anything more, even now. And also, you will observe, my friend, this scheme had the great advantage for Croyland that it promised to get rid of Alfred for ever. Once dead, he couldn't dare to reappear. Croyland had eliminated him and his vices from the family. Croyland had the Abbey to himself. Croyland had the firm to himself. A great inducement. I don't wonder Croyland did his part."

"No, that's all right. He was playing a bit high, of course. I should say somebody else must have had a notion things were fishy——"

"Oh, I should think so," Mr. Clunk interrupted. "The doctor almost certainly. A family doctor, you know."

"Well, anyway we didn't get a hint of it. It was a good risk."

"Dear me, yes. A very sound speculation. I should say Lord Croyland has excellent judgment. He seems to have paid some price for his gains, to be sure. His poor mother, I gather, caused him a good deal of anxiety. But he would have done very well if our friend Harwood had not such an active mind." Mr. Clunk beamed. "I do hope you feel grateful to our friend Harwood."

"I do," Bell frowned. "That's a nasty, filthy brute. And his girl! My Lord!"

"Yes indeed," Mr. Clunk sympathized. "The nastiest creatures. The ways of God are very strange, my friend. Mr. Harwood has been so useful. I tell you frankly, I do not know how I could have done without him. I had quite given up poor Wisberry's death as a mystery which could not be solved here upon earth. Even when Tony found that his father had made a discovery which Garstons had been using, I did not see my way. I could only tell the dear boy to let the matter rest. And still I do not feel that I was wrong. Croyland could have defied us if Mr. Harwood had not given his assistance."

"How much do you suppose Harwood knew?" said Bell.

"That's an interesting question." Mr. Clunk reached dreamily for a piece of sugar. "I incline to think he knew very little to begin with and not a great deal at the end, certainly not the truth. He would have been much more drastic. No. I should say he started with a suspicion there was something in Croyland's past and did not get further than suspecting it was concerned with Alfred's death. I never thought him a man of much power of thought, but very shrewd and sharp in a small way and a bold gambler. He has great faith in his scent for the unpleasant and plays high. It's really wonderful how well he's done."

"I've been after him a dozen times and never got near him," Bell complained. "I can't make a case against him now, nor his woman, that Miss Hurst, either. We've got to let 'em go. They have the laugh of us, confound them."

"I should hardly say that, you know." Mr. Clunk remained calm. "Our friend Harwood has spent a lot of time and a good deal of money on the case, and the only result is that he just escapes penal servitude. Really, I don't think he can be at all pleased with us. But I quite agree we mustn't be satisfied by that. Not at all. I shall consider it a duty to watch for the activities of Mr. Harwood. Yes indeed." He beamed at Bell. "My dear friend, we may be quite sure Mr. Harwood is not a repentant sinner. He won't retire from business —nor the woman. You know, I thought her quite a striking person. She will go far— Oh yes, quite a long way."

"I believe you," Bell nodded. "She's a devil."

"Dear me yes, quite an evil creature," said Mr. Clunk cheerfully. "Ah, we shall meet them again, my friend." He began to hum:

> "*In some way or other the Lord will provide.*
> *It may not be my way, it my not be thy way*
> *And yet in His own way the Lord will provide.*"

Bell was uncomfortable. "Well, of course—putting it like that——"

"There is only one way to put it, you know," Mr. Clunk beamed.

"Yes, all right," said Bell hastily. "I hope I shall meet 'em. With a clear case. But about this one. How do you suppose Harwood got on to it?"

"Dear me, there are various possibilities. I should think it probable he came upon some old scandal about Alfred. He may have heard that Croyland and his mother were on bad terms. He is quite capable of marking down Croyland as a wealthy man of lonely habits who might be blackmailed by a wicked woman. Possibly he discovered that money was going from Croyland to some mysterious destination. Obviously money must have been supplied to Alfred—quite large sums. Alfred would not be easily contented. As soon as Harwood had Miss Hurst working for him in Croyland's confidence, he would certainly discover that a mysterious person was drawing money. I should take it Harwood never knew more than the simple fact. He would of course learn that poor Mrs. Garston suspected Croyland of killing Alfred. Possibly he believed that. At least he inferred that Croyland was paying hush money to someone who knew a secret about the death. He arranged for the theft of Alfred's letters to Miss Morrow and found in them confirmation of the suspicion of murder.

Miss Hurst brought this dear child May Dean into the house that her charm and innocence might extract something more from Mrs. Garston. A really wicked piece of cleverness. But, you see, it's not very deep. The wretched creatures had not thought things out. Most fortunately it never occurred to them that Alfred might not be dead at all. They are quite shrewd and resourceful but they don't grasp the case as a whole. No power of mind is applied."

Bell was restive. A memory of similar phrases used for his own efforts annoyed him. "Wasn't it?" he said sharply. "I don't care so much for running down folks that have given me trouble. It don't make yourself look very clever. Seems to me you thought Harwood was no end of a fellow till you had him beat. Now you say he never knew much. But I remember your telling me that what he did know was the central point of the case. You had a regular row with me because I couldn't get it out of him."

"Naturally," Mr. Clunk snapped. "Well, well, well. I daresay I was rather sharp with you, but really it was irritating. Don't you perceive, he did know very little, but it was the central point? He knew that in the background was an enigmatic person whom Croyland had to finance. If you had got that out of him you would have had the whole case in your hands. I will own that I thought he must have discovered a little more—possibly the identity of the person, at least his whereabouts. I did not suppose his brain work was so feeble. But if the existence of this mysterious person had been pointed out to you, I take it you could have found him. And Alfred Garston would have gone to the scaffold. Oh, I don't complain, my dear friend. The ways of providence are better than our ways. But it was provoking that the wretched Harwood should thwart us."

"He is a hard case," Bell grumbled. "I think you underrate him, you know. I shouldn't wonder if he knew all about Alfred."

"Dear me, no," Mr. Clunk cried. "I'm quite sure he didn't. Do apply your mind!" (Bell wriggled.) "There, there, there, I beg your pardon. But really, my dear friend, do consider—if he had known of the existence of Alfred, there would never have been this diabolical attempt on Miss Dean. Why did Gladys Hurst try to bury her alive? It's quite clear. When Miss Hurst found that Harwood was detained under suspicion of the murders, she wanted to clear him and herself by throwing suspicion on someone else. If she had any notion Alfred was alive she would have put us on his track. That would have been simple, safe, certain. She chose the risk of contriving the disappearance of Miss Dean to make you suspect her and Tony. Obviously Miss Hurst knew nothing of Alfred." Mr. Clunk stopped short and blinked and tapped his teeth. "I said obviously," he murmured. "There is another possibility. She may have wanted to preserve Alfred in order to blackmail him and Croyland afterwards. I hadn't thought of that. It requires you to suppose she is a really able woman. Dear me, yes. I shall watch her future with great interest." He felt in his pockets, found a sweet which was not peppermint and sucked with gusto. "However, she has been very useful. This cruel outrage on Miss Dean cleared up the case for us."

"How do you mean?"

"Well now, let us go back. You will find that in God's good providence it is the work of these two evil people which brought punishment on Alfred Garston and justice for my dear boy Tony. Consider. To Croyland it must have been like vengeance rising from the grave when just as Tony Wisberry appeared to claim his father's rights Harwood threatened a new exposure of Alfred's affairs. Then the letters from Alfred to Miss Morrow were stolen. Croyland saw that suspicions must be gathering dangerous substance. I have no doubt he warned Alfred, and Alfred also was alarmed and came secretly to see him."

"That's right. Alfred was away from Hythe with his car over the night of the murders."

"You have that. Very good. Alfred came into the house at night by the underground passage to avoid being seen by the servants. His poor mother heard something, came from her room and saw him. Probably she cried out. Whether he meant to kill her, we shall never know. He may have meant no more than to stop a cry: we are told she would be very easily killed. My own judgment is that I dare not acquit him of intention. He was a ruthless and reckless man. As he drove away from his dead mother, he was stopped by that unfortunate constable, a man who knew him. Another life had to be taken and he went back to his home—safe. Croyland was left to account for the murders." Mr. Clunk put his finger tips together. "I find it a little difficult to judge Lord Croyland justly. He had been living for many years in the shadow of his mother's belief that he murdered Alfred, though he had saved Alfred from the gallows. It must have been to him a strange kind of torture to be faced with the choice of giving Alfred to justice for his mother's murder or taking the burden of another deadly secret, a share in the guilt of another ghastly crime. It was, of course, a kind of selfishness to help Alfred escape: yet not altogether selfish. The wretched man might believe that he was doing what his mother would desire—as he had been doing for twenty years while she thought of him as his brother's murderer. There is a kind of nobility in the man. Really rather a tragic person, my friend."

"He's had a life," Bell nodded. "I don't envy him his death either—when it comes."

"No indeed," Mr. Clunk sighed. "A strong man. Let God judge him."

"Rather fine, the way he defied us all—taking the hell of a risk to himself. And it wasn't his own crime, not really, not mainly, any of it. Do you suppose he had a liking for Alfred all the time?"

"You know, I should doubt that," said Mr. Clunk thoughtfully. "I should ra-ather doubt it. Probably they were always hostile. Which makes Lord Croyland all the more remarkable. I think he had a liking for his mother. You'll observe that there was a breaking point with Lord Croyland. When Miss Dean vanished he could bear no more."

"That broke his nerve, you mean?"

"Yes, you may say so. Or let us say his conscience revolted at another crime. He cannot have known what had happened to her. Perhaps he suspected Alfred again. I take it he rushed off in that mad way, to demand the truth, to insist there should be no more villainy, to hurry Alfred out of the country—he hardly knew what. He was shaken, mind and soul." Mr. Clunk took another sweet. "A strange night, my friend. That poor child lying helpless under ground—while her fear and suffering drove Croyland to reveal his brother's crimes. Dear me, I wonder if I should have followed Croyland if I had known she was lost. I hope so." He blinked. "Yes, I think so. I had quite resolved to rely on Croyland giving us a clue to Alfred. I believe I should have been strong enough to put everything else aside. Ah, but what an ordeal for her, dear child. How strange

that providence should have found her suffering necessary to do justice? Well, well, well. We can't judge, can
we? Now we see through a glass darkly. Oh, let us be
humble, my friend."

Bell was uncomfortable. "It's a queer business all
right," he said gruffly. "You seem to have seen your
way clear enough, Mr. Clunk. How long ago did you
make up your mind Alfred was the man to go for?"

"My dear friend," Mr. Clunk's voice was very smooth
and sweet, "if you will remember I told you at the very
beginning, before poor Mrs. Garston was killed, when
you were merely dealing with the theft of the letters,
that there must be some present reason for interest in
Alfred. When I found out that the moment of Alfred's
death was the moment of poor Wisberry's disappearance, the moment when it might be convenient for the
Garston firm to dispose of a man's body, I ceased to feel
any confidence that Alfred was dead. When that unfortunate village constable was murdered on the night
of Mrs. Garston's murder, it was clear to my mind that
Alfred was alive and murderous. From that time I
worked and watched to obtain evidence of Croyland's
connection with him. Your unfortunate distrust of me
made it just a little difficult, my friend. But really,
you know, I think we've done ra-ather well." He patted
Bell's knee and giggled. "Yes indeed, very well."

"Not so bad," Bell grunted.

"I'm so glad you think so." Mr. Clunk rubbed his
hands. "Now we shall know each other better, my
dear friend. That's a great satisfaction to me."

"Take it from me, I'd rather work with you than
against you, Mr. Clunk," Bell said with a grim smile.
"I know that much."

"But it's charming of you to say that," Mr. Clunk

tittered. "I hope you will. I hope we shall." And he began to hum:

> "*There's work in my vineyard,*
> *There's plenty to do;*
> *The harvest is great*
> *And the labourers few.*"

"How is the young lady?" said Bell hastily.

"Ah, the dear child!" Mr. Clunk beamed. "She's with us, you know. We thought it would be so much best for her to bring her right away from Limbay to a quiet, kindly household. I do think we are that, you know, the wife and I, just quiet and kindly and homely. Yes indeed. I hope so. I think so."

"Very nice for her," said Bell, looking round the room: at the harmonium, the crowded furniture, the geraniums, the canaries. "Very comfortable, I'm sure. She's getting all right?"

"But you must see her. She comes down for a little in the afternoon. I'll tell the wife." Mr. Clunk tripped away.

He returned with Mrs. Clunk, who smiled and chattered and fussed about the room like a plump little hen, and in a little while the large shoulders of Tony came through the door sideways, for he had May in his arms. He saw Bell and stopped short and looked hugely helpless and bashful.

"Ah, here we are!" Mr. Clunk rubbed his hands. "Come along, come along, Tony. My dear child, here's our good friend Superintendent Bell wants to see if you're really getting well." He patted her cheek. "My dear little girl."

May was blushing. Very large blue eyes looked alarm at Bell. "Oh!" she said, and looked up at Tony.

"That's good enough," Bell chuckled. "I don't have to ask any more about you. Eh, Mr. Wisberry?"

"We're going to be all right," Tony spoke into May's hair.

Mr. Clunk contemplated them benignly. "Yes indeed," he said, and tripped away to the canaries and pursed his lips, and "Sweet, sweet, sweet," he chirruped, and the canaries piped and trilled at him.

THE END

Whether you were keen enough to solve this Crime Club mystery in its early stages, or whether the author succeeded in keeping you in suspense up to the last chapter, Mastermind requests that you add to the next reader's enjoyment by remembering that—

CRIME CLUB READERS
NEVER TELL